W9-ALN-077

DISCARD

THE EX

JOHN LUTZ

THE EX

KENSINGTON BOOKS

KENSINGTON BOOKS are published by

Kensington Publishing Corp.
850 Third Avenue
New York, NY 10022

Copyright © 1996 by John Lutz

Library of Congress Card Catalog Number: 96-076018
ISBN 1-57566-078-4

First Printing: August, 1996
10 9 8 7 6 5 4 3 2 1

Printed in the United States of America

This is the very ecstasy of love,
Whose violent property foredoes itself,
And leads the will to desperate undertakings.
  —Shakespeare, *Hamlet,* Act II, Scene 1

1

The pole-mounted sirens throughout Edwinsville emitted a constant, synchronized wail. There were few people on the rain-slick streets, and the rain driving down from the low, dark clouds discouraged anyone who might have thought about defying the dire warning of the wailing sirens. Lightning fractured the western night sky as wind sheered through the trees and cut along the business loop of State Highway 103 where it became Main Street, knocking over the Alison's Auto Service sign, scattering sheets of plywood stacked behind Builders Hardware and Home Supply. An empty Budweiser can pinged and clattered along Main, airborne as it skipped over curbs and bounced off building fronts, skittering along the wet pavement as if frantically seeking shelter.

On the hill beyond Edwinsville, a ten-foot-high chain-link fence topped with razor wire ran through the thick woods. Except where it stretched away on each side of the ornate wrought-iron gates that were the entrance to the State Institute for Mental Health, little of the fence could be seen, but it completely encircled the large brick building that was the Institute, wherein those wards of the state determined to be potentially violent were incarcerated and, in most cases, treated for their psychoses.

The synchronized, urgent wails of the sirens weren't so ear-splitting on the hill, but the lightning-illuminated black clouds, the steadily increasing wind, and the almost horizontal rain lent the same sense of dread and near-panic that gripped the town below. Patients in identical drab gray uniforms were assembled in the mess hall, where white-coated attendants scurried about trying to calm them. Some of the patients were beyond being calmed and had to be restrained. Others were numbed by what was happening and simply sat hunched over in chairs and on the floor, hugging their knees, keeping their heads lowered, withdrawing into some safe interior space of the mind.

"God's vengeance!" an old man with a shaved head kept shouting as he eluded two attendants—a big man named Sam and a stocky woman named Dora—who were trying to restrain and reassure him. Dora distracted him with a smile and Sam attempted to grab the old man and pin his arms to his sides, but the man slipped away again and leaped nimbly up on a table. "God's terrible vengeance! I warned my wife and uncle when they put me in here! Warned that fool of a doctor why they wanted me out of the way! She didn't sell it cheap—that's what God knows!"

A terrible hammering sound began, and glass shattered as one of the barred windows gave. Large and irregularly shaped hail was driven with the rain, battering the roof and west side of the building in fusillades with each burst of wind. An assault by a thousand machine guns.

Then, abruptly, the rain and hail stopped, the wind ceased, and all was silent except for the distant sirens.

Even the old messenger from God was struck dumb by the perfect stillness, the thick, charged air that made breathing a chore and caused a prickling sensation on exposed skin.

The patients somehow knew before the attendants. Hands rose to lips and temples in horror. Eyes widened. Mouths opened as if to scream but didn't. There was no time.

Outside the Institute a dark funnel cloud had dropped from the night sky and roared eastward. Debris that included trees, and a tumbling and hapless van with headlights still glowing, swirled around the base of the tornado. As it bore down on the Institute, the chain-link fence in the woods coiled skyward like a striking snake and disappeared in the blackness.

The roar became deafening, the lights dimmed, then the west wall of the Institute exploded outward. Over the turmoil and howl of the beast from the clouds screams couldn't be heard. Time and people and stone and earth and sky all whirled together in the dark. There was nothing to do but hold on. There was nothing to hold.

In the aftermath, the warning sirens in the town below were silent. The wind had died down and the rain was reduced to a cool, steady downfall that pattered on the wreckage of the Institute. In the moonlight now filtering through the dark clouds lay a field of wreckage, scattered bricks, jutting wood and wallboard, serpentine coils of chain-link. The only sounds were the rain and the moans of those still alive among the debris. A few shadowy figures were visible staggering about in the night, wandering through another dark and tragic dream.

A hand gripped a splintered two-by-four stud and shoved it aside. What was left of a wooden mess hall table was also moved aside, but slower and with more difficulty.

Loose bricks scraped and clattered, and up from the wreckage stood a tall woman with wild hair and wild eyes. Beneath smudges of mud and a dark trail of blood snaking down from her hairline, her face was strong-featured, with wide-set eyes and prominent cheekbones, a determined sweep of jaw. Under other circumstances she might have been beautiful.

She stood still for a moment, gazing about, her dazed expression gradually changing to a look of comprehension. Then she began slowly picking her way through the wreckage, ignoring the moans and occasional raised hand seeking help.

She was almost beyond the ruins of the Institute building when something stopped her. She glanced down and saw a white sleeve, a hand gripping the pants cuff of her gray Institute uniform. She recognized Sam the attendant, pinned beneath a pile of bricks and splintered wood. Only his head and right shoulder and arm were free. He looked up at her with pleading in his dark eyes.

"Deirdre!" he moaned. "Don't leave this place. Don't do it. Please!"

The tall woman gazed down at him with cold green eyes. She attempted to walk on, but his grip on her pant leg was iron and unyielding.

"Deirdre . . . stay where you belong!"

She stopped trying to escape his grasp, then bent low and attempted to pick up a brick from the debris at her feet. It was actually two bricks and half of another, still firmly bonded by mortar. She used both hands to raise the bricks over her head, then looked down at Sam.

He understood her decision and his fate and merely stared up at her with frightened but resigned eyes. He closed his eyes then, and his face was calm as she hurled the bricks down at his head. Blood black in the night spotted the right leg of Deirdre's gray uniform, and the hand clutching the material slowly released its grip.

She continued on her way, faster now, more resolute in her movements.

Within minutes she disappeared into the dark woods beyond the twisted and uprooted fence.

2

Moonlight softened the already hazy light of the Terrace Top Restaurant in downtown Saint Louis. Though it had rained almost every day since the violent weather of last week, the forecast for tonight was for only a fifty percent chance of light showers, so several diners were eating outside the framed glass wall of the rooftop restaurant, enjoying one of summer's uncharacteristically delightful cool nights.

Christine Mathews sat at one of the outdoor white-clothed tables with half a dozen friends from work. They'd finished dinner and were idly chatting and looking out at the lighted skyline of the city. Twenty stories below and to the east, the Mississippi River lay black and glistening in the moonlight. The running lights of tugboats glowed upstream, and on the far side of the river the *Casino Queen* gambling boat, glittering like gaudy jewelry, was gradually pulling away from its dock in East Saint Louis.

"A beautiful city from up here," Chad Brent, a technical support expert, said from across the table. They had come to the expensive restaurant to celebrate his birthday. Christine knew he had a crush on her. She also knew it was hopeless. Chad was nice enough, and handsome enough, but his timing was off.

Christine, a pretty blond woman in her early twenties, with a somewhat oversized nose she minimized with thick bangs, and with a lush rather than fashionable figure beneath her navy blue dress, looked around the table at Bill and Yolanda and Terry. At Burt and Jennifer. The people at the table weren't exactly intimate friends, but among them was the easy familiarity that grew from working long hours together. And Davison Tire and Rubber often demanded long hours.

The tuxedoed waiter, a young man with sleek black hair, took their orders for coffee and dessert. Christine was dieting as usual and resisted his sales pitch for the chocolate-raspberry special. She ordered only a cappuccino. Terry began talking about the new low-profile radial tire the company was developing. Christine, who was in Accounting, wasn't much interested. She excused herself and stood up.

"Time to feed my habit," she said. She was the only one at the table who hadn't quit smoking to conform to the new company policy.

"It'd be healthier for you to stay here with us," Yolanda told her. She sounded serious. "Those things aren't called cancer sticks for nothing. They're sure to shorten your life."

Chad started to stand. "Want some company?"

Yolanda, who rather liked Chad, smiled and gently pushed him back down. "You'd only live a little while longer than her after sucking in that second-hand smoke, honey."

"She's right," Christine said quickly, discouraging Chad from accompanying her. "Anyway, I'll be back before the coffee comes."

She walked away from the table, toward a garden area that helped to segment the restaurant from the rest of the roof. Maybe it would have been legal to smoke at the table, but she'd seen no ashtrays anywhere, and she knew how smoke bothered everyone since they'd given up cigarettes. She glanced back once to make sure Chad hadn't changed his mind and followed her.

Relieved that she was alone, she stepped between two potted ornamental trees, then through an arched wooden trellis that supported vines growing from large ceramic pots. The tar and gravel surface of the roof crunched beneath her soles as she moved back beyond the line of decorative plants and was invisible from the restaurant, a sinner seeking solitude.

Looking out at the city and breathing in the damp but fresh night air, she felt contentment. A cigarette, then a cappuccino, would end her day perfectly. Nicotine and caffeine. Maybe Yolanda was right about a shortened life span. She fished in her purse for her pack of Winstons and her lighter, found the crumpled package, and almost panicked when it felt empty. But when she drew the pack from her purse and tore it all the way open, she discovered one last cigarette.

She located the lighter in her purse, then moved over to stand at the low iron guard rail to take in the view while she lit the cigarette. The *Casino Queen* had moved well upriver.

A slight sound made her turn, unlit cigarette in one hand, lighter in the other.

From the shadows beneath the trellis, a tall woman emerged. When she moved into the light, Christine saw that she was quite pretty, wearing dark slacks and a light sweater with a bright scarf at her throat. Her shoulder-length red hair hung over one side of her face, reminding Christine, who was a movie buff, of an old-time film star whose name she couldn't recall.

The tall woman smiled at her.

"The places we smokers have to go just to have a cigarette these days!" Christine said. She flicked the lighter and raised it to her cigarette, sensing that the woman was studying her on the other side of the flame.

As she inhaled, exhaled, and dropped the lighter back into her purse, she noticed that the woman wasn't holding a cigarette. She seemed friendly enough, smiling as she moved toward Christine.

"You're Christine Mathews, aren't you?" she asked. "Chrissy?"

Christine was surprised. And curious. She tried to place the woman in memory but couldn't.

"Yes, I am," she said. "Though not many people call me Chrissy."

"So young," the woman said. "I just knew you'd be young." She was still smiling.

"Do we know each other?" Christine asked, beginning to feel an edge of fear.

"I know you," the woman said. "I'm Deirdre."

And suddenly Christine understood. But the tornado, the mental institution, were over a hundred miles out of town . . . It wasn't possible!

But of course it was possible. Merely unlikely.

"You can't—" she said, trying hard not to believe what was happening.

She was cut off as Deirdre leaped toward her with the agility and power of a feral cat and drove an elbow into her stomach, then shoved her backward.

Christine felt the horizontal iron guard rail hard against her thighs, just beneath her buttocks. Deirdre grinned and pushed her again, driving her fist between her breasts, and Christine toppled backward over the railing, trailing a hand just in time to catch the bottom of the rail. Her heart and her horror tried to climb the tunnel of her throat as she lost her hold on the rail but managed to twist her body and grip the tile ledge with one hand, then the other, and hang suspended twenty stories above Sixth Street. She tried to scream but found only enough breath to make a soft whining sound. Her fingers began to slip on the smooth tile.

Then Deirdre was bending over her, smiling down from within the soft frame of her long red hair. *Veronica Lake,* Christine thought inanely. That was who Deirdre reminded her of, though except for the hair, she didn't look like Veronica Lake at all.

"Please!" Christine managed to plead hoarsely. She tried to find a foothold, frantically scraping her toes against the building, but found only rough stone. One of her shoes fell off, and her heart fell with it.

Deirdre reached down with both hands, and for a second Christine thought she was going to grip her wrists and pull her to safety. This was all a joke! A horrible joke!

Instead Deirdre pressed the palms of her hands against Christine's knuckles, pinning her fingers to the unyielding ledge, leaning her weight down hard, pushing, swiveling the heels of her hands to grind Christine's fingers into the tile. Christine couldn't be sure if she was still gripping the ledge or if she remained clinging there only because of the pressure of Deirdre's hands.

Then Deirdre suddenly released the pressure and stood up straight, grinning down at Christine and holding her own hands out as if she were about to soar like Superman.

The abrupt release of Christine's numbed fingers caused them to slip immediately. Christine tried desperately to regain her grip but no longer had any feeling in her fingertips.

It was when she knew for sure she couldn't possibly maintain her hold that she found her voice and screamed.

She screamed all the way to the street.

After a few seconds of paralyzing shock, everyone from the out-door restaurant came running to see what had happened. Led by the tuxedoed waiter, they burst dramatically through the potted foliage.

By then Deirdre was gone.

At least four mornings a week Molly Jones ran the outermost paths of Central Park, then farther. Her distance was a little over six miles, she'd figured, after reading a *Times* article about running and the best kinds of shoes to buy for various athletic activities.

Her own shoes were well-worn Nikes. Not the fancy kind the kids wore, but medium-price, sensible training shoes unmentioned in the article. She was training to live a long and able life, not to slam-dunk a basketball.

She was in the stretch now, approaching the exit onto Central Park South, near Fifth Avenue and Fifty-eighth Street, where she'd shopped for a birthday gift for Michael yesterday at F A O Schwarz. It was a few minutes past noon, and a couple of office workers on their lunch hour, guys in white shirts and brightly flowered ties, with their dark suit coats slung over their shoulders, walked by and gave her the look as she jogged past them breathing hard, her long legs kicking out and her thighs straining with effort. She was running flatfooted now, hearing and feeling the entire surfaces of her rubber soles slap on the packed asphalt. Each stride sent a jolt of pain through her ribs on her right side and stretched the tendons in her calves until they felt as if they were about to tear. The fronts of her thighs ached and threatened to cramp. She was laboring, but she'd make it. She repeated to herself that she'd make it. Her breathing was harsh and ragged, rasping with effort. A man riding a balloon-tire bicycle smiled at her struggle. An old woman dressed in rags glanced at her with gloomy hostility from where she sat cross-legged on the grass, her wispy gray hair a wild tangle, a misshapen plastic trash bag of personal possessions lying beside her like the black and foreboding burden of her life.

Molly reached the park bench where she'd decided to end her run, then made herself take a few strides past it. Discipline. Finally she stopped running and walked in a slow circle, hands on hips, a medium-height, thin woman with a heart-shaped face described as sweet more often than beautiful. She was a bit wide through the pelvis, with breasts she sometimes imagined would fit neatly into teacups. David had told her that about her breasts once, not in any way uncomplimentary, while they were making love.

She spat off to the side. Not very ladylike, but she'd breathed in a gnat or some other minute insect as she'd passed the bench. Probing around the inside of her dry mouth with her tongue, she decided the insect was gone but she needed something to drink, and soon. She stood for a while bent over, still with her fists propped on her hips, then straightened up and used the bottom of her faded *Phantom of the Opera* souvenir T-shirt to wipe sweat from her face.

She let out a long breath and looked around. The office workers and the man on the bike were gone. The old woman was still glaring at her, as if finally she'd found the one responsible for her situation.

Molly felt a pang of pity for the homeless woman, then a thrust of fear as she saw that no one else was around.

The woman stirred on the grass, then began to rise, old bones and sinew demonstrating surprising dexterity and strength.

This was silly, Molly knew. She was a twenty-seven-year-old woman in good shape, maybe a bit winded from her run, but she could still easily outdistance this ancient and decrepit derelict. She had nothing to fear.

Yet she *was* afraid.

Not of the old woman, she realized suddenly, but of something she couldn't quite identify.

A man walking a pair of black poodles on short leashes came into sight from among the trees near the lake. He was moving directly toward Molly and the old woman.

The woman gathered up her bulging plastic bag and, with a final scathing glance at Molly, began shuffling away in the opposite direction. She and the man walking the poodles passed within ten feet of each other without seeming to notice, on the same planet but not in the same universe.

When the man passed Molly, he looked over at her and smiled, then strolled on. She heard him speak sharply to one of the poodles that was interested in something in the bushes and had strained the leash pulling to the side. With a firm tug on the thin leather leash, he drew the desperately curious dog back near him and continued walking.

Molly, seemingly alone now in the sun-dappled park, was still uneasy, and still unsure why. It was as if an unremembered nightmare were plaguing her with a residue of terror. She felt isolated and vulnerable. She hurried toward the brighter sunlight and the sounds of traffic drifting from beyond the trees near Central Park South, breaking into a jog as the shadow of a cloud closed in on the trail and trees around her, darkening grass and leaves.

It occurred to her then that since beginning her morning run she'd had the vague, unaccountable sensation that something was behind her, stalking her.

She remembered the woman who'd been badly beaten while jogging in the park, the victim of a wilding, as it was called. A stockbroker or financial consultant or some such thing. Running along as Molly had been, thinking of stocks or her love life or treasury bills, maybe a friend she was meeting tomorrow for lunch— then all of that had almost ended permanently for her at the hands of cruel strangers.

Fear passed like cool air over the backs of Molly's forearms and the nape of her neck, causing her to hunch her shoulders.

Ridiculous, she told herself. As ridiculous as being afraid of a poor, harmless old woman innocently taking in the sun, perhaps the only friend left for her.

What must it be like, Molly wondered, nearing the end of life and without a human friend?

Without love.

Then her sense of isolation ended abruptly, along with her fear. She was out of the park and on the sidewalk, surrounded by more people than she could count, within twenty feet of hundreds of vehicles streaming past, even a horse-drawn carriage heading into the park.

In the middle of New York again.

The middle of her life.

At the edge of the park, Deirdre stood watching.

It was hot in Manhattan, but still a glorious day. David Jones pushed open the doors of the Hand Building on Third Avenue and stepped out onto the crowded sidewalk. Horns blared as the traffic signal at Third and East Fifty-fourth flashed green, and nothing larger than a deliveryman on inline skates was able to budge because of the gridlocked intersection. David began to walk, glad not to be in one of the yellow taxis baking immobile in the sunlight, caught in a web of progress gone mutant and mad.

He was an average-sized man, fit but not yet muscular despite his regular workouts at Silver's Gym on East Fifty-sixth. With his lean features, unruly sandy hair, and round-lensed glasses with their fragile brown frames, he looked much more the intellectual than the athlete.

Thirty-seven his last birthday, and still the supervisor of the fee reading department at Sterling Morganson Literary Agency, he was beginning to wake up nights worrying about not progressing in life. Not to where he wanted to be, anyway. His job paid reasonably well; it was simply that David had been working at it longer than he'd planned. He'd expected that by this time he'd be an authors' representative at the agency and positioned for an eventual executive position on the board. Morganson had promised advancement but so far hadn't delivered. That was one of the reasons David worked out so hard and diligently at Silver's; an extra five pounds on the bench press, an extra push-up or sit-up, gave the illusion of advancement in life, even if all he really had to look forward to with certainty was another day of overseeing the critiquing of would-be authors' manuscripts, which were usually sent back with kind and encouraging letters explaining why they were unsalable, but maybe next time, if the author learned from his or her mistakes and built on the invaluable experience of having written a novel. Yes, maybe next time.

His musing had soured his mood, and it was too beautiful a day for that. He decided to eat lunch at a sit-down deli three blocks away.

It was a nice walk. No one tried to sell him a Rolex watch or stuck a beggar's cup in his face, burdening him with the guilt of the healthy and employed. A man with a huge dog wearing a kerchief around its neck was holding a sign asking for donations to buy booze for the dog. David thought that one was worth a dollar. It had to be a soul-smearing experience, begging in New York, even if you were working a scam.

He'd finished building his salad and was standing in line to pay the deli's cashier, when a woman spoke to him as if he were an old friend and she was surprised, though certainly not shocked, to run into him here.

"Well, David! Hello!"

The amazing thing was he didn't know right away who'd spoken. Not quite recognizing the voice, though it was disturbingly familiar, he turned around, smiling, ready to bluff recognition if necessary.

It wasn't necessary.

"Deirdre . . ." He said her name softly, his breath snatched away by whatever he was feeling. What was she doing here? Deirdre, his ex-wife, who lived in Saint Louis, a thousand miles away. *You shouldn't be here,* was all he could think. He almost actually uttered the words.

But there she was, standing behind him in line, wearing a gray, businesslike blazer and black skirt, slightly older now, but still, he had to admit, attractive. Almost as tall as his five-foot-ten, her head a mass of red hair he knew was unnatural, her smile bright and wide in a face that had grown somehow stronger. Her green eyes were sparkling with pleasure and something else beneath brows that seemed lighter than when she and David had lived, slept, and made love together. Her wide, full-lipped mouth was exactly the same as he remembered, a feral mouth that seemed always ready to bite, her upper lip sliding sensuously like the sheath of daggers over perfect, large white teeth when she smiled. He found himself staring at her lips and quickly returned his gaze to her eyes. A stranger's eyes, a lover's eyes.

"It's been . . . what, five years?" he asked, still stunned.

"Closer to six," she said. "You never did have a good sense of time." She stepped back, gazing at him with obvious pleasure and disbelief. "This is amazing, running into you here! In a city the size of New York!"

David couldn't quite regain his mental equilibrium; he didn't want to believe this was happening. "What on earth are you doing here?"

"Hey, David!" she said. "You don't seem glad to see me. We were a married couple once, remember? We can at least talk to one another. Don't be afraid. You know me. I never did bite." She smiled. "That is, unless you asked me to."

A bearded man in a gray business suit, standing ahead of David in line, had apparently been eavesdropping and turned to stare. Deirdre ignored him, holding her smile.

David forced a return smile. "It's not that I'm afraid, Deirdre. I'm just . . . well, surprised." He tried to summon cheer that wouldn't seem forced. "How long are you going to be in town?"

"Only about a week. I'm an interior designer for a shoe company in Saint Louis, laying out their stores for maximum efficiency and eye appeal."

This wasn't the Deirdre he remembered. He was amazed and must have shown it.

"Don't look so astounded, David," she said with a grin. "I went back to school after our divorce. There are things we don't know about each other. After all, six years is a lot of water through the dam."

" 'Over' the dam, you mean." Oops! He recalled how she habitually mangled maxims and distorted platitudes. His corrections used to infuriate her. Maybe they still would.

She laughed. "Oh, David. You're still correcting me. I still say things like that a little bit wrong, get them tangled up. It's just like we were still married."

The bearded man turned around again. This time Deirdre glared at him and he turned away.

David was embarrassed. "You're right. I'm sorry. I had no business—"

"It doesn't matter now," she interrupted with a shrug. "I know I used to drive you crazy with my little flaws."

"Well, I wasn't perfect myself."

"Almost, though." She blatantly looked him up and down. "You look good, David. Bigger than I remember. You're lifting weights, right?"

He felt a rush of pleasure at the compliment. "Now and then. How's your husband?" he asked quickly, to assuage his guilt over what was skirting the edges of his mind. "What's his name? Sam?"

"Stan," she said. "Stan Grocci. He's a building contractor. Puts up houses but does some commercial work, too."

"Any children?"

"I'm afraid not." She paused, looked down, then back up into his eyes. "David, Stan and I are divorced."

He was unsettled by the knowledge and didn't know how he should react. What do you say when you find out your ex-wife is divorced again? "I'm, uh, sorry." He was staring at her mouth.

"Me, too. Stan's a great guy, really and truly, but his business was his life. *Is* his life, I mean. He's alive and healthy and doing well. I don't want to make it sound as if he's standing with one foot by the grave."

" 'In' the— No, sorry, never mind. It's my job making me do it, I guess. Bad habit, editing people when they talk."

The line at the cashier's booth had edged forward. The bearded man in front of David paid the Oriental woman at the register and walked away carrying his lunch in its foam container.

David balanced his own foam plate of salad and his soda can and reached for his wallet. Before he could draw it from his pocket, Deirdre had stepped forward and handed the cashier a twenty-dollar bill. "For both of us," she said.

"No, Deirdre," David said, "really, let me—"

"Lunch is on me, David," she cut him off. "For other times' sake. I'm an independent woman now." She accepted her change from the cashier then stood up on her toes and peered across the deli. "Oh, there's an open booth. Come on, let's strike before the iron is hot."

She strode away, elbowing her way through the people still loading their foam plates at the long serving bar.

David hesitated, then followed.

They sat down across from each other in one of the wooden booths that lined the long, paneled walls, their lunches on the table before them. There were framed sports photographs on the walls. The one near their booth was an old black-and-white of Joe DiMaggio swinging mightily at a waist-high pitch, the muscles in his arms corded, his eyes trained calmly and intently on the blurred point of impact where bat met ball.

Deirdre didn't begin to eat, but instead stared as intently at David as DiMaggio stared at the baseball. David was getting uneasy.

Then she looked away from him and began using a white plastic knife to spread mustard on her sandwich.

"So," she said, "you're an editor."

"Not exactly," David said. "I supervise fee readers at a literary agency. People send in manuscripts, and we're paid to read them then write and tell the authors why their work isn't salable."

Deirdre opened her mouth wide and attacked her sandwich in a way that was almost primal. "But you *do* sell them sometimes," she said as she chewed.

For a crazy moment he wondered if she fancied herself a writer and had a manuscript she wanted him to give special attention. Maybe that was what this was about; such things happened in his line of work. "Sometimes," he said, "but not very often."

"Is it a big agency?"

"One of the biggest."

She swallowed her bite of sandwich and licked her lips. "Well, I *am* impressed. All your reading in bed has paid off, and now you're a big executive. I always knew you had brains, David."

"You never mentioned it at the time."

She reached across the table and touched the back of his hand with just the tips of her red-enameled nails. The touch felt like a brand. "No," she admitted, "but I wish now that I had. I wish things had been different for us."

David felt a lump form in his throat. He had to swallow, so he took a sip of his soda to conceal his emotion. "I never did under-stand why you left me, Deirdre."

She shook her head slowly, as if in admonition. "That girl, David. She was barely out of her teens."

Marci, she was talking about. A twenty-two-year-old law stu-dent at Saint Louis University who'd lived in the same apartment building. David had always regarded their affair as more a result than a cause of his problems with Deirdre.

"We were all younger then," he said. "And I was serious when I told you she didn't mean anything to me. She came on to me one day like she was crazy. It was something that happened and was meaningless, then it was over within a month." He stared at his food. "I thought . . . Well, I thought you might have left me be-cause I insisted on the abortion." They hadn't planned on having a child, had little money, and their marriage was clearly deterio-rating at the time Deirdre told him she was pregnant. Abortion had seemed the only logical path to David then. He still wasn't sure if he'd been right.

"I didn't want the abortion," Deirdre said.

David smiled sadly. "So you told me. Then, after you left me, you didn't have to abort the pregnancy, but you chose to anyway." He had always wondered why.

Maybe she still wasn't going to tell him. "Our marriage was about sex, wasn't it? Honestly now, David."

"Not *only* about sex," he said.

"But mostly. You remember how we were. Rough with each other."

He did remember. They'd both been in some kind of dark sex-ual thrall, experimenting, trying anything, sadomasochism, bondage. He'd told himself the marriage was failing and he was trying to hold on to her that way, but on a certain level, he'd known better even then. She'd been the one who suggested many of their activities, but he'd enjoyed what they did, needed it.

"The baby was injured, David. That was why I went ahead and had the abortion. It wouldn't have been born normal."

What she was saying spread inside him like something black and heavy as he recalled the violence of their sex while she was pregnant. "Oh, Christ! Was it something we—something I did?"

"No, not you, David," she said. She touched his arm as if trying to lend comfort. "Someone else, after I left you. Can you forgive me?"

"I'm the one who wanted the abortion," he said. "Whatever happened wasn't deliberate, and your life was your own then. There's nothing to forgive."

"You're a better man than I thought you were six years ago," she said.

"I'm not so sure about that."

"Well, the past is buried and dead." She bowed her head, then suddenly looked up and seemed to brighten. Her eyes were green, wide, luminous with possibility. "Listen, David, why don't you phone me at my hotel? We could get together for a drink. The world has changed for both of us, so maybe we'd both feel better if we talked without emotion about the past and future. We can be friends, I think."

Despite her toned-down appearance, there was sensuality in her every gesture. As she pursed her lips and sipped at her drink through a straw, he couldn't look away from her despite his confusion and discomfort. He wished they hadn't met again, yet he was still sexually attracted to her.

"I don't know . . ." he said.

"If we can be friends?"

"If it's a good idea."

She appeared injured, then smiled. Her wide, red lip slid up over her teeth, almost inverting. "Oh, I get it. The wife. Have you married again? Never mind, don't answer. So what's her name?"

"Molly." It felt almost like a sacrilege, using Molly's name in Deirdre's presence.

"Hmm. I like that name," Deirdre said. "Molly."

He didn't like hearing her say it. Didn't like the indecipherable emotion stirring in the corners of his mind where memory moldered. Memory he thought had been purged of emotion by time. But he'd been wrong. His chance meeting with Deirdre was dissipating the years as if they were mist, striking life into the past. Corpses were rising.

"Molly's young, I'll bet."

"Twenty-seven. Only ten years younger than I am."

"Which would make her eleven years younger than me."

David smiled. "You robbed the cradle, Deirdre."

"Do you and Molly have any children?" she asked.

"One. A boy. Michael. He's three."

"That's absolutely wonderful!" She did seem genuinely pleased.

"We think it is."

"What does your Molly do?" Deirdre asked. "Other than wifely duties?"

"She's a free-lance copy editor. Publishers farm out work to people like her, manuscripts that need help."

"Then you and she have your work in common."

"We have a lot of things in common."

"And Molly and I have something in common." She made a face at her own faux pas. "I'm sorry, David. I shouldn't have said that."

"No, you shouldn't have."

"I guess I'm the leopard that can't change its skin."

David smiled. "There's no real reason for you to change, Deirdre."

"Why, thank you! A compliment!" She seemed immensely pleased.

"Maybe I should have given you more of them six years ago. God knows, I loved you enough."

"Nobody's to blame for the past, David. Life teaches us all. Usually too late. Like I learned too late I shouldn't have left you."

She'd finished her sandwich. Now she patted her mouth with her white paper napkin with exaggerated delicacy, then slid across the booth's bench as if preparing to stand.

"It's been marvelous seeing you, David. Tell Molly I said hello, and that I wish both of you all the happiness in the world. She's lucky, you're lucky. And me . . ." She shrugged. "Well, I haven't been *un*lucky. And I haven't been unhappy the whole time after we parted."

"What about now?"

"Now? Oh, I'm reasonably content these days. Good job, enough money even if I'm not rich. And right now contentment's enough for me. I've learned it's more than most people have." She stood up from the booth, then leaned forward unexpectedly and pecked him on the cheek. It was a kiss like fire. "Bye, David. Take care, hey."

She edged through the crowd at the serving bar, moving toward the counter.

Biting his lower lip, he watched her stride from the deli. Out of his life again.

He suddenly felt much too warm, and the pungent scent of the food was making him nauseated.

He got up and made his way outside, dropping his suit coat from where it was folded over his arm. It landed to form a puddle of cloth on the sidewalk.

"Here, David."

Deirdre picked up the coat and brushed it off, folded it neatly as if she were going to lay it on a bed or chair, then handed it to him.

"I thought—"

"I was about to hail a cab," she said.

"They aren't easy to get this time of day."

"So I've been told, but nothing ventured, nothing obtained."

She smiled and strode to the curb, raising her arm. As if to prove her point, a cab immediately swerved across Third Avenue and coasted to a stop next to her.

She opened the cab's rear door and turned toward him. "Make the rest of your life happy, David!" Then she lowered herself quickly inside and pulled the door closed.

As the cab drove away, David stood staring at the back of her head framed in the arc of the rear window, this woman who was like a stranger but wasn't a stranger. She faced straight ahead as rigidly as if her neck were in a brace. She might have been crying, but he couldn't be sure.

Maybe he was simply imagining her tears because he felt like crying.

5

Deirdre pushed aside the roiling emotions she'd experienced after seeing David. Their meeting had been less and so much more than she'd imagined in the instant their eyes met.

On Broadway, she gazed through the cab windows at the crowded sidewalks and asked the driver to pull to the curb beyond the next intersection. She paid through the little rounded scoop set in the plastic dividing panel, leaving a suitable tip, and climbed out of the cab.

It felt wonderful to be lost in the middle of all the people, all the energy that swirled noisily around her. It was as if she were protected by movement and blaring horns and masses of humanity. And it was true, she told herself, she *was* safe here in New York.

A man with a raincoat slung over his arm almost ran into her, swerving at the last second and smiling at her. She smiled back, and he hesitated, then walked on. Deirdre held her head high, her shoulders back, and joined the flow of pedestrians. Workers hurrying back from lunch, shoppers, sightseers . . . she was one of them, and it felt glorious with the afternoon sun warming her shoulders and glancing brightly off the buildings and the contoured steel of the yellow cabs stuck in the impatient, laboring traffic. There was a strong exhaust smell, but she didn't mind that. It was better than a lot of smells.

A woman carrying a shopping bag emerged from a revolving door and bumped into her. "Oh, hey! Deirdre!"

Deirdre looked at her and smiled. She'd literally bumped into the one other woman she knew in New York. "Darlene! You've been shopping."

"Charging up a storm. I'm happily addicted to plastic." Darlene spoke in a clipped, cultured voice that sounded natural to her but probably wasn't, like a long-ago affectation that had taken root. She was about Deirdre's height but much slimmer, with a long, elegant neck, slender calves like a teenager's, and practically no breasts. She wore her hair combed back severely and neatly braided above the nape of her neck. She had the kind of dark-eyed, delicate features that enabled her to get away with that kind of hair style, Deirdre thought with envy. Darlene looked successful, her own woman, rich. It had been one of the first things Deirdre noticed about her when they'd struck up a conversation at the Port Authority Bus Terminal. That and her distinctive voice.

"I just left an old friend," Deirdre said. "David."

Darlene looked puzzled. A running man brushed Deirdre, knocking her toward the building. She moved out of the stream of pedestrians. Darlene followed.

"I thought I told you about David," Deirdre said. "At Port Authority."

Darlene's soft brown eyes widened. "That's true, you did. He's your ex, am I right?"

"Right," Deirdre said. "He and I had lunch together, a nice visit."

Darlene grinned with tiny white teeth. "That's not the way people usually talk about their ex. Any chance of it becoming more than a pleasant lunch?"

"The bastard got married while I was gone," Deirdre said.

Darlene was still grinning. "That doesn't answer my question."

"Aren't you naughty?" Deirdre laughed. Two women stared at her and had to walk around her. "Walk with me?" she invited Darlene.

Darlene glanced at a silver watch that fit loosely on her thin wrist, then shrugged. "Sure. I've got some spare time before I have to meet some friends."

Deirdre started to walk, and Darlene fell in beside her. They entered the dark shade of a building, where it was noticeably cooler, then emerged into hot sunlight.

"You still didn't answer my question," Darlene reminded her.

"I don't know the answer," Deirdre said honestly. There would be some things they'd never talk about, at least for a while.

Darlene smiled at her. "The way you look, Deirdre, you can make the answer whatever you want."

Deirdre smiled back. "You really think so? I mean, you're the one with the young Audrey Hepburn looks. Men go for the delicate, breakable type. You're built like a model or a ballerina, and I'm built like . . . well, sex."

"I'd trade anytime," Darlene said. "The way the world is now, there aren't many men looking for the kind of woman they'd take home to Mother."

"You're serious?"

"Of course. They want to take you home, but believe me, Mother doesn't figure into it."

"Except with *some* men," Deirdre said. "Mothers can have a terrible influence on some men."

"David?"

"No. Not him at all. David could always . . ."

"What?"

"He was always a good lover."

"Darlene stopped walking, causing Deirdre to barely avoid bumping into her. She raised her elegant thin arm and glanced again at her expensive watch. "I'd better get going or I'll be given up for lost," she said.

"I don't want to make you late for your friends," Deirdre said. She wondered for a moment if Darlene would invite her along.

But Darlene was silent, glancing around. She had such a sweet, clean profile. They moved over and stood on a corner with a cluster of people waiting for the traffic light to change to Walk.

"Are you going to be in town long?" Darlene asked.

"Awhile."

"Me too, this visit."

"Her name's Molly."

"What?"

"That's the name of David's wife. The one who took my place. Molly."

Darlene stared at her oddly, maybe with disapproval.

"They have a child," Deirdre said. "A little boy named Michael."

Darlene was silent.

"I thought you should know."

"I don't understand why," Darlene said.

"You should know about Molly and Michael, as well as about David. But especially about Molly. It will help you understand what's going to happen."

Darlene appeared confused for only a second, then shrugged, as if whatever happened, it would be fine with her. "You said at the bus station you were going to find a hotel. Where are you staying?"

But the light changed and she was virtually swept away by the surging crowd before Deirdre could answer. She smiled helplessly at Deirdre and waved.

Deirdre stood on the corner and watched her disappear in the streams of pedestrians that flowed along Broadway's wide sidewalk like competing currents in a river. For an instant her entire fragile body was visible, striding along with rhythm if not strength. Then only her slender upper body could be seen, and after a while only her head and long, pale neck. And then she was gone.

Darlene reminded Deirdre of a woman who was drowning.

6

"Most men probably feel that way when they unexpectedly see their ex-wife after years have passed," Molly said.

She and David were lying in bed in the sultry dimness of the summer night. It was cool enough that they didn't have the window-unit air conditioner on. She liked it that way, so she could hear Michael if he woke up. Still, she could feel the sticky dampness of perspiration beneath her on the smooth sheet, slowly molding her form to the contours of the mattress.

Beside her, David sighed. It was more a sound of frustration than of weariness.

"I'm glad you told me about meeting her," Molly said. She raised her upper body and strained her neck so she could kiss his cheek. It was damp and warm and he needed a shave. Traces of cologne or soap still lingered with the scent of his perspiration.

She stayed propped up on her elbows for a few seconds, then let herself fall back, her head sinking into her pillow.

"She surprised me, Mol," David said softly.

"Sure she did. It's like your past sneaking up on you while you're thinking about lunch."

"That's exactly what it was."

Molly was suddenly and acutely curious about Deirdre. She'd never even seen a photograph of her, other than a blurred snapshot David had made a show of tearing up and throwing away. A tall woman—at least she'd appeared tall in the photo—with a lot of hair and a fiercely beautiful smile. "How did she look?"

"Oh, the years have made her . . . kind of plain, I'd guess you'd say."

"There was no need for you to worry over telling me about it," Molly said. "So you ran into Deirdre at the deli and talked to her for a while. What were you supposed to do, spit olives at her?"

He laughed softly in the shadows. "I wish that had crossed my mind."

"You're not the first man to see his former wife and experience discomfort. It doesn't mean anything other than that you're human."

"Being human can be a problem."

"You're happy," Molly said, "right?"

She instantly regretted the doubt that had crept into her voice. Or maybe only she had heard it.

"Hell, yes, I'm happy."

The bedsprings whined and she felt his hand brush her cheek, then gently caress her breast through the oversized white T-shirt she slept in. She was aware of a tightening deep inside her and her breathing quickened. The T-shirt was wound around her body so that much of its excess was pinned beneath her. Across its chest, distorted by the twisted fabric, it was lettered FOR SLEEP OR SEX. She'd received it at a bridal shower as a gag gift, but she found it practical and comfortable. The thin cotton strained and stretched, and David's hand was beneath the shirt and sliding slowly toward her left breast. His breath was warm in her ear, then his tongue.

"Wait a second, please!" she breathed.

"What's wrong, Mol?"

"Nothing. Really."

He withdrew his hand and she swiveled on the mattress and stood up. The firm wood floor felt cool beneath her bare feet. She pulled the T-shirt over her head and tossed it in a twisted, pale heap on a chair. Then she slid her panties down to her ankles and stepped daintily out of them, as if relieving herself of shackles. Sounds from the street were filtering in through the screen, cars swishing past outside, faint voices shouting blocks away, the throbbing bass beat of a car radio that faded quickly, a distant siren making exuberant loops of sound. The sheer white curtains swayed slightly in the faint breeze as if in a slow, ghostly dance. She left the window open and switched on the air conditioner mounted in the window alongside it.

When she was sixteen, her father had left her mother and her for another woman. Her mother died two years later, and Molly had never quite escaped the notion that the terrible stress of the desertion had triggered the cancer. Her father had left his new lover, and a few years ago had remarried, to a woman named Verna who owned an art gallery in Detroit. Molly wasn't sure if she'd ever forgiven him, or if she fully understood what forces had moved him. Had there been something lacking in her mother? In herself?

She tried to shake such thoughts from her mind and returned to David's shadowed and patiently waiting form on the bed.

David moved close to her. "What's wrong, Mol? Still thinking about Deirdre?" He kissed her neck. "Well, I'm not. Like she said, the past is buried and dead."

Molly lay very still. "My past with you has been my happiest time."

"Mine, too," David whispered.

"Men leave women," she said softly. "I know it's unreasonable of me to think that way, and it's because of my childhood, but it's the kind of thing that inundates the mind and changes things forever. That's how I feel and I can't help it. Men leave women."

She felt the backs of his knuckles lightly caress her cheek. "Not this man, Mol. Not ever."

She turned to him and they kissed, and his hand found the small of her back and pressed her to him. She could feel his erection hard against her thigh.

"Try not to wake Michael," she heard herself say.

But it was she who moaned and cried out, clinging possessively to him as they made love.

In the morning, while David showered, she made coffee and stuck two slices of whole-kernel wheat bread in the toaster.

He came into the kitchen and kissed her, dripping water from his hair still damp from the shower. Neither of them spoke about last night or about Deirdre. Everything seemed reassuringly normal to Molly.

He cooked eggs and bacon while she quietly finished getting dressed, careful not to wake Michael. After breakfast, she and David would deliberately rouse the child and play with him for a few minutes, then David would leave for work and Molly would dress and feed Michael and walk him to the Small Business Preschool, six blocks away.

"You working on something today?" David asked when they were seated opposite each other at the kitchen table.

"Book on architecture from Link Publishing," she said, salting her scrambled eggs. "I've got the rest of the week to finish it."

He took a sip of coffee and smiled. "What do you know about architecture?"

"What's an architect know about dangling participles?"

"Good point. You gonna finish on time?"

"Easily. It's going to be mostly photographs of European cathedrals. The text is all about flying buttresses, opposing stresses, Gothic spires, that sort of thing."

"Saaay, you *do* know about architecture." His sarcasm was good-natured, and not the sort of remark he'd have made if he felt any tension between them. Grinning, he forked in a final bite of egg, then washed it down with a swallow of coffee and stood up. He was the usual David, all right. She smiled, feeling pleased and secure. "Gonna wake up Michael now?" he asked.

"We can."

She stood up from the table and David followed her into Michael's bedroom. It was a small room, painted pale blue with decals of fish and sea horses on the walls. Toys were piled in a blue rubber laundry basket in a corner. More toys were lined on shelves alongside a narrow dresser. On the top shelf was a penny-stuffed piggy bank Michael's grandfather—Molly's father—had sent him from Detroit last winter when Michael had had the flu. A delicate butterfly mobile dangled from the center of the ceiling, swaying gently in the stirring of air caused by the opening door.

Muffin, the brown and orange cat that was a gift from the previous tenant, uncoiled from where he'd been curled near the foot of the bed, stretched, then left by way of the window that was propped open six inches by a stack of weathered paperback books to allow him access to the fire escape.

Molly and David watched their son sleep for a few seconds. He was fair and blond, as David appeared in his childhood photographs. His round face was set in the blank-slate serenity seen only on children in slumber. He was lying on his side, his knees drawn up, his tiny ribs starkly prominent with each deep and even breath. Mortality was so apparent in the very young. He was perspiring slightly and his downlike hair was plastered to his forehead.

Each morning was like the beginning of a new and fascinating chapter for Molly when she stood alongside her sleeping son. She knew she would nudge him awake, kiss him, and another day would unfold in their journey to his adulthood while they learned from each other. He was her reminder that life was an exploration.

She touched his soft, bare shoulder and he stirred and opened his eyes. Smiled.

"Big Mike," David said, and bent low and kissed him gently on the forehead.

Michael stretched out his arms and David lifted him effortlessly, holding him well away until he was sure he hadn't wet the bed. Then he hugged him, kissed him again, and while Michael was still chortling he handed him carefully to Molly and turned to leave for work.

This must be a ritual as old as the family, she thought. Fathers readying to leave for the hunt on primal, misty mornings lost forever in the past. She smiled. Not a politically correct thought? She wasn't sure. But it was a lovely thought, even if she was soon to begin work herself.

David turned back as if on a whim and kissed her forehead, then ruffled Michael's hair. Michael reached up and ruffled his father's hair right back.

"Have a good day, you two," David said, and left the bedroom.

She heard the floor creak as he walked into the bathroom, probably to recomb his hair, as she sorted through the dresser drawers for something Michael hadn't outgrown.

David laid his folded suit coat on the toilet lid and ran water in the washbasin. He wet his hands and slicked back his hair, then raked a comb through it and checked his image in the mirror. He'd splashed a little water on his shirt but the spots would dry soon.

As he scooped up his coat to put it on, something fluttered from one of its pockets and landed on the hexagonal white tiles alongside the vanity.

A small piece of paper, folded once so sharply that it would be permanently creased. He picked it up and stared at it, trying to remember if it was a note he'd written to remind himself of something. He couldn't recall putting it in the pocket.

He unfolded the paper and saw a phone number scrawled in black ink. Below the number was a message: *Don't be silly. We should be friends. Call me, please. Deirdre. P.S. Say hello to Molly and Michael.*

David crumpled the paper and lifted the toilet lid.

But he paused and stood with his hand above the water. He was slightly surprised that he couldn't release the note. Couldn't press the lever that would remove it from his life.

He glanced at himself in the mirror, then looked away as he stuffed the note into his hip pocket, shrugged into his coat, and left the bathroom.

He could dispose of the note on the way to work, in the subway station, or at the office. There was no rush. This wasn't some kind of goddamned test. Despite a persistent discontent some mornings in the dawn of waking, or at bad times during the day when he would contemplate the futility of his job, he was a settled and happy husband and father, probably less worried about the future than most men his age. Certainly he was more blessed than many he knew. He had unexpectedly run into his former wife yesterday and had an uncomfortable moment, that was all. They were grown-up folks living out their lives as best they could while trying not to experience or cause pain; there was no need for adolescent conflict here.

And no need for him to see Deirdre again before she left town. He would either disregard the note, or he'd phone her and politely repeat his opinion that it would be best if they let the past lie undisturbed. Whatever in its chemistry might tug at him, he could and would ignore.

He called goodbye again to Molly on the way out.

7

Molly backhanded perspiration from her forehead and squinted against the morning sun. Summer continued its relentless assault on the city. She thought it might be hot enough to buckle the sidewalk as she wheeled Michael in his stroller along West Eighty-fifth Street. Small Business was close enough to walk to, but since Michael had become more active lately, it was easier for both of them if she pushed him in the stroller rather than pursue him in his sudden and impulsive rovings. Trash bags and sidewalk grates drew him with irresistible power.

Manhattan's steel and concrete held and radiated the heat like a kiln. Michael seemed comfortable enough, leaning back and calmly watching the traffic and occasional smiles of pedestrians, his chubby right hand idly toying with the colored plastic beads strung conveniently within his reach. His small world was in order; beads properly aligned and easily movable, surroundings familiar.

She noticed her own hands were clenched on the stroller handle. Relaxing her grip, bending her elbows slightly to remove tension, she leaned easily into the weight of the stroller, listening to the soft, rhythmic squeak of one of its front wheels, holding her breath whenever she caught a whiff of garbage from the plastic bags lined at the curb.

Halfway to Small Business, Molly glanced across the street and realized she was looking at the same woman who'd been strolling parallel to them for several blocks. Not unusual in New York, but the woman was diametrically opposite Molly and must have been keeping pace with her almost to the step. There was something eerie about it. If anything, she should have been moving faster than

Molly and Michael, since Molly was leisurely pushing the stroller. The woman was slender, wearing jeans, a tan windbreaker, and a blue baseball cap. She had on sunglasses with mirror lenses that concealed her eyes and altered her features like a mask.

A horn blasted and Molly jerked and stopped the stroller so abruptly that Michael slumped forward and yelped in surprise.

"Eye on the road, lady!" the driver of a dirt-streaked white delivery van yelled at her.

"Outa the street!" someone else shouted.

She realized she'd been so intent on watching the woman across the street that she'd pushed the stroller down the handicapped ramp at the corner, into the busy intersection. They might have been killed.

Relieved but embarrassed, she backed the stroller up onto the sidewalk. Several women in business clothes, and a man carrying an artist's flat, vinyl portfolio tucked beneath his right arm and pressed close to his body, moved around her to stand near the street while waiting for the traffic light to change. One of the women, who was elderly and had strikingly blue eyes and bad teeth, looked over her shoulder and winked at Michael, who paid her no attention. Everyone was still, poised for the change of the light while they stood breathing exhaust fumes. It worried Molly that Michael, who was on a lower level than adults, breathed so much Manhattan pollution.

The light flashed a walk sign, imposing another electronic instruction on the conditioned New Yorkers staring in anticipation. Molly went with the flow of pedestrians and wheeled the stroller across the street and onto the opposite sidewalk.

Then she steered the stroller into a pocket of comparative calm near a restaurant's doorway, propped Michael up straighter in its seat, and peered across the street.

The woman in the tan jacket was nowhere in sight.

Fine, Molly thought. She pushed the woman out of her consciousness and pressed on to Small Business.

When she reached the refurbished four-story building near Broadway, she saw that the usual signs of activity—the arrival and departure of parents' cars as they dropped their children off before work—had already taken place. Julia Corera, Michael's teacher, was standing halfway down the concrete steps to the entrance, beneath the green canvas canopy with its teddy bear design. She was wearing a baggy khaki skirt and a loose-fitting blouse with a wild, tropical plant pattern. There were already crescents of dampness beneath the arms of the blouse.

"Yo, there, Big Mike," she said with a wide smile. She was a heavyset, sweet-faced woman in her mid-twenties, with a perfect mocha-cream complexion and wise brown eyes. She'd heard during the first week of preschool how David referred to his son, and from then on the irony of the nickname had prompted her to use it.

Molly unstrapped Michael, lifted him from the stroller, and stood him on the sidewalk. "Say hello to Miss Corera, Michael."

He grinned and craned his neck, staring up the steps. "Hewo, Yulia."

Julia bounded down the steps and picked him up. Molly wondered if Michael was her favorite or if she was equally smitten with all the children. She'd talked to Julia enough to know that she and her husband, a city fireman, wanted their own children but so far hadn't had any luck.

"Sorry we're late," Molly said.

"That's okay. It's only a couple of minutes." Julia flexed her knees and bounced slightly, jostling Michael. He laughed and tried to grab her ear. "If Michael ever runs away from home," she said, "he can stay with me."

Molly laughed. "You might send him right back."

"Never!"

Molly kissed her son on the cheek. "See you this afternoon, honey."

"Say bye-bye," Julia prompted.

Michael opted for silence, but he smiled and waved to Molly as she paused pushing the unoccupied stroller along the sidewalk and glanced back. A man and woman passing by gazed at him as if he were the most beautiful child they'd ever seen, making Molly almost sob with pride.

Julia and Michael waved to her in unison, then a red Volvo pulled to the curb and a man climbed out on the passenger's side and ushered a girl about three over to Julia. Molly had seen the girl at the school before and thought her name was Margaret.

She watched until everyone was inside the building. The car sat at the curb with its engine idling, a woman behind the steering wheel waiting patiently for the man to emerge. Another family's day beginning. Molly stopped staring and continued down the street.

This was her day not to jog, and she had the architectural manuscript well under control. She decided to take a walk, then stop at the grocery store near the apartment. Muffin was out of cat food. She'd buy that and a few other things to load into the stroller before going home and settling down to work.

David draped his suit coat over the wooden valet in a corner of his office. It was a large office, with crowded shelves of books and manuscripts lining two walls above desk level. David's desk was almost bare, but there was a side table with an IBM clone computer and a stack of manuscripts with letters paperclipped to them. Among the few items on the desk was a framed photograph of Molly and Michael. From where he sat, he could see into the anteroom, where the door lettered STERLING MORGANSON LITERARY AGENCY was open.

After sitting down at his desk, David swiveled his chair to face the computer and booted it up, then checked his E-mail. Nothing urgent. He decided to answer some letters on paper and keyed into the word processing program.

Movement caught his eye, and he looked up to see that fee reader Josh Quinby had entered the office. Josh was in his late twenties, short and not quite overweight, curly-haired, with a mischievous grin. One of those people who become everyone's buddy within minutes. Sometimes that kind of ongoing joviality masked less admirable character traits, but as long as he'd known Josh, David hadn't seen anything other than genuineness. Josh actually was good-natured and mischievous. And everyone's buddy.

Josh stared at him with concern. "You look like Gatsby near the end, old sport. What's wrong?"

"That any way to talk to your boss?" David asked with mock annoyance.

Josh grinned and shrugged. "Sorry, boss. Now you can go ahead and promote me."

David didn't mind Josh's flip manner. They were friends, and Josh was his fastest and best fee reader. Josh was also his confidant sometimes, and David needed someone to talk to about what was happening.

"I ran into my ex-wife in a deli yesterday," he said. "After six years, I hear her voice call my name, I turn around, and there she is. It was like meeting a ghost."

"And?" Josh said, his dark eyes sparkling with interest.

"She wants me to call her."

Josh leaned his back against the doorjamb and ran a finger along his chin. "Hmm. You must have married for a reason, and you must have divorced for a reason. Maybe even the same reason. Did *you* leave her?"

"Vice versa," David said.

"Oh. Then I suppose the question is, did you ever let her go? I mean, all the way?"

"Yes," David said immediately. Then added, "I think so, anyway."

"Then give her a call," Josh said. "Put your mind at ease."

Lisa Emmons, the receptionist and fee reader secretary, stepped into the office, smiled at David, then said, "Morganson wants to see you, Josh."

Josh grimaced, but he was grinning as he left the office. Lisa, a small, intense woman of thirty, attractive with brown hair and eyes, glanced back at David as she left, but he didn't notice. She was five years out of Columbia with an MBA degree, and he knew she periodically looked for other, more rewarding employment. What he didn't know was that he was the reason she stayed at Sterling Morganson.

He got up and closed the door, then pulled the scrap of paper with Deirdre's phone number from his pocket and stared at it for a moment.

He returned to the desk and sat down, dragged the phone over to him, then pecked out the number with his middle finger.

"Windemeyer Hotel," said a woman's voice on the other end of the line.

"Could you ring the room of Deirdre . . ." He suddenly stopped talking, wondering what name she was using. "Deirdre Grocci," he said, figuring she might still be using her ex-husband's name.

After a pause, the operator came back on the line. "We don't have a Deirdre Grocci registered, sir."

"Maybe she's using her maiden name," David said. "Try Deirdre Chandler."

Again a pause, longer. Then: "We have no Deirdre Chandler registered either, sir. We do have a Deirdre Jones."

David was bewildered. "Would you ring her room, please."

He waited while the phone rang six times.

"Your party doesn't answer, sir," the operator cut in. "Do you want to leave a message?"

"No," David said. "No message. I don't really need to get in touch with her."

After hanging up the phone, he sat still. His hands were sweating. After a few minutes, he reached out and adjusted the photo of Molly holding Michael so that it was facing him directly, then sat staring at it.

He inhaled and held air in his lungs until it had a calming effect on him. Controlling his breathing implied he was controlling his life. He wasn't going to call Deirdre again. And probably he'd never see her again. She'd take care of her business in New York then return to her job in Saint Louis.

He tore the note with her phone number into very small pieces and let the pieces flutter into the round metal wastebasket next to his desk.

Then he tried to forget the name of her hotel.

Molly rubbed her knuckles into her eyes, then pushed aside the architectural manuscript and publisher's style sheet. It was quiet in the apartment except for muted street sounds and the faint noise of another tenant's TV tuned to one of the frenetic talk shows that dominated daytime viewing hours. "She's *sleeping* with him, and you don't *mind?*" a woman's incredulous voice inquired. Molly smiled and stood up from her desk.

It was almost noon but she wasn't at all hungry. She walked into the kitchen and poured her third cup of coffee this morning, adding cream and promising herself she'd cut down on caffeine, beginning tomorrow. Idly blowing on the steaming liquid to cool it, she wandered back into the living room, where she'd been working.

"It might not be moral for most people," said a TV voice from beyond the walls, "but it's right for us."

Molly drifted over to the window as she often did to gaze down at the street, at the outside world of selective morality that entered her home by way of a neighbor's blaring television.

She was about to take a sip of coffee when she noticed the woman in the tan jacket on the sidewalk across the street. The woman still had on the baseball cap and sunglasses so her features would be obscured, especially from Molly's angle. Her hair was tucked up beneath the cap.

Molly placed the cup on the windowsill and moved to the side, trying to get a better view of the woman so that when she began walking her face might be visible. Right now she was standing squarely facing a *Times* vending machine with her arms crossed, her head slightly bowed, perhaps reading the front page through the murky glass.

Then she straightened, turned her body slightly, and stared directly up at Molly.

She seemed to be smiling as she looked quickly away and strolled out of sight, in the direction of Small Business Preschool.

8

"What makes you think she was the same woman?" David asked Molly that evening in the apartment. It was raining hard outside, a summer shower that blew intermittently and rattled the loose panes in the windows.

"Same clothes, same size," Molly said. "Same mirror-lens glasses. Why would she be hanging around the neighborhood?"

David tossed his attaché case full of work onto a chair. "Why did a man in a gorilla suit offer me Monopoly money on my way home tonight? Why does anybody do anything in New York?"

"I don't know. Why are you defending her?"

"Defending who?"

Molly watched him but said nothing. It was so muggy in the apartment her skin felt oily. An emergency vehicle siren was wailing somewhere in the city, possibly responding to some crisis brought on by the change in the weather.

"You never mentioned before that you think the sunglasses woman is Deirdre," he said.

"I don't *think* it. But she seems the most likely candidate, considering she's just popped into our lives."

"Who's popped into our lives? Deirdre, or the woman you saw out the window?"

"Let's make it Deirdre," Molly snapped.

"She's not in our lives," David said irritably. "She's in town for a couple of days on business, then she's going back to Saint Louis."

"She told you that?"

"More or less. She has a job there, a house or apartment. Friends. Roots."

"Didn't she remarry?"

"Yes. But she's divorced."

Molly wiped her palm across her damp forehead, noticing that ink from the architectural manuscript had stained the heel of her hand. "So she's single again," she said, regretting the words immediately. She knew she was forcing David into a position where he had no choice other than to defend Deirdre if he was going to defend himself. It was unfair, but she seemed unable to stop doing it.

"Mother Theresa's single, too," he said. He walked over to her and she let him kiss her, but she decided not to kiss him back. Questions and suspicions swirled unsettled in her mind. "Anyway," he said, "neither of us is likely ever to see Deirdre again. And if we do, so what?"

Molly studied his face, loving him, wanting so much not to doubt. No indecision showed in his eyes, in the vertical lines etched at the corners of his lips. "You mean that? The 'so what?' part?"

"Of course." He glanced around, using both hands to loosen his tie. "Where's Michael?"

Molly hadn't finished her scheduled work when it was time to pick up Michael from Small Business. It had happened before and she'd made arrangements. "He's still upstairs at Bernice's. She was watching him while I got some work done." Bernice was a young woman employed irregularly as an office temp. Molly and David trusted her and often used her as a baby-sitter. Bernice was almost on a level with Julia in Michael's affections.

"Why don't you call and see if she'll keep him another couple of hours?" David asked. "We can go to Ching's and have a quiet supper."

Molly didn't have to think long on the suggestion. She'd been working hard, and she'd finally reached the point where she could stop for the day without guilt. And David had calmed her turmoil of suspicion. He was right. Even if the woman she'd seen was Deirdre, she'd soon have to return to her life far away. Deirdre had a job, connections in another city. If she was jealous of the life David had built since leaving her, she should be pitied. Maybe, Molly thought, in Deirdre's position, she'd be curious enough to act the same way, to succumb to voyeurism.

"Wait a few minutes while I comb my hair," she said, forcing a smile, testing his reaction.

He smiled back and the tension seemed to rush from the room. "A gorilla suit, huh?" Molly said.

The next morning in the park, Molly was halfway through her run, breathing hard but jogging easily, when a woman wearing red shorts and a gray sweatshirt emerged from a group of people walking near the woods and veered onto the trail about a hundred yards ahead of her. She didn't seem to have been part of the group near the woods; most of them acted surprised by her sudden appearance. The women glanced at each other while the men watched the jogger who'd materialized so suddenly.

Molly momentarily broke stride. She knew immediately who the woman was. Though she was wearing her blue Yankees cap on backward, she still had on the mirror-lens sunglasses, and there was something unmistakable about the way she moved, quickly yet at the same time with an almost lazy, long-limbed insolence. At the same speed as Molly, she was running with seeming lack of effort, her tanned legs measuring out regular strides. She hadn't looked in Molly's direction before turning onto the trail, nor did she look behind her now.

Surprise and anger added to Molly's energy and speed. A sharp ache in her right side threatened to become a debilitating stitch that would sear through her ribs with each breath. And she was off her pace and wouldn't make the distance if she continued pushing herself so hard.

Then she got mad at herself and decided to end the uncertainty. If the woman was Deirdre and had some sort of psychological problem, or was simply out to antagonize, it was time to confront her. Molly forgot about making the distance to her starting point and lengthened her stride, determined to catch up with the woman.

Anger still bubbled in her at the thought of the woman invading her life and her mind, deliberately appearing before her, wearing the same baseball cap and glasses so Molly would know she was being watched, taunted.

Molly closed to half the distance separating them, and the woman picked up the pace. It was almost imperceptible. Her arms swung in longer arcs, and the white soles of her shoes flashed higher and more vividly. Other than that, there was no change in her motion. Yet the distance between her and Molly began to widen.

Breathing through her nose so she wouldn't become winded, Molly ran even faster. Still without glancing back, the woman increased her own speed and continued to pull away. Apparently she was fresh, and Molly, who'd already run over three miles, was at a disadvantage. Each breath sent pain burning through her right side, as if a hot wire were probing between her ribs, and she knew she wouldn't be able to run for much distance.

If only she could get close enough to catch a glimpse of the woman's face! About two hundred feet separated them now and Molly was still falling back.

She decided to try getting the woman to turn around.

"Hey!" she yelled, but not loud enough. It was difficult to muster a forceful expulsion of air, winded as she was and running fast. She deliberately broke stride, sucking in a long breath then tightening her muscles, tensing to hurl javelins of sound. "Hey! Wait up, you! Turn around, dammit!" Better. Louder.

The woman seemed not to have heard and was running even faster, gaining ground. Soon she was almost out of sight around a curve in the trail, pulling away rapidly, a bright splash of red, her white soles still flashing, her arms swinging.

Then she was beyond the trees and out of sight.

Molly slowed down, kicked angrily at a pebble, then began to walk. Two men jogged past her, chatting casually but breathlessly about the economy, their voices wavering with each stride. A squirrel scurried across the trail ahead of her and scampered in a spiral up a tree to disappear among low branches.

Molly walked slowly, listening to the low, oceanlike roar of traffic outside the park, and the sharper, closer chattering of a jay. The bird sounded frightened and furious, as if it might be protecting its young.

When she neared the starting point of her run, she began jogging again to work off some of her frustration.

Farther along the trail, the woman slowed her pace and fell into an easy jog that was barely faster than a walk. She peeled off the mirror-lens glasses and grinned. Ahead of her, leaning against the trunk of a huge oak tree, Deirdre stood waiting.

Deirdre stood up straight, then began jogging toward her, but she stayed on the grass and at an angle to the trail, in case the winded Molly would begin running again and happen along and see them.

Deirdre kept her eyes fixed on Darlene and smiled, then began to laugh out loud, uncontrollably, as she jogged. The laughter bubbled from her continuously like cold, clear water from a spring. Several people stared at her. A young man and a child stopped and gaped at her peculiar behavior. She didn't care. They didn't understand her. Even people who thought they knew her didn't understand her.

Weren't *they* usually surprised?

Deirdre slowed down. Darlene met her and walked beside her, breathing hard from her run but by no means exhausted. Even though Darlene had assured her she was up to the task, Deirdre was surprised that such a frail-looking woman could summon so much stamina.

"I did what you said," Darlene told her, "stayed ahead of her so she couldn't quite catch up, played with her."

"You must be in terrific condition," Deirdre said.

"I am. I dance."

"Seriously?"

"I'm in ballet. That's as serious as dance gets. If I had to, I could run another five miles right now." She crossed her slender arms as she walked and glanced over at Deirdre. "You think it was right, to play a joke like that on Molly?"

"Why not? She's married to David."

Darlene stared at her in a funny way, as if taking a fresh look. "That's hardly a good reason, Deirdre."

"It's reason enough for me." Deirdre lowered her voice to make it clear that there was no room for argument. "I'd like to come see you dance sometime."

"Sure," Darlene said. She sounded pleased. "I'll let you know."

They were well away from the trail now. Deirdre slowed her pace. Darlene's breathing was perfectly normal now, and the glisten of perspiration was gone from her long, tanned legs.

A man who'd been feeding pigeons rose from a bench in the shade and wandered off. Deirdre walked toward the unoccupied bench, scattering the pigeons as she approached, and the two women sat down. They were in the shade, out of sight of Molly if she happened to jog past on the trail.

Deirdre remembered when she'd first seen Darlene in New York, sitting on a suitcase in the bus terminal, looking at the rack of magazines in a nearby kiosk. She didn't look lonely, but she seemed vulnerable. Deirdre had found herself drifting toward the magazine rack, knowing it wasn't magazines that drew her. But it was Darlene who struck up a conversation, asking Deirdre if she was new to the city. As if Darlene couldn't tell.

"Molly yelled something at me when I started to pull away from her," Darlene said, bringing Deirdre back to the present.

"Was it my name?"

"I don't think so." Darlene gave her that funny look again. "I thought you two hadn't met. Why would she think I was you?"

"She saw me once. She knows what I look like, more or less, wearing the cap and sunglasses I asked you to put on."

"Then that's why she was trying so hard to catch up with me. You didn't explain that part of the joke."

Deirdre watched a pigeon peck persistently at the hard earth, somehow knowing there was something beneath the surface worth getting at. "It wasn't exactly a joke that we played on Molly."

"No, I guess not." Darlene, too, was studying the pigeon. "I think what we did to her was cruel, Deirdre."

"You agreed to it."

"But I didn't know then why you wanted to taunt her. Just because she's married to David, that's no way for you to behave. No way for you to win David back."

"David will never know about it."

"Yes he will. Molly will tell him."

"He won't believe her. I can make sure of that."

"Is that your plan?" Darlene asked. "To drive a wedge between them?"

"I hadn't thought about it, but that wouldn't be a bad plan."

"I disagree," Darlene said. "Why don't you face up to the fact that your relationship with David is over and get on with your life?"

"That phrase about people getting on with their lives is the worst kind of psychobabble," Deirdre said. "Unless we decide to commit suicide, none of us has any choice other than to get on with our life."

"It's *how* we get on with life that's important, Deirdre. We can accept fate and be content, or we can fight it and be miserable."

"It isn't that simple!"

Darlene looked around, embarrassed. "*Shh*. You're raising your voice."

"You're the one talking too loud," Deirdre said. "People are staring."

"They're staring at you, not me." Darlene stood up from the bench. "I'm going now."

Deirdre suddenly felt guilty, unworthy. Darlene was one of those people who could do that to her. It was something she hadn't counted on. "I suppose you're mad at me now."

Darlene looked down at her, smiled, and shook her head. "No, it isn't that. If I don't leave, I'll be late for dance class."

"You're always dashing away somewhere so you won't be late."

"I lead a busy life."

"Busier than mine."

"It doesn't have to be that way, Deirdre. You'll meet people, have fun. You'll see."

"I'm not even sure that's what I want."

"What *do* you want?" Darlene suddenly raised a forefinger to her lips. "No! Never mind, don't tell me. There's no time." She began walking backward, grinning at Deirdre. "We'll get together soon."

"When?"

Without answering, Darlene lifted her arm in a wave, then spun gracefully to face the direction she was going.

Deirdre sat and watched her walk away. After about fifty feet, Darlene began to jog. She ran with beautiful long strides and perfect balance, her head held high and not bouncing at all. All that ballet, Deirdre thought, as Darlene passed from sight.

Deirdre continued staring after her. There was something about Darlene she didn't like, she decided.

And she knew what it was.

Darlene was beginning to treat her the way other people often did. As if there might be something wrong with her.

Didn't she know that could be dangerous?

Silver's Gym in midtown Manhattan was crowded that evening. All of the Nautilus equipment was in use, and four exhausted-looking women were riding the stationary bicycles side by side. Two men were waiting for David to finish his bench presses with the free weights so they could use them. Herb Mindle, a psychiatrist whose office was nearby, was spotting for David, as David, on his back on the padded bench, struggled to raise the heavy barbell for the fourth time and set it in its supports. He was doing three sets of four with the weights near his maximum capacity, trying to build bulk.

"You're there!" Mindle said, staying back but ready to jump in and support the weight if David's strength failed.

David let out a long *whoosh!* of air as he let the barbell drop into the cradle of the bench's vertical supports.

"Want to use this thing?" he asked as he sat up and wiped his face with a towel.

"No thanks," Mindle said. "I'll spot for these guys."

David got up and walked toward the locker room, noticing that the clock over the door read seven-fifteen. Molly was expecting him at eight.

He showered, dressed, packed his workout clothes in his small blue nylon duffle bag, then left the gym. Mindle, just standing up from having done his sets of bench presses, waved to him as he went out the door. The women on the stationary bicycles were still at it.

He was three blocks away from the gym, walking along the crowded sidewalk toward his subway stop, when he heard Deirdre's voice.

"David! Again! My God, I don't believe it!"

He couldn't hold down his pleasure at seeing her, but he knew this seemingly chance meeting had to have been planned. "Listen, Deirdre, this is more than coinci—"

He stopped talking as he noticed the man who was obviously with Deirdre. He was tall, balding, a businessman of some sort, apparently, with his muted checked gray suit and conservative tie. He was slender through the chest and shoulders but had put on weight around the middle so that his stomach bulged noticeably over his belt beneath his unbuttoned suit coat. His face was bland and amiable, and he wore thick glasses without frames that made his eyes look immense and strangely innocent.

"David!" Deirdre almost squealed with pleasure. "I was sure we'd never meet again!"

Before he could move, she'd leaned forward and pecked him on the cheek. Her red hair looked particularly wild and attractive in the summer breeze, and she was wearing a simple but low-cut beige linen dress and matching pumps. When she moved in close to kiss him, a disturbing and not unpleasant scent of perfume and perspiration came to him.

"Where are you going?" she asked.

"Subway station, then home." He'd sounded curt, surlier than he'd intended. The man glanced at him.

"Oh!" Deirdre said, stepping back. "This is my very good friend Craig Chumley. Craig, meet David Jones, my ex."

Chumley looked surprised. "As in ex-husband?"

"Uh-huh! He sure is." She seemed oddly proud of David. She squeezed Chumley's arm. "Well, what'd you think, my ex would be old and bald as a cucumber?"

Chumley laughed, a bit ill at ease, perhaps because he was one of those men who tried to disguise baldness with long strands of hair plastered sideways across their heads, like loosely thatched lids at the mercy of the wind. He had yellowed teeth and oversized bicuspids that gave him a faintly canine look when he laughed.

"Craig and I were on our way to dinner," she said. "He promised to show me the Rainbow Room. Ever been to the famous Rainbow Room, David?"

"No."

"You really oughta take Molly there sometime. Hey, why not tonight? You want to join us? Four's company."

David smiled. He was feeling better every second. Maybe it was Chumley's presence, but today Deirdre seemed not at all threatening to his libido.

"Four's more likely to be a crowd," he said, looking at Chumley, who was rocking back and forth on the heels of his huge wingtip shoes, like a man testing the precariousness of his situation.

"Well, maybe some other time. Maybe I'll call you." Deirdre lowered her voice, as if trading a confidence. "You know, David, I wrote a note and a phone number where I could be reached in New York and slipped it in your jacket pocket when we met the other day. Did you find it?"

"No," he lied, "I hardly ever use my suit coat pockets."

"I knew at the deli you'd refuse to call if I suggested it, so I thought I'd let you think on it. I hoped you'd make the first call and we could talk. The past isn't so threatening that we need to be afraid of it, David. We definitely should be friends."

"The past doesn't seem so terrible or threatening to me," he said.

"Why, David!" she said with a dazzling smile, pretending, or perhaps actually believing, he'd complimented her.

Chumley glanced at his wristwatch, caught David looking at him, and shrugged as if in apology for being ill-mannered.

"We have reservations," he explained, a helpless victim of time.

"So have I," David said, looking directly at Deirdre.

"We'd better get on to the restaurant," Deirdre said, "or they'll give our table to some celebrity." She took Chumley's long arm. "You call me, David, hear? Friendship is olden and golden and shouldn't be tossed on the trash mound."

He didn't answer.

"Nice meeting you, Dave," Chumley said, and held out a long, pale hand toward David.

David shook hands with him. "Enjoy the Rainbow Room."

"Oh, we will!" Deirdre said.

She surprised David by kissing Chumley full on the mouth. Seemed to surprise Chumley, too.

They were holding hands as they walked away toward East Fifty-fourth Street.

David watched them until they'd disappeared in the throng of heat-weary people who had dropped in elevators from one plane of their lives to another and, like him, were wending their way from work to home. Chumley was definitely a welcome addition to the Deirdre equation. Whatever temptation she might be to David, whatever wiles she might have worked, any involvement was less likely now. David felt safe from her. From himself.

Twenty minutes later he was on the subway, roaring through darkness toward Molly and Michael.

Molly was sitting quietly in the apartment living room, the back of her head resting against the sofa's thick upholstery. The room was eclectically and comfortably furnished: overstuffed sofa, well-stocked bookcases, framed museum prints on the walls. A console TV with a VCR on top sat against the wall opposite the sofa. Near the double-window was Molly's desk with a green-shaded banker's lamp, reference books, a ceramic coffee mug stuffed with pencils next to the architectural manuscript.

Her body jerked against the soft back and arm of the sofa as a key grated in the lock. Her mind had wandered; she'd been thinking about this morning, the woman in the park.

She set aside the *New York Times* she'd been reading when she'd lost concentration. The door opened and David came in. He dropped his blue duffle bag on the chair where he usually tossed his attaché case.

"Hi, Mol." He walked around behind her, leaned over the sofa, and kissed the top of her head, her hair. She stood up as he went to the closet by the door and hung his suit coat on a hanger. He removed his tie, the paisley one she'd given him last Christmas, and draped it over the back of the chair.

Molly had parted her lips to tell him about the woman in the park when he said, "I ran into Deirdre again. There was a man with her."

She listened as he described his meeting with Deirdre and Craig Chumley.

"She'd left a note with her phone number in my coat pocket," he said. "I told her I hadn't found it, but I had. I didn't bother calling her."

"Apparently she wasn't offended," Molly said.

"More disappointed, it seemed. I do think she simply wants to exorcise some old demons, to be friends. Enough time's passed that it's possible, I suppose."

"Who's this Chumley?" Molly asked.

David shrugged. "Just a guy she met through her job, is the impression I got." He walked into the kitchen. She heard water run in the sink. Silence. He returned to the living room holding a glass of water. His upper lip was wet and glistening. "They were on their way to the Rainbow Room for dinner. She invited us to join them."

"Both of us?"

"That's what she said. I doubt if Chumley was keen on it, though. He seemed relieved when I declined." He walked over and kissed her lightly on the lips, looked down at her with an adoration so obvious that she feared it was feigned. "Listen, Mol, I think both of us have reacted a little extremely to Deirdre popping up here in New York."

"Maybe," Molly said, wondering where this was going.

"She's not going to be in town that long," David said, "and she's tied to her job back in Saint Louis. I guess what I'm trying to say is, if she and this Chumley want to have dinner with us, maybe we should accept."

"I'm not so sure, David . . ."

"I know how you feel, honey, and I don't blame you. She's my former wife and you don't want her in the same orbit, even the same solar system, that our family's in."

"Try galaxy."

"I feel the same way, and she really isn't in the same galaxy, except she's just a visitor—like in *Star Trek*. Couple of days and she'll be beamed back to Saint Louis via TWA."

Molly didn't know quite what to make of what he'd just told her. Another chance meeting on the street, and this time Deirdre had a man in tow.

"I want to make sure we understand each other about Deirdre," she said.

"And I want you to understand she doesn't seem to harbor any sort of malice toward you or me."

"Why is she so intent on seeing you?"

"She's curious about me. About us." He took another sip of water then swirled the liquid around in the glass for a moment, staring down at it. "Mol, after the divorce she met someone, got pregnant." Half a lie, he thought. What difference did it make who had fathered the dead fetus? "He . . . well, he physically abused her and injured the baby. It had to be aborted. The incident still haunts her."

"God, that's terrible."

"I think all she wants is to have a quiet dinner with us and Chumley, talk for a while, and lay the past to rest. Can you understand that?"

"I should be able to, I suppose."

"Neither of us has anything to fear."

"Neither of us?"

"That's right. She and Chumley are in at least the early stages of a hot romantic relationship. They're into French kissing in public."

"How reassuring."

David grinned. "Poor Chumley. Deirdre can be very moody. There's no way for him to know what he's getting into. Anyway, if they ask us to dinner again, how about it?"

"Is this some kind of test?" She waited for his reply.

Instead of answering, he said, "Have I mentioned Deirdre's hair is red now? I guess she wants to jazz herself up, make herself look younger, but to tell you the truth she's still kind of worn-down and ordinary."

Twisting the truth to protect her; what had she to fear from this older woman? Molly couldn't help smiling. She went to him. "David, David . . ." She kissed him then backed away a step and stared at him. "Okay," she said, "if they invite us again, we'll go. But I'm not sharing any dip with her."

Molly watched him tilt back his head and finish his glass of water. She realized she'd been holding her breath, as if she'd been the one drinking. She moved closer to him and pressed her head into his shoulder. He hugged her, and she felt his hand gently patting her back. There was no reason to tell him about the woman in the park now, no point in pushing him on the subject. He might consider her paranoid about Deirdre, and he might be right. New York was undeniably well stocked with leggy women who jogged and wore baseball caps and sunglasses.

"Michael at Bernice's again?" David asked.

She nodded, prodding his chest with her forehead.

"Let's get him," he said, "then the three of us can go out and have some supper. Sound okay?"

"Sounds fine." She remembered the last time he'd suggested dinner under similar circumstances. It had been for just the two of them. She liked it better this way.

"Any preferences?" he asked.

"Anywhere but the Rainbow Room."

They settled on hot dogs from the vendor down the street.

David had been so reasonable she knew *she'd* been unreasonable. He could do that to her; it was one of the few infuriating things about him.

But he was right, she knew. She'd become unsettled about a woman she'd never met, who might indeed have nothing to do with the jogger Molly had seen in the park. *Probably* had nothing to do with her.

Not that it mattered, since Deirdre would soon be leaving New York to return to her home.

The only thing remotely bothering Molly now was a persistent feeling that she'd shied away from a fear she should have faced. And maybe she should have had more faith in David.

More faith in herself and the two of them together.

10

Molly met Traci Mack the next afternoon in Egan's, the lounge of the Darville Hotel on West Forty-fourth Street. Traci was the Link Publishing editor of the architectural manuscript. Molly had worked with her before, and the two women had become friends.

Traci merely glanced at the first half of the thick manuscript, *Architects of Desire,* with its yellow Post-it flags sticking out from between the pages. As the waiter brought their drinks—a glass of chardonnay for Molly, a martini for Traci—Traci stuffed the manuscript into her black leather attaché case and leaned the case against the legs of her chair. She was a tiny, fortyish woman with graying hair and a droll expression that seldom changed. Her eyes were dark and always narrowed into slits as if she were myopic, and she had a round face, underslung jaw, and long upper lip that made her resemble a turtle. Molly had never seen the diminutive Traci in anything other than sacklike black dresses of the sort often worn by heavyset women to disguise bulk. Traci must have owned half a dozen similar outfits. Her idea of getting dressed up was to wear a sash or a belt.

Molly sipped her wine and looked around Egan's. There were about a dozen other customers scattered about the lounge. It was upscale but functional in the way of hotel bars, with small, marble-topped tables and a long bar with a large-screen TV mounted above it. A soap opera was on the TV but fortunately there was no volume. Beyond the far end of the bar was an archway and a sign indicating that it led to the lobby. Molly and Traci were at one of the small marble tables near the window. It was cool in the lounge; bright and bustling Manhattan streamed past in the heat on the other side of the glass.

"Thanks for the first half of the manuscript, Mol," Traci said in her rasping voice. "Gonna have the last half by the end of next week?"

"Guaranteed," Molly said. A man in threadbare clothes walked past close to the window, glanced inside, and locked gazes with her, then moved faster as if ashamed of his misfortune. Something about him gave Molly a chill. They were separated by much more than a pane of glass, yet his world waited for the weak the way a lion waited and watched the herd for potential victims. That was how Molly was trying not to feel—like a victim.

Traci sat back, sighed, then smiled as she lifted her martini. "Enough of business. What's going on in your life?"

Molly told her.

Traci leaned back in her chair and looked thoughtful. "I've got to tell you, Mol, I don't think it's ever a good idea for wives and ex-wives to get together unless it's at hubby's funeral."

Molly laughed.

"I'm editing a mystery novel about that very situation," Traci said, "and it doesn't turn out well for the wife."

"Are you warning me that life might imitate art?"

"Maybe."

Molly had to ask. "So what happens to the wife in the novel?"

"The husband and the ex kill her then say she ran away. But she's really in the freezer of a neighbor who's on vacation. They dispose of her body little by little. What they can't get the neighbor's German Shepherd to eat, they get rid of with the trash compactor and the U.S. Mail."

Molly winced and tried to ignore the knot in her stomach. "Well, David and I have a strong marriage. If it can't survive us sitting through dinner with a sad, lonely woman who's only in town for a little while, I'll be surprised. Besides, she happens to be eleven years older than I am. What do I have to fear from a woman fast-approaching menopause?"

"Hold on, there!" Traci said, grinning.

Molly was embarrassed. "Oh, sorry . . ."

"People live longer and stay young longer these days. And a thirty-eight-year-old can be quite a sexpot." Traci used her tiny red plastic-sword swizzle stick to toy with the olive in her martini. "I thought you told me Deirdre was in love with some guy named Chalmers."

"Chumley," Molly corrected.

"Whatever. He's a man. She doesn't sound so sad and lonely to me."

"Or like any kind of a threat," Molly pointed out. "I admit I was hesitant at first, but now I'm looking forward to meeting both of them."

Traci speared and ate her olive. "That's amazing."

"I don't think so," Molly said, "among reasonable people."

"I don't believe I've ever met a reasonable person," Traci said. She raised her glass in a mock toast. "But anyway, I do commend you."

Molly ignored the toast. "I guess I see it as a test for our marriage," she admitted. "If it's as strong as I say it is, simply acknowledging Deirdre exists should do no harm. It will only make us stronger. Maybe all of us."

"I hope you're right." Traci finished her drink and placed her glass on its cork coaster. "Well, I'd better get back to Link. The author of *Sane Sex for Singles* is coming in to the office and I want to meet her." She dropped some bills from a pocket of the black dress onto the table to cover her share of the check. "I'll leave you to go home and finish the other half of our flying buttresses manuscript." She bent down and picked up the leather attaché case. "Good luck with your dinner Saturday night. Whatever Deirdre is, you're a young and attractive woman with a nice figure. Wear something that'll knock her and her boyfriend dead."

"Deirdre told David we're dressing casual," Molly said. "I don't think anybody wants this to be a big deal. In fact, that's the whole idea, that it's no big deal. Then everyone will be reassured."

"Maybe," Traci said. "But take my advice and wear something tight."

11

Deirdre walked into Rico's Restaurant wearing a tight black knit halter dress and black spike heels. Her hair was a vibrant, fiery red, and her makeup was as bold as her walk.

Rico's was a modest restaurant done in dark woods and reds, with candle holders in the center of each table providing most of the illumination. It was intimate rather than fancy. Deirdre was the brightest thing in it. She was knock-dead gorgeous. Every male head in the restaurant turned to follow her progress as she made her way to the corner table where Molly and David waited.

Molly had gone light with her makeup and hadn't done much with her hair, and she was wearing jeans and a white blouse. She'd noticed at the restaurant, too late, that Michael had drooled chocolate milk on the right shoulder of the blouse just before she and David had left to walk to Rico's.

As Deirdre approached, smiling, Molly told herself not to feel inferior. She was younger than this woman—and she was the one who had Michael. It was a plan, Deirdre showing up here dressed like that. It was a goddamned plan and Molly was determined not to let it work.

But she *was* intimidated and couldn't entirely deny it.

David stood up from the table, letting his napkin slide from his lap to the floor.

"Where's Chumley?" he asked.

"He sends his regrets," Deirdre said, looking directly at David. She hadn't yet looked at Molly. "He had to work late tonight. He's in the import-export business, you know. Maybe his ship came in."

David seemed to come out of his daze. "Molly, this is Deirdre." He stooped quickly and picked up his napkin.

A waiter seemed to spring from the floor and pulled a chair back for Deirdre, who sat down with a calculated show of leg and cleavage. "You're as young and pretty as David said," she told Molly. Then to the waiter, before Molly could acknowledge the compliment: "I'll have a vodka martini on the rocks with a lime twist."

The waiter nodded and retreated.

Deirdre smiled and looked from Molly to David, waiting for conversation but not at all ill at ease. Molly told herself again not to be intimidated by this woman.

David picked up the glass of beer he'd been drinking, then set it back down. He nervously wiped his damp fingers on his napkin. "You and Chumley seemed to be getting along well when I saw you yesterday," he said to Deirdre.

"Craig's a dear. I'm lucky to have found him." She turned to Molly. "And you're lucky to have found David. Unbelievably lucky. Oh, he's not perfect—and believe me, I know all about him—but I think he's turned into a real winner."

The waiter returned with Deirdre's drink. She hesitated until he was gone, then she raised her glass. "Well, here's blood in your eye."

"That's— No, never mind," David said.

They all sipped from their drinks while the silence at the table stretched to awkwardness.

"Deirdre's in the shoe business," David finally blurted out.

Molly stared dead-eyed at him.

"Well, not anymore," Deirdre said. "That is, I won't be for long if things work out right. Craig Chumley's offered me a job as his assistant. Everything about it sounds wonderful. I haven't said yes yet, but I'm considering it."

It took Molly a few seconds to absorb what that might mean. She sat stunned for another few seconds before she could speak. She glanced at David, who looked down at his lap. "But don't you have friends, a home, obligations in Saint Louis?"

Deirdre seemed not to notice her discomfort. "Nothing I can't walk away from," she said. "Of course, the cost of living's a lot higher here in New York than it is in the Midwest. I'll just have to sit down and figure it all out. Run it up the flagpole and see if it salutes."

Molly felt David's hand come to rest on hers as he spoke. "I got the impression yesterday, Deirdre, that there was something . . . I mean, some affection between you and Chumley."

"Oh, there is. He's a wonderful man. That's certainly something else I'll have to take into consideration." She picked up a menu and studied it for a few seconds. "Is the cannelloni good here? One thing I don't have to worry about is my figure. Not yet, anyway."

"All the pasta's good here," David told her. He ran his forefinger around the rim of his glass. "Deirdre, this is kind of a bombshell."

"You mean my figure?" She laughed. "No, you mean the cannelloni."

Molly kicked the side of David's leg, hard, under the table.

"What I mean," David said, showing no sign of pain, "is that the kind of move you're talking about is a major step for anyone to take. You seem to be doing it almost on a whim. New York can be a hard city to live in."

Jewelry and bright red enamel flashed as Deirdre made a casual backhand motion of dismissal. "Don't worry about me, you two. I always jump before I leap."

"But you don't know anything about the import-export business, do you?" Molly asked.

"What's to learn?" Deirdre said. "Import, export. In and out, in and out . . . I'll be an expert in no time."

"Yep," Molly said. She felt David's foot nudge hers beneath the table.

"Let's stop talking about me," Deirdre said. "Tell me about Michael." She leaned forward with her elbows on the table. More cleavage. "Does he look like David?"

"More like Molly, actually," David said.

"He looks exactly like David," Molly said.

Deirdre smiled directly at her. Great, even white teeth, Molly noticed. Though it was oddly carnivorous, it was a smile that dazzled. "He could do a lot worse," Deirdre said. She beamed her full attention at David. "One thing I'm going to need is an apartment. Do either of you know of a good one that's available? Is this a decent neighborhood?"

"We like it," David said.

Molly thought it was good that no one at the table was carrying a gun.

The waiter approached to take their orders.

Molly caught his attention first.

"I'll have the cannelloni," she said.

That night Molly stood before the medicine cabinet mirror in the bathroom and assessed her image. She was preparing for bed and was wearing only her FOR SLEEP OR SEX T-shirt and panties. She was attractive enough, she thought. Not the potential watermelon queen of the state fair like Deirdre, but she knew she appealed to men—at least some men. David. She thought. No, she was sure.

She pulled up the front of her shirt and rubbed a hand across her slightly protruding stomach. Normal, she assured herself. Even Deirdre would have a slight stomach paunch. Maybe even a few stretch marks like the ones in the mirror. Surely any thirty-eight-year-old woman would have given some ground to gravity and age. She pinched the excess flesh around her waist. According to that cereal commercial on TV she needed to lose weight. But then they were trying to talk her into buying cereal instead of doughnuts.

Okay, they'd eat fewer doughnuts.

Dissatisfied with herself, she let the T-shirt drop. She ran some cold water, bent over the washbasin, and began vigorously brushing her teeth.

She'd closed the bathroom door only halfway. It was pushed all the way open and David stood in the doorway looking in at her. He was wearing only his T-shirt and jockey briefs.

Okay," he said, "it didn't go well. It's a shame Chumley wasn't there. He seems like a nice enough guy, and they're obviously crazy about each other."

Molly leaned closer to the washbasin and spat. "If the woman were a fish, she'd be a piranha."

David smiled. "I thought you were going to say shark."

"No. Sharks are honest predators. They take big bites then swim on." She wiped a washcloth almost viciously across her mouth and dropped her toothbrush back in the porcelain holder. "Piranhas take small bites, but lots of them."

"Come on, Mol. She isn't that bad. I'll admit she's a little flaky. In fact, a lot flakier than she used to be. But at heart she's a decent enough person."

Molly put the toothpaste back in the medicine cabinet and held his gaze in the partly opened mirrored door. "Then why did you two divorce?"

"Incompatibility, like the divorce decree said."

"Weren't you the one who decided to end the marriage?"

She saw guilt cross his face for an instant. He'd lied to her.

"Yes," he said, "at a certain point. But legally which of us left the other would depend on whose lawyer you asked. And maybe I wasn't such a decent sort myself in those days."

"She left you, didn't she?"

"At a certain point, maybe." A brittle, defensive note had found its way into his voice. "It's hard to say now. And it doesn't matter now."

"Jesus, David!"

She switched off the light and walked into the bedroom, aware that he was close behind her. She got into bed, didn't look at him as she heard the sheets rustle as he climbed in beside her, felt the mattress give beneath the weight of his body and heard the bedsprings whine. She wondered if there was some way to get bedsprings to be quiet; she was sure they could be heard next door or in the apartment below. She lay facing away from him, silent. He settled down and was silent, too. The window was open but the air conditioner was off. Sounds of nighttime traffic wafted in. Someone shouting far away. What might have been a gunshot. The city kept getting more dangerous.

"Did I hear Michael?" David asked.

"No." She knew he was only trying to forge an opening so they would talk. All right, if that was what he wanted.

Still facing away from him, she said, "That abortion story you told me, was that true?"

"Of course! Deirdre's been through a lot, and she feels middle-age sneaking up on her. She's jealous of you, Mol."

Molly wasn't convinced. "Some older woman!"

"It really doesn't matter," David said.

"Do you think she's had cosmetic surgery?"

"I don't know. Or care."

"Sometimes you can tell if you look closely. Around the eyelids."

"To tell you the truth, Mol, I think you're acting a little paranoid about this. It's the younger woman who's supposed to be a threat to the older one."

Molly sat up in bed and switched on the reading lamp. "I can't believe it! You're actually defending her!"

David stayed down. Not rising to the bait, she thought.

"Not really defending her," he said. "I'm just trying to inject a modicum of reason into this conversation."

It angered Molly when he did that, tried to take the high philosophical and moral ground. "I don't want to see her again. I don't want you to see her again."

He still didn't move, his face pressed sideways into his pillow, slightly distorting his words. "We probably won't run into each other again. And if she and Chumley want to have dinner with us, we can politely decline. Is that good enough?"

"It would be if I didn't think you were just trying to please me." She switched off the light and settled back down, lying facing away from him again in the dimness. A breeze pressed in through the open window, swaying the curtains. Shadows danced.

He moved closer, she could hear the sheets rustle, feel the warmth of his breath on the back of her neck. "What's wrong with doing something just to please you? I love you, Mol. I enjoy doing things to please you."

"I do things to please you, too, don't I? Wasn't I polite to Deirdre? I mean, under the circumstances?"

He moved in closer, snaked an arm over her, kissed her cheek. "You're always polite. I told you, you're civilized. It's one of the things I love about you."

She didn't answer.

"Mol?" He kissed her cheek again, then used a finger to toy with her ear. She forced herself to lie still and not respond. "What are you thinking about, Mol?"

"Architecture," she said.

12

Deirdre stood hunched close to the public phone, as if to keep her conversation as private as possible, though she was alone on the dark street of shabby office buildings and closed shops. There wasn't much light except for the corner where the phone was, and where some faintly glowing show windows cast pale dim illumination over the sidewalk half a block away. A red neon sign near the intersection said that used watches were sold there. There was a faint but ripe smell of sewage in the night air.

"I've decided to stay in New York," she told Darlene. "To live here."

"That would be a mistake, Deirdre." Darlene's voice on the phone was firm and positive. "You must not have thought this all the way through."

"Oh, but I have. And I know this is the place for me. That I absolutely belong here."

Darlene laughed. "I'm not sure anyone belongs here. New York is a hard city. It will allow you anything and forgive you nothing."

"Like the rest of the world."

"No, much harder than the rest of the world. Most of that world, anyway."

"*You* more or less live here."

"I'm used to it."

"Then I can get used to it," Deirdre said.

"What about your job in Saint Louis? What will you do for money here in New York?"

"I have a job lined up."

"What sort of job?"

"Import and export. In and out."

Darlene was quiet. Deirdre could imagine her sitting in her apartment, maybe with a cup of tea beside her, with her legs curled beneath her and her hair and makeup perfect. Like in a movie. Maybe she even had a white telephone.

"Listen, Deirdre," Darlene finally said, "it isn't that I don't like your company—"

"Oh, sure."

"C'mon now, Deirdre, give me a break. I'm only trying to keep you from making the same mistake made by a lot of people unfamiliar with how New York can be for them. It's a dangerous city."

"Everywhere is dangerous. I learned that early. Horrible things can happen to you even at home in your own bed."

"I wish I could change your mind."

"You try," Deirdre said, "but you can't change the way I think. The way I am. Or arrange my life so it's like yours. You'll have to have the wisdom to accept what you can't arrange."

"Where are you calling from?" Darlene asked.

"It doesn't matter."

"What are you going to do now?"

"I'm going to the movies. In New York, you can go to the movies almost any time of the day or night. It's wonderful."

A man in a grimy green muscle shirt, cut off so his protruding stomach showed, appeared a few feet away from the phone. He looked like a small, chunky Burt Lancaster, only with darker hair on his head and more hair on his body. Even his stomach was dark with hair. He grinned and Burt Lancaster was there even stronger, only uglier, with much coarser features.

"You don't know the parts of town that are dangerous," Darlene said on the phone.

"You about done talkin', sweetheart?" the man asked. Above the grin, his eyes consumed her.

"Who said that?" Darlene sounded alarmed.

"Don't worry. It's just some guy waiting to use the phone."

Burt Lancaster grinned wider.

"Deirdre, listen—"

"Sorry, Darlene, I've gotta hang up. The gentleman wants to make a call. I'll phone you back later about New York."

She replaced the receiver and started to walk away from the

phone. Burt was suddenly in front of her, still with the toothy grin. Didn't he know he was overdoing it?

"This is a bad neighborhood, sweets. Interesting things can happen to a looker like you."

"You're in the wrong role," Deirdre said. "Even the wrong movie."

"Role? Movie?" He shook his head, then glanced up and down the dark street. "You're gonna play the scene just like I tell you, so you might as well accept that fact. You might say I'm gonna be your director." His hand touched his crotch. "You really wouldn't mind that at all, would you?"

Deirdre's right arm shot straight out so the heel of her hand slammed into the man's nose.

He backed up several steps, his fingers clutching his broken nose. There was blood on his shirt and dribbling down onto his hairy stomach.

For an instant rage almost propelled him toward her, then he seemed to notice what was in her eyes. It wasn't the fear he'd expected. It was something else entirely. He stood still.

She stepped toward him, and he moved away.

"I was only trying to be nice to you," he said, spitting blood.

"You've already been very nice to me," Deirdre told him. "Maybe you can be even nicer."

He stared at her with uncomprehending eyes, then turned and walked quickly away.

She stood still. He glanced back twice to make sure she wasn't following.

When he saw that she was smiling, he walked even faster and crossed the street.

She shrugged and shook her head. "Men!" she said softly to herself.

13

David was sitting in his office Monday morning, staring idly at his desk photo of Molly and Michael, when Lisa walked in.

Her glance followed his gaze, and she looked quickly away from the photo with a momentary expression of pain. David didn't notice.

"Someone in the outer office wants to see you," she said. "A woman named Deirdre."

David felt his body tense.

"Something wrong?" Lisa asked.

"No . . . no, nothing."

"So you want me to send her back here?"

"No," David said. He didn't want Deirdre to see his office, didn't want any more familiarity than was necessary. Or maybe he didn't want to be alone with her. "I'll go out front and talk to her."

As he entered the anteroom, Lisa was sitting down at the curved receptionist's desk, preparing to busy herself with paperwork. It was a sparsely but comfortably furnished area. Lisa's desk was near oak double doors to the main offices. There was a black leather sofa, a low table with a smoked glass top with glossy magazines fanned out on it like a colorful poker hand full of face cards. On the wall behind the sofa was a glass-covered collage of dust jackets from books sold by the agency.

Deirdre was seated on the sofa with her legs crossed. She was dressed down from Saturday night at the restaurant but still looked glamorous in very tight jeans, a green blouse, and low-heeled shoes. Her perfume, not so much sweet as a musky, primal scent, came to David as she stood up and smiled at him. There was no sound in the reception area other than muted laughter somewhere outside in the hall.

Deirdre took a step toward him. "I guess you're surprised to see me, David, but I wanted to kind of clear the atmosphere. I got the impression at the restaurant that Molly was a little aggravated by the situation."

From the corner of his eye David saw Lisa look up from her paperwork.

"No, no," he said to Deirdre, "she'd just had a hard day and was a little touchy."

Deirdre's smile wavered slightly as if she were nervous. "I need your help, David. A favor."

"Well . . ."

"A woman I met, Darlene, told me about a furnished apartment near here that's for rent. I have a key and I'm supposed to go by and look at it. The rental agent should meet me there, but this is the big city, and I guess I'm a little scared to go alone. Anyway, I don't even know what to look for in a New York apartment."

"The agent gave you a key?"

"Well, I sort of talked him into it . . ."

David swallowed as he realized where the conversation was headed. "Listen, Deirdre, I'm not sure—"

She'd moved closer to him; she extended her arm and brushed his chest with the tip of her middle finger, somehow making the gesture extremely intimate. "It *is* lunchtime, David, and when I realized I was near your office, I thought, My God, I *do* have a male friend in the big city! I was sure you'd take ten minutes to walk around the corner with me and look at this place. I'd feel a lot better if a man—if you—okayed the apartment before I made any kind of commitment."

David saw that Lisa was staring at Deirdre curiously now, her paperwork forgotten. Deirdre swiveled her head a few inches and stared back. Immediately Lisa turned her attention to the papers on the desk.

"I don't know . . ." David said. He wanted to go with Deirdre, but something in the core of him told him to refuse.

"Ten little minutes out of your life is all I'm asking, David."

Deirdre smiled again, this time with subtle challenge. "Are you afraid Molly wouldn't approve?"

"It isn't that," he said. He glanced over at Lisa, who was studiously not paying attention.

"Now, David . . ."

"All right," he heard himself say. "Give me a minute while I save what's on my computer."

"Sure," Deirdre said. "Better safe than worry. And thank you, David! You don't know how reassuring this is."

She watched him as he disappeared through the oak doors behind the receptionist's desk.

Now Lisa did look up from her paperwork. "There's a copy of *Home Companion* on the coffee table for you to read while you're waiting," she said. "It might give you some decorating ideas."

"Thanks," Deirdre said. "I see it right next to a copy of *Mind Your Own Business.*"

Only seconds after Deirdre and David had left the office, Josh wandered in and stood at the desk near Lisa.

He gave her his amiable grin that always made her think he should be the host of a TV game show. "Looking out for your boss, Lisa?"

Obviously embarrassed, she glared at him. "I've got a feeling he needs looking out for. Did you see that woman?"

"Did I ever."

"She wants him to help her look for an apartment."

"No kidding? I think she might be his ex-wife." He placed his palms on the desk and leaned close to her, still grinning. "You jealous?"

She pretended to stab at him with a pencil and he faded back neatly to avoid the sharp point. "Find something to do, Josh."

"An apartment . . ." she heard him say as he walked back toward his office. "A *pied-à-terre.*"

"Be quiet, Josh."

"A love nest . . ."

14

It was a corner apartment on the thirty-fourth floor of a stone and glass building on Second Avenue. The hall was white and carpeted in beige. At the end of the hall was a tall, narrow window, but most of the illumination was provided by brass sconces set high on the walls to reflect light off the white ceiling. The apartment doors looked like darkly grained wood but David suspected they were steel.

Deirdre handed him the key. The small cardboard tag attached to it by a string read 34F. After making sure they were at the right door, he fit the key into the deadbolt lock above the doorknob, turned it, then pushed the door open. Stale air wafted toward the hall, as if the apartment had been unoccupied for a while.

"You'd better go first, David," Deirdre said behind him.

He stepped into the apartment. The living room was bright, small, and uncluttered, with abstract prints on the walls, a low-slung modern sofa and angular slate-topped tables. A black, lacquered wall unit held a large-screen TV, a stereo, and some crystal animal figures. Half a dozen books that appeared never to have been read were propped between large onyx bookends in the shape of charging bulls that seemed to be squeezing the books together.

A loud metallic click made him turn.

Deirdre had locked the door behind them.

David looked back to the apartment's interior. "Hello!"

No answer.

"I don't guess the rental agent's here yet," Deirdre said. She began to walk around slowly and hesitantly, like a wary trespasser, touching objects randomly and gently as if to reassure herself that they really did exist. "Look at all the light streaming through that window!" she exclaimed. "It's beautiful! I love this room!"

"It's well furnished if you like modern," David said. He didn't like modern and thought the apartment looked like a futuristic art gallery.

"Darlene said the man who lives here sells and demonstrates electronics. He needs to sublease because he travels all over the world and he's going to make his home base in London for a while. He's smart like you are, David."

"If I were smart, I wouldn't be here."

"Don't you believe it," she said.

He trailed behind her as she walked to a short hall and glanced into the kitchen gleaming with white cabinets and appliances. She gave the black and white tiled bathroom the same cursory examination. The open door at the end of the hall led to the bedroom. She entered and he paused in the doorway, then followed.

The bedroom contained only a king-sized bed, a dresser, a chair, and a small triangular table with a lamp and heavy glass ashtray on it. Beyond the foot of the bed was a wide window whose light was barely muted by gauzy white ceiling-to-floor curtains.

"You *did* say a rental agent was supposed to meet you here, didn't you?" David asked.

"That's what I thought someone said to me, but they might have been mistaken."

He knew that the odds on a rental agent showing up were slim.

Deirdre walked to the wide window and located the pull cord. Rollers rasped in their traverse-rod track as she parted the curtains.

"Just look at this view, David!"

He dutifully walked across the bedroom's plush rose carpet and stood at the window.

The view was toward the river and Queens. Afternoon sun highlighted the tall buildings so they were deceptively beautiful. The ornate steel suspension of the Queensboro Bridge was visible. Far below in the shadowed and sun-hazed canyons, tiny cars and foreshortened pedestrians crawled along in symmetrical puzzle-patterns of activity.

He heard, then felt, Deirdre move close behind him.

"What do you see, David?" Her voice was soft.

"New York. Too many people hurrying and not knowing where they're going."

He felt her fingertips on his shoulder and he turned.

"Now what do you see?"

She was standing even closer than he'd thought and had unbuttoned her blouse almost all the way down. She wasn't wearing a bra and her large, firm breasts parted the fabric. One erect nipple was visible.

David opened his mouth, about to say her name, then her lips were closed over his, warm and writhing, soft and insistent. He felt the velvet wedge of her tongue.

With an effort of will and physical strength, he broke away from the kiss.

"Not a good idea, Deirdre." He was breathing hard.

Desire glowed like fever in her eyes. "It was once. It can be again. Besides, you want to."

"That doesn't make it a good idea."

He started to walk away from her but she blocked him with the length of her body, smiling up at him. She kissed him again. He resisted again, but not as determinedly.

"Listen, Deirdre . . ." He hated the wavering note in his voice.

He felt her hand work between their bodies, find its way inside the front of his pants. She began to manipulate him, gently, so that it seemed such a natural thing to do. They had been intimate in a way never forgotten.

"At least once, anyway," she breathed. "Don't make me beg, David."

Under the warm pressure of her fingers he felt himself go from tumescent to rigid. He threw back his head and stared straight up at the ceiling. His body cried to do what his mind was rejecting. "Jesus!"

"That sounds like a prayer, David. It can be answered." Her hand continued its clever, expert work. She knew him; their bodies knew one another. Forever familiar. "We both want the same thing, the very same thing . . ."

The tightness in his body grew taut, and something in him gave.

He lifted her and carried her to the bed. Laid her down and bent over her, kissing her breasts as she pulled at his shirt. He raised his head then, and they virtually tore each other's clothes off.

Pale and nude, beautiful as memory, she lay before him, gazing up at him with amusement and lust. "Want to hurt me, David? Want to whip me with your belt?"

He felt the mood shift.

"I'm not into that anymore, Deirdre."

She gave him the most lascivious grin he'd ever seen. "Honestly?"

"Yeah, honestly. Straight sex is gonna have to be good enough." He bent lower, kissed her.

When their lips parted, she gripped his earlobe and twisted it playfully. "Want me to hurt you? You been a bad boy?" She gave his ear an extra twist.

He gripped her hand and lowered it. "Straight sex, Deirdre."

She pulled him down to her, on her. He kissed her lips again, her breasts, her stomach, the dark, wet center of her. She spread her legs wide, guided him up to kiss him again, then wrapped her legs around his waist as he entered her.

She made a deep, throaty sound and he began thrusting, slowly at first, spanning warm interior spaces, then faster and more violently as his passion took him. Her long, powerful legs clamped tightly around his waist like a trap. "Hurt me!" she moaned in his ear. "Hurt me, hurt me, hurt me, David! Please!"

He gripped her wrists and bent her arms back behind her head, watching her grimace and narrow her eyes. Her lips tightened, baring her teeth. He felt the core of her throbbing, then her fingernails clawing, digging painfully into his back. Her body arched with a power that surprised him. He knew she was climaxing as she whispered hoarsely in his ear. "Mine, mine, mine, MINE!"

She went limp beneath him and her legs fell to the sides as he thrust into her violently and emptied himself.

She kissed his ear, the one she'd twisted, as he slowly disengaged himself from her and rolled gasping onto his back.

Neither of them spoke.

He tried to analyze what he felt but couldn't; his mind was still floating somewhere above body and desire, connected by only tenuous neural threads.

Finally, after he'd caught his breath, he stood up and went to the window, where he stood staring again at the teeming riddle of

Manhattan. The scratches on his back felt like wounds from a lioness.

From behind him on the bed, he heard Deirdre say, "That was lovely, David. Aren't you going to thank me?"

Twenty minutes later, as they were leaving the apartment, David knew how he felt: guilty and ashamed. Deirdre, he noticed with dread, looked smug. He couldn't deny that he'd wanted her desperately, uncontrollably. Couldn't deny it to her or to himself.

He held the door open for her and she edged past him into the hall, brushing him with her hip, glancing briefly up at him with a sated kind of lust that slumbered.

Behind them, and behind the louvered doors of the bedroom closet, a videocassette ran out of tape.

There was a soft click, a whir, and in the dark closet a pinpoint of red light winked out.

15

Molly emerged from Small Business among a swarm of parents and children. She carried Michael with one arm and used her free hand to guide the stroller down the stone steps to the sun-washed sidewalk.

When Michael was strapped into the stroller's canvas seat, he and Molly both waved to Julia, who was standing in the shade of the canopy watching her charges depart with their regular guardians. The responsibility she'd carried all morning was now divided and dispersed; Molly wondered if Julia felt as suddenly free as she appeared.

As Molly pushed the stroller along crowded West Eighty-fifth, she found herself glancing uneasily from time to time across the street. Through the intermittent and glaring stream of noisy traffic, she half expected to see the woman in the blue baseball cap and mirror-lens glasses.

But there was no sign of the woman.

When they reached the apartment building, Molly entered the lobby then wheeled the stroller directly to the elevator. She pushed the button for the floor above hers, where Bernice Clark lived.

Bernice was a thin, thirty-five-year-old woman with a huge mass of tightly sprung brown hair that made her seem even frailer than she was. She'd been out of work except for occasional jobs arranged by Modern Office Temps since Molly had met her. Bad luck had left her harried but cheerful. Irrepressible optimism ran in her blood; a firing squad would have to fire into her smile to erase it. Molly felt comfortable leaving Michael with her.

Bernice looked paler than usual this afternoon as she let them into the apartment. She unstrapped then scooped up Michael from the stroller and kissed him on the cheek. He grinned, and when she placed him on the hardwood floor, he swaggered directly to the TV, where Martin and Lewis's *Jumping Jacks* was playing without sound. Jerry Lewis was mugging and twitching around while Dean Martin stood calmly and stared at him with that odd combination of amusement and disdain. Michael plopped down in front of the screen and became engrossed.

The apartment's floor plan was identical to Molly and David's, but it was furnished more sparsely and cheaply. Near the old console TV was a cushionless chair that seemed ready to collapse. Its cushion was lying on the floor near the window, as if Bernice had been sitting on it staring outside. The place smelled slightly and pleasantly of pine-scented cleanser and wax. There was no sign of dust along the baseboards or on the scarred hardwood floor. Bookshelves fashioned from planks laid across stacks of bricks contained only knickknacks and dog-eared paperbacks, along with a few bound uncorrected proofs that Molly had given Bernice. An ornately framed round mirror hung on another wall, centered over a polished mahogany half-moon table, leftovers from more prosperous times.

"I appreciate you watching Michael," Molly told Bernice. "It wasn't in my plans to work almost every afternoon, but suddenly the publisher needs the manuscript I'm editing by next week."

Bernice ran her fingers through her mass of hair. "Hey, no problem. We live in the same building, and I'm getting paid, aren't I?"

Molly grinned. "And worth every inflated dollar." She looked more closely at Bernice's pasty complexion and the tiredness in her eyes. "You look pale today. Are you feeling okay?"

"Sure. I just need some sun." She glanced over at Michael. "Maybe I'll take our guy swimming at Koch Pool, if it's okay with you."

"Sure, just keep a close eye on him. And make sure he doesn't get too much sun." Molly looked at Michael, still lost in *Jumping Jacks*. Lewis had parachuted from an airplane and was drifting toward the ground, clutching his chute's lines, squirming around and looking terrified. "What about a real job?" she asked Bernice. "Having any luck with those résumés you sent out?"

"Not much. But there's always hope. And thanks for printing them on your computer for me. They make me seem so employable that even I might want to hire me."

A siren sounded close outside, then a fire engine's loud, rude air horn blasted twice to help clear a path through traffic. The wail of the siren moved away, fading until it was absorbed in the usual muted turmoil of the city.

"That reminds me," Bernice said, "there was another false fire alarm while you were gone the other day. Third one in the last few months, if I'm counting right. It's getting so half the tenants don't pay much attention or bother to leave the building."

Molly could understand why. She and Michael had heeded the alarm once. Another time it had sounded in the middle of the night, and she and David had hurriedly gathered up Michael and obediently trudged downstairs to stand in the street until it was determined that there was no fire. Her fear was that if a fire did break out, too many tenants would ignore the erratic alarm that so far had meant nothing but inconvenience.

"The management company ought to repair the wiring," she said.

Bernice grinned and shook her head. "They'd rather stall. They figure if there really is a fire someday, they can redecorate the apartments of all the dead tenants and charge more rent. Hey, there's Muffin!" She pointed toward a spot near Molly's feet.

Molly wasn't surprised. She stooped and picked up the cat, who purred and snuggled warmly against her side. "He leaves by way of the window we keep propped open a few inches for him, then gets back into the building when people enter and roams the corridors. I hope nobody thinks he's a pest."

Bernice reached out and stroked Muffin. "In this city there could be lots worse things than cats roaming the corridors."

At Sterling Morganson, David looked away from his computer monitor and drew in his breath in surprise.

Deirdre was standing in the corridor outside his open office door, watching him.

16

Deirdre walked into the office. She looked clean and fresh and was still wearing her tight jeans, but now she had on a gold blouse tucked in around her narrow waist, emphasizing her breasts. Open-toed, high-heeled sandals flashed red enamel that matched her fingernails.

She smiled; there was something possessive in its white glitter. "I told that girl up front I was coming back here, David."

He tried not to show his annoyance, but he didn't get up from his desk chair. "What do you want?"

"Oh, I've had what I want, David. I only came here to tell you I'm not sorry for what happened. I was weak. We both were. It's the kind of thing that simply happens, and there shouldn't be any recriminalizations or guilt."

He couldn't believe he was hearing this. And he didn't want anyone else to hear. "My God, keep your voice down!"

Quickly he stood up and closed the door, then sat back down so Deirdre wouldn't reach for him.

He hadn't seen Lisa standing in the hall only a few feet from the door.

It chilled him to think what it might mean if Deirdre decided to make any kind of scene, what it might do to his life.

"And why *shouldn't* there be any guilt?" he asked.

"Because love doesn't take circumstances into account. Love makes us all go round, and we can't help it."

He stared at her; she'd meant what she said. "I *do* feel guilty, Deirdre. I'm in love with Molly, and I feel responsible."

She shook her head as if in mild frustration at not being able to make him see some simple and obvious truth. "But you shouldn't feel responsible, either. We think we're in charge of our lives, but that's a joke on us. We're really all like pieces in a game, and destiny moves us when and where it wants. It's not like we don't have free will, but it's up to us to make the most of our destiny, whatever situation it puts us in. Don't you believe in destiny, David?" She seemed somewhat taken aback, as if she'd just discovered he might not believe in the Bill of Rights.

"To an extent, I suppose. Or maybe it's just a handy excuse for people to do what they want." He leaned back in his desk chair, causing it to squeak surprisingly loud in the quiet office. He couldn't read her eyes. "I take it *you* believe in destiny?"

She moved toward him as if drawn. Her voice was fervent. "Oh, yes, David! I sincerely believe certain things were meant to be. I think this afternoon proves it."

"I think we'd better forget this afternoon."

"But we can't, and you know it."

"What about Molly?"

"Molly has her own destiny."

"It includes me, Deirdre."

She shrugged, as if resigned but tolerant. "I can accept that for now."

He wanted to leap up, grab her by the shoulders, and shake understanding into her. But he knew he wouldn't. He shouldn't.

"I'm not talking about for now," he said. "We're going to have to avoid seeing each other."

She laughed at him as if he were a bright child who would eventually see things her way. "Are you afraid of losing control again? I'm not. I'm a Taurus—I know how to accept and control my destiny. That's something everyone should learn, David. The world would be so much happier."

"I don't like losing control."

"Of course you don't. But the only thing we have to fear is being afraid, David."

"It isn't fear," he told her. "Or guilt. At least I don't think so. What we started today can only lead to trouble." He looked at his hands, gripping the edge of the table where his computer glowed. "No. I guess, to be honest, I am afraid. I'm afraid of loss. I don't want to lose what I have."

She seemed amused. "You won't lose me. I promise."

"You know that isn't what I meant."

She walked over to the bookshelves and examined a stack of manuscripts. Then she moved near the desk and ran her fingertip lightly over the brass frame of the Molly-and-Michael photo. "What you're really afraid of, David, is destiny. But maybe you're right. Either way, surely we can remain friends. Molly shouldn't object to that."

"Friends?"

"That's all I'm asking for now, David."

He didn't answer her. He knew it was futile.

She walked to the door, then turned around and smiled at him. "David the Virgo."

As she went out, she bumped into Lisa.

David watched the two women exchange a look he didn't understand, even though he could almost see the charged arc of emotion. Without a word, they walked away in different directions, as if nothing had happened.

David wondered if Lisa had overheard any of his and Deirdre's conversation. It was obvious that Deirdre thought so.

He looked again at his hands gripping the edge of the computer stand, so hard now that his fingertips were white. It was as if he needed something solid to anchor him in the familiar and manageable world. Strong currents were running and he didn't understand them. But he knew that an undertow was drawing him inexorably toward where he feared to go.

He forced himself to relax his grip and watched his fingers gradually loosen, slide slowly, then release their hold on the firm, hard wood.

David stood that night before the medicine cabinet mirror in the bathroom. He was wearing only Jockey shorts and was holding a white T-shirt. After getting Molly's hand mirror from the top of the toilet tank, he turned his back to the medicine cabinet.

It took him only a few seconds to find the angle where he could hold up the hand mirror and see his back in the larger mirror.

Deirdre hadn't scratched his back with her fingernails, she'd gouged it. Four parallel tracks of congealed blood on each shoulder blade ran toward each other, not quite meeting at his spine.

They were so uniform there was little doubt she'd deliberately marked him as if to claim him. That would be unmistakable to Molly.

He put down the hand mirror and worked his T-shirt over his head. It was one of his larger ones and draped loosely from his shoulders. Then he picked up the hand mirror and checked again in the medicine cabinet mirror to make sure no fresh blood was seeping through the shirt.

His eyes met the eyes of his reflection. There was something different about the man staring back at him. He hoped Molly wouldn't see it.

He shook his head hopelessly at his image, parting his lips as if to lecture himself. But neither he nor his reflection had any knowledge to impart.

With a sad smile, he laid the hand mirror back on the toilet tank and left the bathroom.

In the dim light of the bedroom he settled down on the bed beside Molly. The air conditioner was running and he felt cool air pass like liquid over his bare legs.

The sheets rustled as Molly moved close to him. She kissed him on the mouth, and in the tautness of her lips he felt rather than saw her smile.

David kissed her back, then yawned and maneuvered her around so that she was facing away from him and they were lying on their sides molded together spoon-fashion. He reached back and adjusted his T-shirt, then lay with his arm thrown over her and patted her wrist.

"Kinda tired tonight, hon," he murmured. "Only cuddle, okay?"

He felt her body tense. "Sure," she said into the darkness, "we've got the rest of our lives."

He knew she was lying there awake, staring at the shadowed wall, and hoped she couldn't feel the vibration of his quickened heartbeat.

In the morning, he wondered which of them had fallen asleep first.

17

Deirdre had eaten supper at a deli near the movie theater. Now she sat alone in the dark, watching Esther Williams do underwater calisthenics. At least that's what they looked like to Deirdre. She thought she could do what Williams was doing, and look better doing it. She might even be a better swimmer.

Well, no, she had to admit. Maybe not a better swimmer. But Williams was a strong-looking woman like Deirdre, an athlete with curves. And probably, if you took swimming out of the mix, not as good an athlete as Deirdre. Maybe even if you left swimming in. Deirdre was sure she could have beaten a young Esther Williams at the decathlon. Or in a martial arts tournament. She smiled at the idea.

Deirdre loved to sit alone at the movies, secure in the darkness, lost in the world on the screen. She had always been fond of dark, safe places: movie theaters, closets, basements. But at the movies was the best place of all to be, with not only security, but a world that was as real as her own, brilliant and actual before her, claiming her eyes and her mind.

Everything in Williams's world was so perfect, so beautiful. Problems and people moved in and out of her celluloid life, but always things worked out for her no matter how menacing her antagonists or how gloomy the outlook. The screenplay took care of her like benign fate.

The music swelled. The screen was now filled with dozens of beautiful women in one-piece bathing suits diving through flaming hoops into the spacious pool. The camera followed some of them underwater, where they smiled as they kept their form, legs tight together and toes pointed, and rose toward the surface like graceful mermaids.

Deirdre preferred old movies. They drew you *into* their world and held you there. The new movies came out of the screen *at* you, tried to startle you with abrupt, jarring images like on MTV and with sudden loud noises. Sometimes they posed questions without answering them, and she would leave the theater perplexed rather than reassured. But tonight, she knew as she watched the aquatics and troubled love affairs, that by the end of the last reel everything would be resolved. As it might at least possibly be in her own life. If it happened to Esther Williams, why not to Deirdre?

She sat transfixed by the movie until the final credits had run and the house lights came on to reveal the dinginess of the theater and the flawed humanity of the patrons rising from their seats or filing up the aisles toward the lobby and exits. A very thin man who looked unhealthy, with a yellow-white beard, glanced over at Deirdre as he passed in the aisle. He grinned toothlessly and winked. She gave him an angry look and he walked on. He was nothing like any of the men who had courted Williams.

When almost everyone had filed from the auditorium, she rose from her seat and walked up the aisle.

The lobby was like an air lock between the predictable and perfect parallel world of the screen, and the tawdry and sometimes surprising world outside the glass doors. Deirdre stood and watched people stream past outside. Some of them were well dressed, obviously tourists or Broadway theatergoers. Others were shabby and had a furtive air about them and walked hurriedly, as if something might be pursuing them. Three teenage boys jumped and bounced past, yelling at each other and grinning. An old woman laden with shopping bags waved a cab over and climbed into the back, glaring after the boys as if they'd been the final straw that had made her hail a taxi rather than walk the rowdy, unsafe streets. A slim woman with graceful, slender legs, wearing high heels and a light blue raincoat, strode past.

Darlene!

Deirdre ran to the nearest glass door, opened it, and stepped out to the middle of the sidewalk. Someone bumped into her and didn't apologize, but she hardly noticed. She was staring at the

woman in the blue raincoat, who was standing on the corner waiting to cross the street.

"Darlene!" she called. But apparently the woman didn't hear
her.

Deirdre began walking toward her, preparing to call Darlene's
name again when she was closer.

Then the woman turned around and hurried to the other side
of the cross street to take advantage of the still unchanged traffic
signal. Deirdre saw her face for a few seconds and realized with
disappointment that she wasn't Darlene. Her eyes had been fooled
by some other woman who from a distance, and at a glance from
a certain angle, resembled a youthful Audrey Hepburn. Only this
woman wasn't so young. Maybe even in her mid-fifties.

Suddenly Deirdre was acutely, piercingly lonely. She knew now
that she'd felt that way since the end of the movie. That had to be
why she'd so wanted the woman to be Darlene.

She decided to go for a walk, to be among the crowds of people in Times Square. She'd heard that lonely people could be even
lonelier in a crowd, but she knew that it wasn't always true. So
much of conventional wisdom was wrong. Tonight, she'd feel better surrounded by fellow human beings.

Before setting out, she decided to call her hotel and see if there
were any messages. If everything had gone smoothly, like in the
movies, the real estate agency would have called to give her the
final go-ahead. The agent had said that there should be no problem because the apartment was vacant and had been for almost a
month. But you never knew.

Back in the lobby, she asked an usher for directions to a public phone, and he told her there was one near the rest rooms but
for movie patrons only. He remembered her, though, and gave her
permission to use the phone. Kindness from a stranger. A hopeful
sign.

The hotel switchboard operator had her hold the line for a
minute, then returned and said yes, there was a message for her.

Deirdre smiled as she listened to the message read over the
phone.

She hung up and smiled at the usher as she was leaving the lobby
for the second time. Developments had shaped this world so that
for now it was like the world of the movie screen. The dynamics

were the same, as Deirdre's present and near-future were concisely and benignly scripted by fate. The times when such convergences occurred were rare, and she appreciated and savored them.

The apartment was hers. Of course there was the problem of money, but Deirdre was sure that one could be resolved. It was in the stars for her, just as it would have been in the world on screen.

On the teeming pavement, she walked fast. People got out of her way.

18

Molly wheeled Michael in his stroller from the elevator the next morning and stopped near the bank of tarnished brass mailboxes. The apartment building's lobby was almost small enough to be called a foyer. Gray tiles flecked with black ran halfway up the walls, which were painted an industrial green. There was no doorman, and the intercom had been painted over so many times that it was obviously inoperable. The finely cracked gray marble floor was littered with crushed cigarette butts, a crumpled McDonald's wrapper, and marred with dark scuff marks from heels. Molly noted with some alarm what looked like a crack vial whose glass had been ground under someone's shoe to a fine, reflective powder that glittered like diamond dust.

She fished her key ring from her purse and unlocked her mailbox. Above the bank of mailboxes with their sometimes functional doorbell buttons, someone had painstakingly but obviously altered black felt-tip graffiti reading "fuck you" to the less objectionable "book you."

Nothing in the mail much interested Molly. There was a statement from Apple Bank, an appeal for a donation to a charity she'd never heard of, a pamphlet without a postmark that warned of an imminent global reckoning with God, and a mail-order catalog of remaindered books.

She slipped the mail into her purse. The elevator doors opened, and an elderly man she remembered from standing in the street with the other tenants during false fire alarms emerged. He smiled and nodded a good morning to her, then held the street door open while she pushed the stroller outside into bright sunlight.

It was going to be another hot day, but the morning was still comfortable. As she pushed the stroller along West Eighty-fifth on the way to Small Business, she found herself looking around tentatively, half expecting to see the woman with the mirror-lens glasses.

But if the woman was nearby, she was staying out of sight.

Nor did Molly see the woman in the park later that morning as she jogged her usual course along the sun-dappled trail, listening to her own deep breathing and the rhythmic light touch of her rubber soles on the warm asphalt. She was running well, with spring in her step. This was why she jogged, this feeling that through determined and relentless exertion she could overcome all obstacles and keep her world in balance and control.

But she experienced a surprising surge of anxiety as she approached the place on the trail where she'd seen the woman yesterday.

When she passed that point and had jogged several hundred yards farther, she relaxed.

If she didn't want the woman—Deirdre, she still suspected—to upset the morning even in her absence, she decided she'd better concentrate on finishing her run.

She slowed her pace and regulated her breathing, settling into the mental and physical groove she knew would allow her to go the distance. She felt secure enough now. There were other joggers on the trail, people walking, even a pair of lovers in each other's arms on a blanket. She could hear the hum of traffic, and through the trees glimpse the fleeting bright yellow of a cab passing on one of the park's gently curving streets.

Deirdre and Craig Chumley were in the back of the cab. Chumley was clenching his jaws as Deirdre, leaning down and to the side, performed oral sex on him.

He groaned and the driver glanced again in the rearview mirror. Chumley, and Deirdre, knew the driver was aware of what was happening in the back of his cab. Neither minded; he was simply part of the fantasy.

Deirdre raised her head. Her eyes met the driver's boldly in the mirror and he looked away. She saw the curve of his cheek as he smiled and concentrated as best he could on his driving. He was probably never surprised by what went on between his passengers.

She wiped her wrist across her mouth and leaned back in the upholstery, letting her head drop to the side to rest against Chumley's shoulder. The lush green trees, the oncoming traffic, the people in the park, slid past outside the window like a bright dream. Chumley made no move to zip his fly.

"God!" he said softly, "you didn't have to stop!"

"I'm sorry," she told him. "I . . . well, I've got a lot of worries lately."

"Such as?"

She hesitated, as if she really didn't want to burden him with her problems. Then: "There's this apartment I found. It's perfect! All I have to do is get the money for a security deposit and I can have it."

"So?"

"I'm afraid somebody else is going to want it and snatch it away from me."

Chumley tucked in his chin and gazed down at her in surprise. "For God's sake, Deirdre, why didn't you say so earlier? I can give you an advance on your salary."

"That's a wonderful idea!" Then she backed away and looked at him, suddenly concerned. "But are you sure you can afford it?"

He smiled. "Of course! The company's healthy enough for that. We've had a good quarter." He pulled her back to him so her head was against his shoulder again, then tenderly brushed a strand of hair up off her forehead. "Besides, I trust you, Deirdre."

She resisted his efforts to hold her and sat forward again so she could twist her body and look into his eyes. As the cab struck a pothole, the suspension bottomed out, and she almost slipped from the seat. "That's wonderful of you," she said. "I won't forget this. I really won't."

The cab rocked as it rounded a corner, and this time she let the momentum take her and collapsed far back in the seat in great relief, beaming.

The cabby glanced again in the mirror. "Back to the office?"

Chumley pretended not to have noticed the hint of sarcasm in his voice. "No, just drive around the park some more for a while."

Deirdre wrapped her arms around Chumley's neck and kissed his cheek. Her eyes met the driver's again in the rearview mirror. She winked.

Then she grinned at Chumley and slid down again to sit on the cab floor.

Molly was seated cross-legged on the living room floor that evening, playing with Michael, when David came home from work. They both waved to him then went back to using Michael's See 'n Say, a toy that made appropriate animals sounds when a cord was pulled. "This is a sheep," said the See 'n Say as David tossed his attaché case in the chair then hung his coat in the closet just inside the door.

"Not me, I hope," he said, over the *Baaaaaa* of the See 'n Say.

"You're early," Molly said.

"One of our fee clients is driving me nuts, claiming we won't try to market his manuscript because it's political dynamite. He's convinced Charles Manson engineered both Kennedy assassinations."

"What do you think?" Molly asked, smiling.

David crossed the room and picked up Michael, then kissed him and playfully jostled him.

Molly stood up and looked at both of them with pride and a possessiveness edged with worry.

"Why don't we see if Bernice can watch Michael, then let's go to Rico's for dinner?" David said. "This time just the two of us."

Pleased, Molly thought the offer over. "Better yet, why don't the three of us go?"

She wasn't sure he was going to agree, but he grinned and handed Michael to her. "Okay. Just give me a minute, then we'll leave."

She watched him walk toward the back of the apartment, then go into the bathroom. A minute later she heard water running.

In the bathroom, David was standing shirtless before the mirror, twisting his torso this way and that to examine the scratches on his back.

He stared at them for a long time before deciding they looked better. They were scabbed over evenly and there was no swelling. He wouldn't have to worry about infection.

The hunger Deirdre obviously felt for him was something he couldn't quite fathom, but he had to admit to feeling flattered somewhere within his agony of hating the circumstances that had entrapped him in the Fifty-fourth Street apartment with the wide bedroom window.

Of course, Deirdre considered it destiny and wanted him to think of it the same way. But wasn't that how all adulterers thought?

A loud knock on the door made him jump.

"Hey," Molly called through the door, "you okay in there?"

He hurriedly struggled back into his shirt. "Sure. Be right with you!"

When he emerged from the bathroom, they were standing by the door to the hall.

"Better not keep us waiting any longer," Molly said jokingly. "We're starving, and it's alarming what hunger can do to the disposition."

19

Molly stopped the stroller by her mailbox in the lobby the next morning and glanced out through the rectangle of glass in the street door. Early as it was, the sun was glaring on West Eighty-fifth Street.

"Go!" Michael exhorted from his seat in the stroller. "Let's go!"

"Ease up," Molly told him with a smile.

"Wanna walk," he said.

She didn't pay much attention to him; he hadn't used his no-compromise voice that might lead to a show of temper.

Michael was getting too big for the stroller, and she dreaded when she'd have to walk with him to Small Business. He was still young enough to be subject to sudden impulses and outbursts of speed, taking adults unaware, and there was so much danger to run toward in Manhattan.

"Walk next year, maybe," she told him, and unlocked and opened the brass door of the mailbox.

She leafed through the mail. Nothing but junk and a postcard from a friend who was traveling in South Dakota. The card featured a color photograph of Mount Rushmore. Molly couldn't look at Mount Rushmore without thinking of the Hitchcock movie *North by Northwest*. Average people suddenly pulled into dangerous situations through no fault of their own was a recurring theme in Hitchcock movies. Molly was glad it didn't happen that often in real life.

She closed and locked the mailbox door and turned around.

Gasped and dropped the mail.

Deirdre was standing in the lobby, smiling at her.

She was wearing jeans and a faded red T-shirt and had on brown cotton gloves, the kind sold in hardware stores for working in gardens.

"This must be Michael!" she said, and bent down and touched his cheek with a brown cloth glove finger. "He really does look like David!"

"What are *you* doing here?" Molly asked.

Deirdre picked up the mail while she was bent over to be on Michael's level, then straightened up and handed it to Molly.

"Sorry," she said, "I didn't mean to scare you."

Molly stood holding the mail, staring at her, puzzled and not at all liking her presence so close to home. "If you've come to see David . . ."

"Oh, no, that's not it," Deirdre said. "The fact is, the darnedest thing has happened."

"Darnedest thing?"

"Yes. David might have told you, I've been having some trouble finding a decent apartment. Well, a real estate agency recommended an apartment in this building, on the fourth floor. I looked at it and loved it. It was perfect! It wasn't until I'd signed the lease this morning and started moving in what little stuff I have that I noticed the name 'Jones' on one of the mailboxes, just saw it out of the edge of my vision. Such a common name, though, I figured it couldn't be *my* Joneses. But one of the neighbors said yes, David and Molly Jones! It's a tiny world, isn't it?"

Molly was thunderstruck. Her mind couldn't grab on to what she'd heard. "You mean you're moving into *this* building? *Here?*"

"Sure am. Right this very moment. Craig's helping me."

The street door opened, letting in a wave of warm air and Craig Chumley. He was wearing a blue workshirt and paint-spattered jeans, clumsily backing into the lobby carrying a large cardboard box that had once held cartons of Cheerios.

Still smiling, Deirdre said, "Oh, Molly, this is Craig."

Chumley grinned; his teeth looked yellow in the lobby light, the long bicuspids lending him an amiable but wolflike expression. "Hi, Molly. Sorry I couldn't make it to dinner the other night."

Molly ignored him completely, still staring at Deirdre. *"Here?"* she asked again in disbelief.

"Yes, we're neighbors! I didn't plan it this way, but when I found out, after having met you, I didn't see any problem. At least not enough of a problem to try breaking my lease. Even if that was possible. Which of course it isn't."

"Whatever's in this box," Chumley said, "it's getting heavier by the nanosecond."

Deirdre laughed. "Oh, sorry!"

She hurried to the elevator and pressed the Up button. The elevator was still at lobby level from Molly and Michael's descent, and the door opened immediately. She entered, and Chumley carried the box in and stood beside her. He didn't put the box down but continued holding it in front of him. Molly could just see his paint-spattered jeans and the top of his balding head.

"Bye for now, neighbor!" Deirdre said as the door slid shut.

Molly stood motionless, gripping her mail hard enough to kink the postcard from South Dakota.

"Wanna walk," Michael demanded from the stroller.

David sat at his desk at Sterling Morganson, pressing the cool plastic phone to his ear and staring at the letter he'd been composing on his computer monitor. It was a reply to a fee client in Idaho who'd inquired about a special rate if, instead of one novel, two were submitted for appraisal and possible marketing. The glowing screen seemed to recede, the letters merging to form wavering white lines on the deep blue background.

"What?" he asked, his voice incredulous. "You're sure about this? She's moving in now?"

He listened intently to Molly for several seconds. A part of his mind was grasping the true import of what she was saying; something fundamental and problematic had happened, and his life was changed. His heart got colder and heavier with every word she spoke. He didn't see Lisa pause in the doorway and stand watching him.

"I'll talk to her," he said at last. "But it won't help. She has a right to live where she wants, and if she signed a lease there might not be much she could do to get out of it even if she tried. Just like we can't get out of our lease."

His face became paler as he listened.

"Dammit, Mol, I don't like it any more than you do but—"

Another pause. He adjusted the receiver so it wouldn't hurt his ear.

"But I don't *know* what to do," he said. "We've got a situation here. Have *you* got any ideas? Mol? Molly?"

Lisa moved back into the hall and hurried away as he slammed down the receiver.

He sat quietly for a moment, his mind lurching in numbed shock as it struggled to assess the perils and possibilities in what he'd just heard.

Then he picked up a bound manuscript from his desk and hurled it against a wall.

The noise must have attracted Josh, who looked into the office holding a half-full glass coffeepot. His gaze panned the office, took in the manuscript on the floor, then fastened on David.

"Want some coffee, boss?"

David sat hunched over his desk, his face buried in his hands.

"No," he said between splayed fingers. "Not unless it contains strychnine."

"You're in luck," Josh said, and entered the office.

20

Molly sat that afternoon with Traci Mack at a table in Midnight Espresso, an Upper West Side coffee shop on Columbus Avenue. Behind the counter two women were serving coffee from complex steel urns, near a rack of upside-down bottles of colorful flavorings for lattes and cappuccinos. Alongside the counter was a display of gourmet coffee beans for sale, ground or whole, in white six-ounce bags. August heat had infiltrated the coffee shop with the frequent opening and closing of the door, and the scent of brewed coffee permeated the warm air. Several customers stood at the bar sipping coffee, while others sat at tables.

Molly and Traci were at a small table near the door. Traci's black leather attaché case, with another ten copyedited chapters of *Architects of Desire* inside, was leaning against the curved wooden legs of her chair. She was wearing one of her sacklike black dresses, this time with a silver pin on it resembling a chalked outline of a body. A gift from her mystery author, she'd told Molly.

She wiped frothed cream from her upper lip, put down her cappuccinno, and looked at Molly. "So what's new with you and the ex?"

Molly told her.

Traci stared at her in surprise. "You're kidding! She's actually moving into the same building?"

Molly gazed down despondently at her caffe latte, as if it were a crystal ball that had disappointed her. "She's probably already moved in by now," she said, "cooking up poison recipes on the stove."

Traci sat back in her chair. "Hmm. Your attitude's changed since the last time we met."

"Well, the circumstances have changed."

"What's David say about this?" Traci asked.

Molly looked up at her. "A situation, he calls it. We're just going to have to live with it."

"It would be an understatement to say you seem less than happy about that."

"Because it seems there's nothing I can do about it."

"You could move," Traci suggested. Another sip of cappuccino, another wiping away of the white foam mustache with the back of her curved forefinger.

"I'm afraid not," Molly said. "We've got our own lease, and it runs for another six months." She gazed out the poster-cluttered window at New York suffering in the relentless heat, then sighed and took a sip of her latte. "Maybe I'm making too much of it. You know how Manhattan apartment buildings are—neighbors exist in the cocoons of their lives and hardly ever see each other. Maybe it'll all work out."

Traci raised a hand and toyed with the silver pin. "It doesn't work out in the mystery novel I'm editing."

Molly found herself getting irritated. "Life doesn't always imitate art," she said defensively. "David and I have a strong marriage."

"Sure, I know that, Mol. But do you want it tested this way?"

"I've thought about that," Molly said, "and I have to admit, I shouldn't be afraid of being tested. David and I love each other, we've got Michael, and whatever was between David and Deirdre is over. That's why they divorced."

"You sound as if you're trying to persuade yourself."

Molly made a helpless gesture with both hands. "I have no choice other than to believe that's the way it is. Besides, I told you Deirdre's romantically involved with Craig Chumley."

"All true enough," Traci said. "But on the other hand, men are men."

"Jesus!" Molly said in disgust. "You sound like one of those gynocentric feminists."

Traci was unflappable. "Just speaking from experience." She

sipped again at her cappuccino. "What's this Chumley guy look like?"

Molly thought about that. Chumley certainly wasn't a standout and was difficult to describe. Of course she'd only seen him in work clothes, and behind a cardboard box. "Average-looking," she said. "Maybe even dorky-looking. Tall with thinning brown hair, a little overweight in the wrong places. In his mid-forties, I'd guess."

Traci cocked her head to the side. "Odd that the woman you describe would glom on to somebody like that, even if he is near her age."

"What are you getting at?" Molly asked.

"Maybe she's using him."

"Oh, she's probably wearing him out!"

Traci laughed. "That's not exactly what I had in mind, though you might well be right. Hell, I'm pushing forty and I wish I had somebody to wear out."

Molly sat frowning. She found she wasn't at all comforted by having confided in Traci. She should have known better than to tell her everything.

Traci leaned forward with her elbows on the table, her wrists bent and her fingers laced off center so they were diagonally twined. "Don't look so severe, Mol. I'm interested in your dilemma. As a friend."

"It doesn't help," Molly said, "to have your friends predicting doom."

"I'm not predicting it, Mol. In fact, I'm hoping like hell this mess all works out for you, however that's possible." She suddenly raised her head and sniffed, like an animal testing the wind. "What's that perfume you're wearing?"

"Is it overpowering the scent of the coffee?" Molly asked. "I was distracted this morning and put it on twice. It's Oscar."

"De La Renta or Madison?"

Molly made herself smile. Traci's humor could crush you if you let it. "Very funny. David likes it."

Traci lifted her tall cappuccino mug. "Then for God's sake, keep wearing it." After she'd taken a sip of coffee and replaced her mug on the table, she said, "I almost forgot, a woman phoned Link today and asked for you. I told her you sometimes did work for us but you were free-lance and didn't have an office there."

"She leave a name?"

"Darlene, I think it was."

"Did you give her my phone number?"

"No, I thought you might not want me to do that."

"Could have been an editing job."

"If it was, she'll figure out a way to get in touch." Traci grinned. "Anyway, right now we don't want to share you."

Molly ran a fingernail back and forth on the table, thinking. "I'm sure I don't know any Darlene."

Traci shrugged dismissively. "Well, she knows you."

21

The same afternoon heat that made the Midnight Espresso coffee shop uncomfortable made Koch Public Recreational Swimming Pool almost unbearable anywhere but in the water. Only dedicated sunbathers appreciated the searing afternoon glare. They reclined on loungers and on beach towels spread on the pool's concrete apron. Occasionally people climbed trailing water from the pool or rose from where they lay baking on towels, the hot, high sun puddling their shadows at their feet as they walked to and from the snack stand with drinks whose ice was melting almost before they could take it into their mouths and chew on it, or cup it in their hands and rub it over chest or shoulders.

But it was only the relatively few adults who seemed to be suffering severely or taking precautions against sunburn. Most of the swimmers and sunbathers were teenage or younger.

Bernice was seated with Michael in the water at the shallow end of the crowded, noisy pool. She'd obeyed Molly's instructions and lavishly applied sunblocker on Michael. Then she'd smeared it liberally on herself. But she still preferred to keep both of them submerged to limit exposure to the sun. Besides, the water was blessedly cool compared to the hot, rough concrete surrounding the large, rectangular pool.

The only problem was that almost everyone else felt the same way. The pool was too crowded to swim more than a few strokes in any direction without bumping into someone. Or to dive, which was what Bernice enjoyed most about coming to Koch.

She watched a prepubescent girl in a two-piece black bathing suit pinch her nose between thumb and forefinger then leap from the diving board and create as large a splash as her light body would allow. Bernice couldn't actually see the girl enter the water. Her view was obstructed by the splashing and turmoil of dozens of scantily clad bodies of every hue among the glittering blue water and white foam of the pool.

She reached down with cupped hands and dribbled water over her shoulders. "Lots of people had the same idea we did this afternoon," she said to Michael.

Too busy playing to acknowledge her, he concentrated on the small red plastic boat he'd brought. He grinned as he made the boat skip over the glinting water then suddenly dive straight down.

Bernice kept a watchful eye on him, but she also sneaked glances at the deep end of the pool, waiting to see if the activity around the diving board would subside.

There continued to be a line of people waiting to dive, especially from the low board, which Bernice preferred. The impact of hitting the water from the high board had once made the top of her swimming suit slip down, and she'd had to hurriedly work it back up and refasten it underwater to avoid embarrassment.

Apparently the red boat had gone to war. It had resurfaced, and Michael was making gun sounds in the back of his throat and slapping his hand down ever closer to it, splashing water as imaginary shells closed in. The boat was rocking, threatening to swamp.

It was then that Bernice noticed there were only three people waiting to dive. She decided to take advantage of the lull.

"Michael, if we get out and go to the other end of the pool for a few minutes, will you promise to stay on the towel while I dive?"

He docked the boat next to his small chest and smiled up at her, squinting into the sun. "Promise."

She gave him a hug, feeling him trying to pull away from her. "What a good boy!"

Making sure he had a grip on his boat, she picked him up and carried him from the pool to where their towels lay on the concrete, along with her blue rubber thongs and the bottle of sunblocker. She slipped her feet into the thongs, carefully hooking the strands of rubber between first and second toes, then picked up everything and went with Michael to the deep end of the pool.

That end of the pool was only slightly less crowded. The only place there was room to spread out a towel was well away from the water, which was fine with Bernice. It kept Michael all the farther from danger and allowed her plenty of time to dive, surface, and get to him even if he did decide to wander toward the pool.

She spread out the large Miami souvenir towel with the sunset-and-flamingo design, then made sure Michael was happy seated on it, pouring a thin stream of water from his toy boat.

"Promise me again to stay here until I come back?" she asked.

He was watching the water from the boat making dark patterns on the pale concrete. " 'Course," he said, without looking up at her.

Confident he was busy with the boat and would obey her, she slipped her feet from the thongs and hurried over the sun-heated concrete to the diving board.

After waiting for one other diver, she got up on the damp rubber matting of the board and glanced over at Michael.

He was still on the towel, watching her now. She waved to him and he waved back. A few men and teenage boys looked her way, but the frail, almost bustless woman in the yellow-flowered two-piece suit didn't hold their interest.

With a final glance at Michael, she walked to the end of the board, sprang twice for height, then did a fairly neat jackknife, entering the water clean and not making much of a splash.

After the heat of the sun, the cool envelopment of the water felt wonderful. She reached the slightly angled bottom of the pool, pushed away with her hands, and quickly surfaced, stroking to the side of the pool and checking on Michael even before she climbed up the aluminum ladder onto the concrete. He was still safely on the towel, as he'd promised.

Bernice smoothed her wet hair back where it had worked from beneath the rubberband behind her head and started to walk over to Michael. Then she noticed there was another lull around the diving board. And he was preoccupied playing now with the plastic bottle of sunblocker.

"One more dive, Michael!" she yelled over to him.

He glanced her way, smiled, then pretended the sunblocker bottle was another boat, steaming toward the red toy one at the edge of the towel. Bernice hurried to the diving board.

Still wet and cooled down from her first dive, the water didn't feel so luxurious when she entered it after her second dive and cut toward the bottom. She'd attempted a swan dive, and she knew she hadn't been nearly vertical on entry and would have scored low if anyone had been judging.

Again her palms found the smooth concrete and she turned in the cool silence and began her rise to the surface.

She was surprised when her progress was stopped.

Then she realized something—someone—was clutching both her ankles, keeping her from rising.

Worried but not panicked, she twisted her body to see downward. Through the blue murkiness she could actually see the hands, the long pale fingers, encircling her thin ankles, but she couldn't make out the face of whoever was doing this to her.

She bent down lower, contorting her body so she could reach the strong fingers and try to pry them from her ankles. But her buoyancy prevented her from reaching the hands.

She'd assumed someone, probably a teenage boy, was playing a joke on her. But the grip of the fingers was so powerful, seemingly as unbreakable as steel bands. Maybe he didn't realize how strong he was.

Enough is enough! she decided.

She tried kicking herself free, but the hands allowed all the lateral movement she wanted without permitting her to rise. She knew she was merely wearing herself out.

Sitting in the sun on the warm, damp towel, Michael stared at the pool and wondered why Bernice hadn't come up yet. Then, as a skinny black girl in a green suit bounced twice on the edge of the board and dived, he turned his attention back to his boats.

Beneath the water, Bernice decided to change tactics and was paddling upward as hard as she could, trying futilely to provide lift for herself and whoever was keeping her from rising. She was aware of a slim girl in a green suit shattering the surface above her head and sliding past only a few feet away, her eyes clenched shut as she gracefully arched her body and began a smooth arc up toward bright sunlight and air. Bernice's chest began to ache as she realized her increased efforts were only causing her to rise a few feet then sink back toward the bottom of the pool.

She understood then that this was no joke, and she panicked, flailing desperately with her arms and hands, writhing and trying to kick free as she strained every muscle and ounce of will toward the dim light above.

Still, she could not rise.

The white boat with the sunblocker collided with and sank the red plastic boat at the edge of the towel.

Michael looked around again for Bernice but didn't see her.

He wasn't alarmed. He picked up the white boat, now the sunblocker bottle again, and tried to remove its lid.

Bernice hung suspended beneath the water, her arms spread wide as if she were about to embrace a lover. The last of the air in her lungs had escaped through her slack mouth and was curving away in a graceful string of bubbles.

The cruel hands had finally released their grip on her ankles, and she slowly began to rise.

Deirdre gripped the tile lip of the pool and easily hoisted herself up and out of the water.

Someone screamed. Several people began to shout.

Deirdre snatched up her towel and started drying herself off.

Then she walked around the hot concrete apron to the other side of the pool to join the growing tide of people streaming around a confused Michael to see what had happened in the deep end.

22

Molly wished David would arrive.

She sat on the sofa hugging Michael to her. He'd stopped crying. At first she was relieved, then his silence began to bother her. She wondered if his young mind had finally grasped what had occurred. But that was impossible, she realized; most adults hadn't grasped the immensity and banality of death. He lay inertly against her as she held him even tighter.

Molly had finally stopped crying too. The police had brought Michael to the apartment an hour ago, two uniformed officers with sad and respectful expressions. The taller of the two, who wore an inadequate mustache and looked barely out of his teens, told Molly they'd found Bernice's purse and identification in one of the lockers at Koch Pool, and several people said they thought she'd been with Michael, whom someone noticed seemed to be unattended. When they brought him to this address, Mrs. Esslinger, downstairs, had informed them which apartment Michael lived in.

And the police had told Molly what happened to Bernice.

She cried on the phone when she called David at work to tell him. And she'd cried for a long time afterward. But now the shock, the merciful deadening of the senses, had set in, and her tears had dried as the hard fact of death was assimilated and the grief turned inward.

The door opened and David entered. He carried his suit coat slung twisted almost inside out over his shoulder, and the wind had mussed his hair. His eyes appeared puffy, as if he'd been crying too. Maybe he had, Molly thought. She'd never seen him cry.

He dropped his coat on the chair and came to her, then touched the side of her neck gently.

"You okay now, Mol? You sure Michael's okay?"

She met his eyes and nodded, then looked away from him. She guessed she was okay. Her eyes were so dry now they burned, and her throat felt constricted.

"Nobody seems to know what happened," she heard herself say. "Someone said they saw her go off the diving board, and she just never came up."

David leaned down to kiss Michael, who smiled slightly but didn't move. "Maybe she hit her head on the bottom of the pool," he said, straightening.

"No. The police said there wasn't any sign of that. They think maybe she blacked out and drowned. Or maybe got disoriented underwater." Molly sighed. "Hell, David, she was a good swimmer. She went to some lake in New Jersey last summer with her mother and an aunt, showed us photos of her diving off a dock. She bragged to us that she'd won a bet by swimming across the lake, remember?"

"I remember," David said. "How did Michael get home?"

Molly told him.

"Has someone notified Bernice's mother?"

She nodded. "I told the police that her mother lived in Teaneck, and they said somebody there would talk to her." She could feel moisture soaking through her blouse from Michael's tears or saliva. He'd loved Bernice and he'd miss her in whatever way three-year-olds grieved. She'd miss Bernice too. How many friends had Bernice had, with her small family and her temporary jobs? It seemed she had never sunk the kind of roots that would sustain her into middle and old age, as if her life had been predicated on a premature death. There were people like that; you could see early death on them in their childhood photographs, something in their eyes, their stances, their uneasy look of impermanence. As if a part of them knew they were only travelers passing through, their stays briefer than most. It was all so unfair and sad.

Her grief expanded in her, almost choking her, and she began to cry softly. "Goddamn it, David!"

She felt the cushion shift as he sat down beside her. He rested a hand on her thigh. Michael moved against her, and she saw his bare feet dig into David's stomach down near his crotch. David didn't seem bothered by the small feet. He raised his hand from her thigh and cupped it around her shoulder, hugging her.

"It happens," he said. "Stuff like this just happens. It's shitty, but that's how the world works."

A sad laugh that surprised her broke through her sobs. "You sure are a comfort."

"I guess I'm not much help. This kind of thing throws me. I'm sorry, Mol."

She reached up and squeezed his hand gripping her shoulder. "It's okay, David. I'm just all . . . I don't know. Things are so screwed up lately."

Then she began sobbing harder. It made her furious that she couldn't stop. Within a few minutes she'd set off Michael, who began to wail.

Molly wiped at her eyes and saw David lean back against the sofa. His body slumped and he clenched his eyes shut. He looked haunted and years older.

She tried to get some work done the next day but couldn't. David had gone to work as usual, but he still looked strained and tired. She doubted if he was getting much accomplished either.

She'd kept Michael home. He slept most of the day. Slept so much, in fact, that she'd become worried and phoned the doctor, who'd told her it was probably Michael's way of dealing with Bernice's death. Molly wasn't to worry about him unless signs of physical illness or prolonged depression appeared. It was difficult to notice signs of depression in someone when they were asleep, she thought. But she didn't mention that to Michael's pediatrician.

Molly had sat at her desk, her work spread before her, waiting, but she'd barely touched it. She'd spent most of the day gazing out the window—rather, *at* the window. At nothing. Not even at the bluebottle fly that buzzed against the pane and crawled along the window frame. Her focus was inward. On grief and mortality.

Julia had agreed to come to the apartment and baby-sit Michael that night, while Molly and David were at the mortuary. This was the only night for visitation. Bernice's funeral was scheduled for the next morning.

Molly began dressing for the visitation early, before David got home from the agency. She'd taken a long, cool shower, then chosen her simple navy blue dress to wear, with matching shoes. Her only jewelry would be her wedding ring.

David came home and kissed her hello. He acted very subdued and put on his charcoal suit, a white shirt, and gray and maroon tie.

Dressed for mourning, they sat on the sofa in the living room, waiting for Julia. Michael was asleep again. The TV was on CNN, but the sound was little more than a murmur. Neither Molly nor David moved to increase the volume. In near silence they watched a tearful woman interviewed in the rain, then tape of a military plane crash that had occurred last year and been caught with a bystander's video camera. Molly watched the sleek jet fighter skim low over what looked like a runway, then dip a wing that caught the ground. The plane pinwheeled and disappeared in an orange fireball. The backs of spectators' heads could be seen as they moved toward the crash site, then the tape went black.

The phone rang.

David sprang to answer it before it woke Michael.

Molly watched his brow knit and his expression darken as he listened to whoever was on the other end of the connection.

"All right," he said. She recognized that tone of voice, the one he used when he was trying not to show irritation. "Sure, that's the breaks. And you're positive she's okay? All right, yes. No, really, we can work something out. Sure. Okay, good luck."

She waited while he hung up the phone.

"Damn!" he said. "This is just what we need!"

"Who was it?" Molly asked.

David glanced at the phone with loathing, as if it were a snake that had just sunk fangs into him. "It was Julia. She said she can't baby-sit Michael tonight. She just got a call that there was a fire a few hours ago at her mother's house in Brooklyn."

Molly tried to feel something. She knew that under ordinary circumstances she would, but tonight she felt nothing. Her emotions had been frayed and numbed by Bernice's death. Now more tragedy for Julia. Julia's mother.

Then a rush of shame almost made her blush. She wasn't the only one in the world with grief.

"Is her mother okay?"

"Yeah," David said. "Nobody was hurt, thank God. But this leaves us without a baby-sitter, and we've got to get to the funeral parlor within an hour."

Molly felt a twinge of guilt at being secretly relieved that she wouldn't have to view Bernice's body. Or maybe the body wouldn't be on display, a custom Molly despised. She realized she didn't even know Bernice's religion. Either way, Molly had had enough of death and didn't want to visit with it this evening. "There's nothing we can do about the situation, David."

"Of course there isn't!" he said angrily.

Her grief and the way her life had been knocked off center the last few weeks welled up in Molly. Tears were hot in her eyes. She damned herself for her weakness, but she began to cry.

David approached her cautiously and laid a hand on her shoulder. The hand felt like a bird that had lighted there and might any second fly away. He was unsure of her reactions these days. Well, so was she.

"I'm sorry, Mol," he said gently. "I get frustrated, angry, and I say things I don't mean."

Molly didn't trust herself to try to speak, so she nodded. She managed to stop crying and wiped her eyes with her fingertips. Hell on the makeup. "That's not why I was crying," she said, only half lying. "I just thought about Bernice being gone. It doesn't seem real. I should have remembered, death is something people learn to look away from."

Even me, she thought.

"I don't like to admit she's gone, either," David said. He removed his hand from her shoulder and glanced at his wristwatch. "Maybe we could take Michael with us."

Molly was horrified. "No, David! We're not taking a three-year-old child to a funeral home where someone he loves is laid out."

"People do, Mol," he said with a gentleness that surprised her.

She refused to be anything other than adamant. "People, maybe. Not us. Not our child!"

David couldn't quite throw off his irritation. "We don't have a lot of choice. The funeral's tomorrow. This is the only night for visitation."

"Michael's sleeping," Molly said. "Dreaming God knows what, but at least he might have some relief from his grief. I'm not going to wake him up and take him to see Bernice's— I'm not going to do it!"

Someone knocked three times loudly on the door. It occurred later to Molly that it was almost on cue. As if it were the result of eavesdropping.

She and David exchanged glances, then David crossed the room and opened the door.

Deirdre was standing in the hall.

David stepped back and she moved in.

"I heard about your baby-sitter," she said. "I just came down to tell you I'm sorry. I feel for you. I know how awful it must be—"

She stopped talking and regarded them more carefully.

"Did I come at a bad time?"

Molly looked off to the side. "Christ!"

David bowed his head and looked embarrassed. Molly could have kicked him.

"We were about to leave for the funeral home," he said, "when the woman who was going to watch Michael for us called and canceled."

Deirdre glanced around. "Where is Michael?"

"He's asleep."

"Well heck," Deirdre said, "I'll watch him for you. How much trouble can he be if he's asleep. He won't even know you're gone."

It made sense, but Molly didn't want it to happen. She felt almost panicky. "David, I—"

"It'll be okay, Mol." He glanced again at his watch, frowning. "He's sleeping, like Deirdre said."

Deirdre smiled and flipped her hair back off her shoulders. "I'll just curl up on the sofa and watch television."

Molly shook her head. "No, really—"

"Don't you worry," Deirdre said. "He'll be snug as a slug in a rug."

David shifted his weight nervously. "We're gonna be late, hon."

Molly was beaten, resigned. "All right," she heard herself say in a defeated voice. "All right . . ."

David nudged her toward the door, and Deirdre followed.

"Anything I need to know about how the TV works?" she asked.

"No, it's easy," David said. "The remote's right there on the table."

When they were in the hall, Deirdre leaned against the doorjamb, smiling at them. "Don't you worry, you two. Everything's gonna be just fine here."

"We won't be gone long," Molly said. She realized it had sounded almost like a warning.

"Be gone as long as it takes," Deirdre said. "And please, *don't* worry."

She closed and locked the door, still smiling as she thought back on this evening.

After a moment, Deirdre went to the window and watched Michael and Molly climb into the back of a taxi. As the cab pulled away, she could see Molly's pale face as she craned her neck to glance worriedly out the rear window. Like a ghost watching her life recede.

Deirdre tiptoed into the bedroom and stood gazing for a long time at the sleeping Michael. He was frowning in his sleep, his closed eyelids pulsating as he dreamed. He looked so much like David when he frowned. She closed the door softly and went back to the living room.

This might be my apartment, she thought. My life. David might be my husband, Michael my child. Destiny had decided otherwise, but destiny could be manipulated. Fate could be tricked.

Sitting down on the sofa, she aimed the remote at the TV and pressed the power button.

My favorite button, she thought with a grin.

After tuning to a Roseanne rerun, she sniffed at the sleeve of her blouse. Then she walked into Molly and David's bedroom and chose a perfume from the array of bottles on Molly's dresser. She dabbed some on her wrists. You never could tell who might show up at the door unexpectedly—maybe even Molly and David, returning home with changed minds about attending Bernice's visitation.

Deirdre touched her fingertip to the bottle again and pressed it here and there to her blouse. She bent her left elbow and held the material of the blouse's cuff to her nose.

Better, she thought, smiling at herself in the mirror as she replaced the cap on the bottle. Hardly detectable. Though she was sure neither Molly nor David had noticed. It was something only she'd be aware of, because she knew and they didn't.

She'd returned from Brooklyn only an hour ago, and she still smelled like smoke.

23

The next morning, a cab pulled to a halt at the curb where the taxi had picked up Molly and David the previous night. The sun hadn't yet burned away the clouds and it was a softly lighted, hazy morning, not yet oppressively warm. Passersby on West Eighty-fifth stepped along with energy and enthusiasm; their posture and expressions were unlike the heat-intensified weariness they would display at the end of the workday.

Craig Chumley climbed out of the cab and slammed its door. As it drove back out into the stream of traffic, he put on the gray suit coat that he'd been carrying and straightened his tie. Then he drew a miniature aerosol can from his pocket, sprayed some breath freshener into his gaping mouth, and entered the building.

Deirdre's doorbell worked only some of the time, so he ignored it and rode the elevator to the fourth floor, then walked down the hall and knocked on her door.

It took her a while to open the door. She looked delicious and prompted the familiar tightening sensation in his heart and groin. She was wearing makeup, and her red hair was arranged in its characteristically tousled look that quite correctly hinted at wildness in her nature. But she hadn't finished dressing for work and was barefoot and wearing a green robe with a sash pulled tight around her slender waist. She was obviously surprised to see him at her door, and for a second she appeared annoyed.

But she quickly recovered and smiled, then leaned forward and pecked him on the cheek.

Chumley was mollified. She stepped back as an invitation for him to enter, then closed the door behind him as he stepped inside.

It was the first time Chumley had been in her apartment since he'd helped her move in. Things were still untidy from the recent move. There was a hodgepodge of furniture, most of it obviously secondhand, lined along the walls, as if Deirdre still hadn't decided where to place it. Near the living room window was a small wooden desk on which sat a calendar, a phone, a blue mug stuffed full of pens and pencils, and a green-shaded banker's lamp. Chumley could smell coffee, but she didn't offer him any.

"This is a pleasant surprise," she said, not exactly in a voice bursting with sincerity.

"I thought you might want to go out for breakfast before work this morning," Chumley said.

Now she seemed pleased. "Sure. Sounds fine." She was staring at him with those luminous green eyes, that pinpoint of something in them that intrigued him and suggested danger.

"We have things to talk over," he said, as if he needed a reason other than personal to come here. As if he didn't want to take her into the bedroom and mess up her makeup and hair and fuck her until they were both crazy. "The shipment of watches from Taiwan is coming in today."

"Okay," Deirdre said, "but you're a little early. I haven't been awake all that long. Give me five minutes to finish getting dressed."

Chumley grinned. "I'd rather give you five minutes to get *un*dressed."

She smiled and wagged a finger at him as if he were a crude and naughty boy. "There's a time and a place for many things. Morning in my apartment, before going to work, is neither time nor place for what you have in mind."

"Don't be so sure," he said. "I might have something in mind that you'd like very much."

She gave a backhand motion that seemed to brush him off, as if the matter had been settled. "Oh, I don't doubt that in the slightest! But I have to finish dressing, and we need to leave. You know that."

"I know that," Chumley admitted.

He watched the sway of her hips beneath the green robe as she walked from the living room. It had been years since a woman had reached him as she had, had so excited him. She wasn't a ripe and eager girl—only a few years younger than he was, would be his guess—but there was a sensuousness to her that was eternal.

"I won't be long. Make yourself comfortable," she called to him from what he assumed was the bedroom.

He considered walking back there to join her, then thought better of it. That would be pushing her too far. And she was right; they should tend to business. There'd be plenty of time for play later today.

The apartment was quiet except for the intermittent humming of traffic from the street below. Somewhere in the building water ran. There were very faint voices, a muted thump as if a shoe had dropped.

Chumley slipped his hands into his pants pockets and walked over to the window overlooking the street. Traffic had picked up and the sun had come out full strength and spoiling for a fight with the city's air-conditioning resources. It was glaring off the windshields of cars and causing pedestrians to squint or shield their eyes. Summer was getting down to business, too.

Turning away from the window, he glanced in the direction Deirdre had gone, then began idly wandering around the living room. He knew so little about her, and he wanted to know so much more. He ran his fingertips over the threadbare back of an armchair, lifted a book, *Astrology and Eros,* to examine a slip of paper sticking out from between its pages. The paper was blank. He replaced it and carefully laid the book on the coffee table exactly as he'd found it.

He went over to the desk by the window, switched the green-shaded lamp on and off as if to test it, lifted the phone, and listened for a dial tone. As he replaced the receiver, he noticed that one of the desk drawers was open about four inches. He hooked a forefinger in it and gave a gentle tug. The drawer slid easily and silently on its runners. He opened it wider. Inside was a worn shoe box. He touched the cardboard lid, then began to lift one end of it to peer inside.

The floor creaked behind him and he knew she was in the room. Letting the shoe box lid drop closed, he shoved the drawer shut with his hip, hoping she wouldn't notice.

But it slid closed just as easily as it opened, and made a noise as if it had been slammed. He turned around.

Deirdre was fully dressed now, wearing a green dress almost exactly the shade of her robe, and black spike high heels. Her face was a furious mask that shocked him.

"What the fuck do you think you're doing?" Her voice was level but full of rage.

He was embarrassed at having been caught, but he was puzzled by the intensity of her reaction. After all, he'd only been nosing around to kill time, not removing pearls from a wall safe.

"I was, er, just looking around," he said. "Passing time while I waited . . ."

"You mean snooping!"

Chumley wanted desperately to defuse this. "Hey, take it easy, Deirdre. I didn't mean anything by it. I mean, I didn't think you'd mind, considering what we are to each other . . . what we've . . . Hell, I'm sorry! I'm genuinely sorry!"

She let out a long breath and stared at the ceiling, then back at Chumley. She seemed calmer now, more in control.

"I'm sorry too," she said. She ran her hand through her thick hair.

"Look, Deirdre—"

"It's just that I've got this thing about people who snoop. Always have felt that way. It's not because I have anything to hide."

"Of course not. Never thought you did. I don't even know what I was looking for . . . if I was looking for anything. I suppose I was curious because . . . well, I don't know much about you, Deirdre. Not really."

She stared hard at him. "All you need to know, I hope."

Another tender spot, Chumley thought. He shrugged. "All right. That's okay, I understand. You happen to be a private person. Hell, I admire that." He was always on the defensive with her.

She seemed to have regained her composure completely now, as she crossed the room toward him, smiling apologetically. She kissed him lightly on the lips, surprising him.

"I really am sorry," she said. "I shouldn't have gotten so upset. Can you forgive me?"

"Easily," Chumley said, relieved. "Let's forgive each other."

"Done!" she exclaimed. She kissed him on the mouth again, this time with more passion. "There! Sealed and delivered with a kiss, like so many things in life."

Chumley licked a minty taste from his lips and grinned down at her. "You taste like toothpaste."

She reared back and pretended to be offended. "You don't like it?"

"Toothpaste never tasted so good," he told her. He was off guard again, though. You couldn't press certain women. Not women like Deirdre, anyway. And why should he press her? Why should he be impatient? "I'll tell you what," he said, "why don't you take the day off? Enjoy the beautiful morning."

"But why?"

"The morning's my gift to you. If you feel like it, come in to work later." He touched her shoulder gently. "I want you to, Deirdre. Really."

Her smile was wide. "If you're certain, Craig . . ."

"I am."

"Okay, but I *will* be into work later today. I promise."

"You don't have to promise, Deirdre."

She leaned forward and kissed him on the mouth again.

He didn't mention toothpaste.

Almost everyone was seated for the ceremony at Halstadt Funeral Home in Brooklyn. David and Molly sat in one of the pews toward the back of the narrow, hot room, far away from Bernice, resting as if asleep in her coffin near the altar in the front of the chapel. Though it was still early, the chapel was warm, and David could feel perspiration at his white collar. He reached up and straightened his tie, turning his head slightly as he did so.

And saw Deirdre standing in the doorway of the chapel behind him.

He stopped breathing. What was she doing here? Why wasn't she at work?

She was wearing a green dress and black spike heels, standing with her feet far apart so it pulled the material of her dress taut across her muscular thighs. She smiled at him.

He looked away. Swallowed, aware of Molly sitting beside him and staring toward the front of the chapel.

He couldn't help it. He turned his head again to look back at Deirdre.

She was gone.

Not far, though, he was sure.

What was in her mind? What kind of trouble might she cause?

David decided he'd better see if he could find her and talk to her, try to prevent . . . whatever might happen if he didn't.

He nudged Molly with his elbow. "Gotta get out of here for a few minutes," he said. He smiled at her. "I'll be right back."

She nodded, perhaps assuming he was uncomfortably warm, or that he had to use the lavatory.

He stood up and excused himself as he slid past the knees of the mourners seated between him and the aisle.

The plushly carpeted, hushed main room and reception area of the mortuary was deserted. David looked around for Deirdre but didn't see her.

He walked to one of three small rooms with quiet conversation areas, "consolation rooms," he'd heard one of the mortuary employees call them.

In the first room was a woman trying to comfort a sobbing teenage boy. David withdrew awkwardly, then more cautiously stuck his head into the second room. It was identical to the first, with the same plush green carpeting, small traditional furniture, and a table with a coffeemaker whose glass pot was half full.

Deirdre was alone in the room, standing next to the coffeepot. She smiled at David.

He felt his anger surge as he entered the room. "Dammit, Deirdre, what are you doing here?"

"Calm down, David. And come here."

"You didn't answer my question."

As he stepped closer to her, she suddenly reached out and gripped his left wrist. He heard a distinct *click,* and was astounded to look down and see that she'd attached one of the bracelets of a bulky set of handcuffs.

He could hardly find words. "What the hell are you doing?"

"I came here to see you," she said. Without warning she deftly moved behind him, twisting the arm with the cuffed wrist behind his back. She wrenched his free wrist around suddenly and attached the second bracelet so his wrists were cuffed behind him. He'd been paralyzed for a moment by her strength and decisiveness.

He felt an indignation that almost instantly became fear. *What if somebody walked in on them? How could he explain?* "Jesus, Deirdre, this isn't the place—"

"Oh, it's exactly the place," she said firmly. She shoved him aside and closed the door of the consolation room. "And the time," she said with a grin. She lifted the green skirt of her dress and he saw she was wearing nothing beneath it.

In a panic, he moved toward the door then stopped.

"You're not going out there with handcuffs on, are you?" Deirdre asked. "Here. I'll open the door for you." She took a step toward it and extended her hand toward the knob.

"Wait!" David said, then lowered his voice. "At least lock it," he said, motioning with his head toward the lock button centered in the doorknob.

"That would take away most of the fun," she said.

She knelt before him and reached for his fly. As he tried to turn away, she clutched his testicles. She didn't squeeze, but he knew she might. He stood still and she worked the zipper, then reached in with her other hand and found what she sought. She took him in her mouth.

"Ah, damn it, Deirdre, don't." His gaze darted to the door.

A minute later she stood up, laughing. "Apparently you don't think this is such a bad idea at that, David." She stroked his erect penis.

He knew she was determined and the smartest thing now was to get it over with, to let her satisfy herself. As she backed him against a wall, he offered no resistance.

In her spike high heels she was the right height to move in on him, raise herself slightly, then envelope him warmly. He felt a thrill he hadn't expected as she plunged along the length of his erection, groaning sensuously. She was still for a few seconds, then began to grind her hips.

"You're harder than I can ever remember, David. It's sex and death. They go together, don't they? Bernice is laid out there on her back in her coffin, so beautiful. Almost like a doll. Did you ever have sex with Bernice, David?"

"That's sick, Deirdre!" He groped with his fingers at the flocked wallpaper behind him, strained against the handcuffs, then gave it up.

"Sex is the opposite of death," she said, increasing the pumping motion of her hips. "But then heads is the opposite of tails. Sex and death are opposite faces of the same coin."

"Deirdre!"

She slapped him. Hard. "Quiet, David! You don't want someone to hear us and come in here, do you? Remember, I left the door unlocked."

The grinding and thrusting of her hips became harder, violent. The handcuffs were clinking against the wall behind David. A stack of plastic foam cups next to the coffeemaker vibrated to the edge of the table then fell to the floor and rolled in a tight semicircle.

David looked away from the white cups, at the white ceiling, and was suddenly lost in everything but sensation. Deirdre's hands clutched his upper arms as she lay her cheek against his, expelling short, hard and hot breaths, moaning.

He reached orgasm but she didn't stop.

"Deirdre . . ."

"*Quiet, quiet!*" she whispered, and rested her forefinger across his lips. Its sharp fingernail cut into the tip of his nose.

He felt himself go soft inside her, and finally she pulled away and stepped back, smoothing her dress. She glanced in an oval mirror hanging on a wall and cocked her head to the side, touched a hand to her hair. She might have been alone in the room.

"Deirdre," David said breathlessly, "unlock the cuffs." He was desperately afraid again that someone would walk in on them.

Maybe even Molly! Come looking for him!

"The cuffs!"

"Deirdre smiled at him in the mirror, then turned around. "I didn't bring a key, David."

"Oh, my God!"

Then she came to him and kissed his cheek. "I'm only joking. Do you really think I'd leave you here like this?"

"Yes," David said.

She frowned and shook a finger at him. "David?"

"All right, no, you wouldn't leave me like this. Unlock these, Deirdre, please!"

She moved around behind him and he heard the key enter the handcuffs, felt the sudden release of pressure as they clicked open. He pulled his arms around in front of him and stared at his hands. They were quivering. Guilt tore at him. In a way, he knew, he'd aided her in what had just happened. He didn't want to do this to himself or to Molly, but he couldn't help himself.

Deirdre was standing by the door. "Zip your pants, David. And clean yourself up. This is kind of a place of worship, and cleanliness is the next best thing to Godliness."

Without looking back at him, she walked from the room, leaving the door standing open behind her.

He rushed to the door and closed it.

Then he zipped his fly, straightened his shirt and tie, and opened the door again, slowly.

Deirdre was gone. The entrance area outside the consolation rooms was still deserted.

He managed to make his way to the rest room and followed her advice.

At Glory and Resurrection Cemetery, the morning sun was beginning to make the mourners uncomfortable despite the fact that they were gathered in the shade of a temporary canopy. Molly felt a rivulet of perspiration trickle down her ribs beneath the same navy blue dress she'd worn the previous night to the visitation. She didn't like the idea of wearing the same dress, but it was the only dark outfit she owned that wouldn't have been stiflingly hot.

Only a few dozen mourners had made the journey from the mortuary to attend the funeral. A short, gray-haired woman with puffy eyes had introduced herself near the coffin the night before as Bernice's mother. She seemed to be benefitting from physical as well as psychological support from a lean, dark man with sunglasses, standing next to her and supporting her. Bernice's uncle, if Molly remembered correctly.

The pallbearers had rested Bernice's burnished steel casket on a bier. The grave was dug but covered with sagging, impossibly green artificial turf to spare those gathered the trauma of seeing into the yawning cavity in the earth that was about to receive Bernice's body and claim it for the rest of time.

Molly wiped her eyes and leaned on David as the minister, a young, prematurely bald man with acne, finished the service with a prayer: ". . . shall dwell in the house of the Lord forever."

She didn't remember anything else about the prayer. "Forever," was all she could think about. *Forever.*

David hadn't spoken at all during the drive to the cemetery and was standing motionless, as if lost in his own thoughts. Maybe Bernice's death had affected him more than Molly had thought. Men were that way, keeping their feelings bottled and corked and then breaking down in private, as if grief and loneliness had to be synonymous. He'd missed the first part of the service in the mortuary chapel, and when he'd returned to sit beside her again in the pew, his face was pale and thoughtful.

The minister tossed a handful of earth onto the artificial turf, then nodded to the mourners as a signal that the funeral was over. With a sad smile, he moved toward Bernice's mother to give final consolation.

David started to leave, but Molly gripped his arm and stopped him. He seemed startled for a second, which surprised her. Then he smiled down at her and looked all around him, as if coming out of a dream.

When the minister had walked away, she went to where Bernice's mother was still standing with the slim, dark man.

"If you need any help," Molly said to her. "I mean, with Bernice's things. We live right downstairs from her apartment and we'll be glad to do what we can."

"That's nice of you," the mother—Iris, Molly remembered now—said. She might have had a slight accent, though Molly hadn't noticed it the night before. Molly wrote their phone number on a slip of paper from her purse and gave it to her.

"She was on her swim team in high school," Iris said. "Did you know that?"

"No," Molly heard David say. He had joined them and now seemed himself again, free of his thoughts of death.

"We could have had an autopsy, but I couldn't bear to think of that being done to her. She's dead. She'll stay dead forever, no matter why she died."

"I understand," Molly said. "I think you made the right decision."

"In the water," Iris Clark said, "she was a natural. Like a beautiful and graceful dolphin."

"I'm sorry," Molly said again, not knowing what else to say. The lean man might have been looking at her. She could see only her own twin reflections in his glasses.

He took Iris Clark's arm, nodded to both Molly and David, then turned and led Iris to one of the waiting black limousines.

Molly felt David's arm encircle her waist as they walked toward the last of the three limos.

"On her high school swim team," Molly said.

"Freak things happen," David said glumly.

Forever.

Molly began to cry.

24

After Deirdre described what had happened at the funeral home, Darlene looked horrified.

"That was a terrible thing to do!"

"Why?" Deirdre asked. "Just because angelic little you wouldn't do it?"

They were walking along crowded Fifth Avenue. Darlene was wearing tight slacks that showed off her slender, shapely dancer's legs, and a white pullover with a scoop neck that made her own neck look even thinner and more delicate. She and Deirdre had met in front of the public library, near a stone lion that guarded so much knowledge. Deirdre's high heels were making regular clacking sounds on the concrete as she strode along the sidewalk. Beside her, Darlene walked quietly in soft soles.

"I certainly wouldn't do it in a mortuary," Darlene said. "And don't tell me about all the Freudian relationships between sex and death. That's no excuse."

"I don't need an excuse. Anyway, Freud was a fool."

People glanced at them as the two women approached, then the crowds on the sidewalk parted to let them pass. Darlene had such a confident stride that folks automatically made way for her, sometimes even stepping wide to get out of her path. Deirdre was jealous. She couldn't help but notice the deferential way people always treated Darlene, as if she were some kind of royalty.

"Why *did* you have sex there?" Darlene asked.

"Because I wanted to, and so did David."

"You made him want to. I've been thinking a lot about your

situation, Deirdre. What you wanted, what you still want, is to control David entirely. To possess him sexually and in every other way."

"I never made a secret of that. Not with you, anyway. Propriety is the spice of life."

"Don't spring those cutesy puns and malapropisms on me, Deirdre."

Deirdre didn't like being talked to in such a manner, but an apology here might be the wisest choice. "Okay, I'm sorry. It's an old habit."

"I don't like it. And I don't approve of sex with a married man in a funeral home. It's inexcusable."

"But we both enjoyed the risk. This might be impossible for you to understand, but for some people sex is best when it's dangerous. It's much more of a thrill."

"Does that explain why all those poor people died of AIDS?"

"It explains some of it, I bet. I didn't realize you had such a social conscience."

Darlene stopped walking. Deirdre continued for a few steps, then stopped and turned. They moved into a doorway so they wouldn't be knocked down by the relentless mass of pedestrians.

"I care about *you*, Deirdre," Darlene said. "I don't want you taking those kinds of risks, sinning that way. I care about your body and your immortal soul."

Deirdre was astounded. "Are you some kind of religious freak?"

"No."

"Then don't be so judgmental."

Darlene looked down at the cigarette butts and crumpled gum and candy wrappers littering the pavement. Then she looked up at Deirdre. "Okay," she said seriously, "maybe you're right. From now on I'll try not to judge."

Deirdre felt better. She reached out for Darlene, but Darlene moved away. Almost as if she were afraid.

"You're not scared of me because I like wild sex, are you?" Deirdre asked.

"Of course not. And who says I *don't* like wild sex?"

Deirdre laughed. "I can't imagine you . . . actually doing it."

"Well," Darlene said, "I actually do. I have male friends."

Deirdre glanced across the street at a corner coffee shop. "Let's go over there and have something to drink."

"I can't and you shouldn't," Darlene said. "You've missed enough work today. Your boss might object."

"Not Chumley. I've got him trapped around my finger."

"Deirdre!"

"Oh. Sorry."

"You're so manipulative."

"Aren't you being judge—"

"Yes, I am. My turn to apologize. But you really should get to work."

"Chumley truly won't care if I'm another hour late. Because I took time off today, I plan on working very late tonight. It's already arranged."

"Be that as it may," Darlene said earnestly, sounding old-fashioned the way she did sometimes, "I can't go across the street and have a drink with you. It's impossible."

"Why?"

"It just is." Deirdre thought she was going to glance at her watch again, but she didn't. Instead she moved out of the doorway, into the throng of passing pedestrians. "Sorry, Deirdre."

"Wait a—"

"Bye! Don't do anything I wouldn't do."

And she was gone.

Maybe you're sorry, and maybe you're not, Deirdre thought.

She was hurt and disappointed. She had wanted to talk with Darlene, to find out exactly what she thought that Freud had said about sex and death. She wanted to set Darlene straight about Freud.

Then she glanced at her watch, the way Darlene so often did, and began striding briskly to work.

Sex and death indeed!

25

"You're killing me!" Chumley moaned.

Behind him nighttime Manhattan glittered outside his office window. It was a large office with gray file cabinets along one wall. On another wall was a sales chart, a bulletin board plastered with memos and shipping schedules, a Minolta copy machine on a table with folding legs. Cardboard storage boxes were stacked in a corner. It was an office not for show, but where work was done.

Two gray steel desks, one larger than the other, matched the filing cabinets. On the large desk sat a black multilined phone, file folders, a wire Out basket, a fancy gold and black marble pen set, and framed photos of a smiling, middle-aged woman and two preteen girls wearing smaller but brighter versions of the same smile.

Chumley was seated in his desk chair rolled out from behind the larger desk. Deirdre, her skirt hiked to her waist, was straddling him, moving her hips with increasing speed and force. With each pump of her hips the chair squealed as if in pain. Sometimes it was Chumley who groaned, not in pain. After hours had never been so good for Chumley.

He had his head thrown back now and was moaning softly. Deirdre knew the moment. She grinned down at him, cupped his face in her hands, and kissed him violently on the lips. His body arched and trembled beneath her and she rode him as he reached orgasm.

"Jesus!" Chumley moaned, and his body relaxed. Went completely limp.

Deirdre lifted herself up from him just enough to work her hand down between their bodies. She kissed him again, hunching her shoulders, then used her hand to bring herself to climax. She'd been close, and it took her less than a minute.

Her breathing was only slightly hard and not at all ragged, but Chumley's chest was still heaving as he sucked in oxygen. Laughing deep in her throat, she leaned forward and probed his ear with her tongue. He turned his head away.

"I've had it, Deirdre," he gasped. "Whew! . . . Sorry."

She planted her feet on the floor and rose up off him, letting her skirt fall back into place then smoothing it down over her thighs. She leaned back with her hips against the edge of the desk. Chumley, fully dressed but with his pants and boxer shorts down around his ankles, remained sprawled in the chair, slowly winning the struggle to regain his breath.

"You are something," he said between gasps.

She smiled at him, then picked up her panties from the floor and stuffed them in a pocket of her skirt. She was looking out the window behind them. The blinds were raised high and the drapes opened wide. Hundreds if not thousands of lighted windows faced them. And some that were not lighted. Those were the ones that interested her, people staring out at the world from darkness.

Chumley was breathing more evenly. The desk chair, tilted as far back as it would go, gave a final *eeeek!* as he dropped forward in it.

"We should do this at your place," he said. "In a bed. We keep this up and you're gonna kill me."

"It's possible."

"Your place next time?"

She yanked her belt around so it was aligned with her skirt. "I kind of like this, with the window behind us and everybody in New York with a telescope watching."

Chumley laughed. "You're an exhibitionist."

"Only sometimes."

Chumley bent low, then pulled up his shorts and pants as he managed to climb out of the chair. It was an awkward maneuver. He rebuttoned his shirt, fastened his belt, and straightened his clothes. Then he stooped and picked up his tie from the floor. Also on the floor were a goose-necked desk lamp, a jumble of file folders and papers, and various other items brushed from the desk during their sometimes violent lovemaking. Chumley picked up the In basket, which had been lying near his tie, and set it on the desk next to the Out.

He looked around and shook his head. "We made a hell of a mess here."

"Worth it?" Deirdre asked.

"Worth it."

She picked up an ashtray and laid it on the desk. "Don't worry about the mess. You go ahead home and I'll straighten things up and put everything back where it belongs. There's a place for everything, and I know where."

"You live in a conveniently compartmented world," Chumley remarked, smiling.

She tilted her head, thinking about that. "Sure. That's how the world should be."

"Well, since you came on the scene, this place is certainly getting more organized."

She flashed him her wicked grin. "Not to mention more fun." Then she put her hands on her hips and looked at the folders and papers scattered on the hardwood floor. "But now's the time for organization rather than fun. Time to pay the pauper."

" 'Piper,' you mean."

"Whoever."

"You're too good to me, you know that?"

"Uh-hm, part of my job."

He tucked in his shirt, then rolled down and buttoned his sleeves and put on his tie, making sure the wide end overlapped the narrow. He knew his wife could be on the alert for any sign of irregular behavior in the city. When it came to that kind of thing, women had radar.

"Presentable?" he asked.

"At least." She brushed off his suit coat and handed it to him.

He worked his arms into the coat. She stepped in close and buttoned it for him.

"You are something!" he told her again.

She smiled up at him. "You already said that."

"Well, I think it's worth repeating."

She kissed him lightly on the lower lip, then nudged him toward the door. He hesitated, looking back at her.

"Don't be late," she said. "We don't want questions."

He nodded, then went out the door.

Deirdre picked up the still-glowing goose-neck lamp and placed it on the desk, then gathered some papers from the floor, rearranged them, and placed them in the In basket.

When she'd decided that Chumley was gone from the building and enough time had passed that it was unlikely he'd return, she went to the door and shot the deadbolt into its shaft. She rolled Chumley's chair into the kneehole of his desk, then lowered the blinds. The office suddenly seemed smaller, quieter.

Still in her stockinged feet, Deirdre walked to the file cabinets and opened one of the bottom drawers. Squatting effortlessly so that her buttocks rested on her heels, she quickly found the hanging file folder she sought and lifted it from its steel tracks, then stood up and nudged the long drawer shut with the side of her foot.

She carried the folder to the copy machine and set to work, smiling.

26

Molly scooted over toward the window to make room for Michael. David sat across from them in the booth at the Choice Deli, on the corner two blocks down West Eighty-fifth Street from their apartment. The Choice had been at the same location for decades. Though the walls screamed for plaster-patch, their coat of rose-colored paint was fresh. The counter stools and booths were only a few years old, gray vinyl with a sparkling silver design salted throughout. A tall, slowly revolving glass display case near the cash register dated back to the fifties and somehow made the thick cream pies and cheesecakes look like delicious confections from childhood.

The waiter came over and they ordered an omelet for Molly, scrambled eggs and milk for Michael, a toasted corn muffin for David. Molly scooted the steaming coffee cup that the waiter had left, so it was well out of Michael's reach, and stared at the back page of a Saturday *Times* the man two booths away was reading. A young woman from the Village had been raped and murdered near the East River, full-column news because it was in the area of Sutton Place, where the wealthy of New York didn't factor possible murder into their plans.

The pretty, young victim was smiling mischievously in her photograph, as if someone had just told her an off-color but amusing joke. On that sunny day she'd been psychologically a million years from unexpected violent death, but in reality closer than she'd known when the camera's shutter was tripped. The city had been waiting.

Michael stared up at Molly over his mustache of milk. "I'm hungry."

"Everybody's hungry," David said.

Molly patted Michael's wrist. "The food will be here soon," she assured him. David handed him a pencil and he began scrawling crude stick figures on his napkin, his eyes sharply focused and his lower lip tucked in with childish concentration.

Molly glanced out the window at the wet street. It had been drizzling from low, dark clouds since early morning. The sky looked like an upside-down gray bowl arcing inches above the tops of buildings. Along with the heat and almost tropical humidity, it helped to produce a claustrophobic feel to the city.

"Thank God it wasn't raining yesterday at Bernice's funeral," Molly said.

"This isn't your morning to run, is it?"

David changing the subject yet staying with the weather. Very adroit.

"Tomorrow," Molly said.

He picked up the *Times* he'd wrestled from the corner vending machine and folded then started to read the front section. The smiling young woman who'd met her death near Sutton Place again stared at Molly from her newspaper photo.

The waiter arrived with their breakfasts, and David had to lay the paper on the seat beside him to make room.

When their coffee cups had been topped off and the waiter had left, Molly spread butter on Michael's toast, then, at his insistence, jelly. He beamed when she gave in to his demands, then promptly stuck his elbow in the jellied toast as he reached for his milk.

David observed this and grinned. "He'll clean up okay with a little soap," he assured Molly.

"Deirdre called and offered to baby-sit him today while I work," Molly said, using her napkin to wipe jelly from Michael's arm.

"Take her up on the offer?"

"No. Julia called with the same offer. I told them both no. I think we should keep him home for a while, watch him for . . . you know, effects." She lowered her voice to pronounce the last word, knowing even as she did so that it was silly. Michael was sitting right beside her and would hear. But he wouldn't know that the effects she referred to were his possible reactions to Bernice's death. Molly was worried about what the experience would do to him. Three-year-olds could accept these things with a matter-of-factness that eluded some adults. Yet on a deeper level the trauma and grief could leave a lasting scar.

As she forked a bite of omelet into her mouth and chewed, Michael glanced up at her, possibly wondering about his fate for the day.

"I'm going to the gym to work out later this morning," David said. "When I get back, I can keep an eye on him while you work. Maybe we'll go out, find something fun to do."

Michael had resumed eating and didn't look up from his scrambled eggs, but he grinned.

"I thought you worked out yesterday," Molly said.

"Upper body." He bit into his toasted corn muffin. "Lower body's scheduled for today."

That didn't seem right to Molly, but she said nothing. David, as far as she knew, had never been on an alternating workout schedule. But then she wasn't privy to what went on at Silver's Gym. She'd been there only once, to meet him before leaving to join friends for dinner. She remembered it as a functional, depressing place, with old equipment and a darkened and smoothly worn wood floor. But men seemed to like that kind of atmosphere where they worked out. Possibly it made them think they were sacrificing more and so should see greater benefits.

". . . about the fire?" David was saying.

"What?"

"Did Julia say anything more about the fire at her mother's apartment?"

"She told me it was deliberately set. The arson investigators said an accelerant had been used, and they found an empty wine bottle in the basement that had contained gasoline. It was lucky nobody was killed. Well, not only luck was involved. Unlike our building, when the fire alarm sounded, everyone knew there was probably a fire."

"Maybe they'll lift some fingerprints from the bottle," David said. He took a sip of coffee.

"No. According to Julia, the fire took care of that. The bottle

was blackened and in pieces from the heat. Gangs, is what the police think. There's a lot of gang activity in that neighborhood, and
a sixteen-year-old kid who's been in that kind of trouble before
lives in the building."

Michael demanded more jelly for the second half of his toast.

"It's a shame kids get screwed up in those gangs," Molly said.
"It must be a tough neighborhood."

She used her knife to scoop grape jelly from its plastic container.
"You do what you must to survive, I guess."

Don't we all? he thought. Or was he only telling himself the sur-
vival of his marriage and reputation depended on his cooperation
with Deirdre? She was a potent exterior force, but maybe his com-
pulsion was his own. Their relationship was one he knew was
drowning him as surely and fatally as Bernice had been drowned.
He realized it yet seemed unable to find the strength to swim toward the surface.

He could only struggle and sink deeper.

As he was going to do later that morning.

27

The basement was almost completely dark except for yellow pools of light spread by bare overhead bulbs. Visible in the dimness were jumbles of ductwork above, and junk below. There were ripped screens, an old sawhorse, an upside-down tricycle without wheels. A row of wooden storage lockers faded into the blackness, its walls constructed of slats with two-inch spaces between them, solid wood doors with hasps for padlocks.

In the dim light of a paint-splotched lightbulb back near the boilers, David had Deirdre pressed against a wooden wall of one of the storage lockers. He was standing. Her wrists were bound above her head to the slats with one of David's old silk ties. Her skirt was hiked up and her legs were locked around his waist.

Beside them was the duffle bag containing David's workout clothes for Silver's Gym, where he'd told Molly he was going. Later, he would slip out through a side door of the apartment building and actually go to Silver's and work out. Though right now he doubted if another workout was necessary.

He was thrusting into Deirdre, causing the loosely nailed slats of the storage locker to slam together. Something fell inside the locker with a sound like glass breaking on the concrete floor.

"Too much . . . noise, David!" Deirdre moaned desperately between thrusts. "God, too much . . . noise!"

He didn't let up. "You're the one who . . . insisted on doing this down here . . ."

Getting winded, he paused and took a deep breath, then leaned forward and bit her earlobe, hard. Punishing her for making him need her. Her arms strained against their silken bondage.

"Shit, David! Don't draw blood!"

He drew his head back to look closely at her in the musty dimness. Her eyes were puffy and dreamy with lust but still held their glint of calculation. She was losing herself only ninety percent.

"You never minded before," he told her. "Besides, turnabout's fair play." He bit her ear again, but not nearly as hard. She tried to move her head away but couldn't, her movements restricted by her upraised arms.

"I'm a working girl now. I have to wear earrings." She giggled. "For those I need ears."

He'd stopped biting her and resumed driving himself into her, watching her eyes lose focus and become slits and her lips tighten and withdraw over her perfect teeth. She was his a hundred percent now.

And he was hers.

He felt her body tense and her legs clasped him more powerfully. After a few more strokes he pressed hard into her, holding himself tight against the bulge of her pubic mound and grinding her against the raw wood slats as he spilled into her. He heard himself moan. He held her pinned against the slats afterward, hard enough to make the old wood boards creak with the strain, as he valued every second.

Finally he withdrew from her and she lowered her legs and was standing on her own. He quickly untied her wrists and slipped the silk tie into a pocket.

They kissed long and feverishly, then smiled at each other, eyes serious, and began reorienting themselves to the postcoital world as they rearranged their clothing.

"I love dark and dusty old basements," Deirdre said, rubbing her wrists. "I've had more fun in them than anyplace else."

David checked to make sure he'd zipped his fly. "I don't like Molly being right upstairs."

Deirdre gave him a lascivious grin. "I kind of do." She spread her legs slightly and held her wadded panties to her crotch beneath her skirt. "Wow! You must have come a gallon, the way you're running out of me. It's lucky I only have to make it to my apartment in this building, or I'd leave a trail."

He winced, not only at her indelicacy but at her casual attitude about them all living beneath the same roof, the wife, the lover, the cheating husband. It was one of those moments when David gained some perspective and was terrified.

There was a soft scratching sound from another part of the basement, and he and Deirdre stood still for a few seconds.

Then she kissed him and said, "Only a rat."

"So there's another one down here."

"You're far too hard on yourself, David. We're not the only two people having an affair, and Molly's not the only wife who's in the way. You should learn to embrace your destiny the way you hold me."

"It isn't just Molly. What about Michael?"

"I don't want to see him hurt any more than you do. But his world isn't going to come to a close. Did you know the children of divorced parents are a majority in public schools now?"

"The statistics don't bear that out, Deirdre."

"Well, there are liars, darned liars, and statisticians. Anyway, sometimes people have to recognize reality and give in to its power. It's like this big roulette wheel that spins and decides whose lives get mingled and changed. This time it's you, me, and Molly. She might not like it, but it's fate."

"Another thing she didn't like was you being our baby-sitter the other night."

"That's just because she's too suspicious. She's paranormal."

He felt to make sure his underwear had soaked up his sperm and her wetness, and the front of his pants was free of telltale spots that would have to dry before he could leave the basement. "You mean paranoid. And why wouldn't she be? She's got a lot of stress in her life lately."

"We can't help that."

"Can't we?"

"You're not down here with me against your will, are you, David?"

He spread his fingers and raked them through his hair, scraping his scalp with his nails. "I'm not sure I've got any will left."

She laughed loudly, causing his heart to skip as he glanced around nervously. Hardly anyone came down to the dusty, gloomy basement, but if someone they knew *did* happen to discover them here, it would add another layer to his guilt and fear and might be devastating. Deirdre's roulette wheel in the sky, jolting his future again.

"It sure seemed like free will a few minutes ago," Deirdre said. "That's the part you don't understand. The choice is yours but you can't help yourself, David. You can't help loving me."

"I can't help fucking you."

"That's close enough for now."

She moved directly in front of him then reached out and laced her fingers behind his neck, leaning back slightly so he was supporting her. She stared into his eyes with a gloating but desperate gleam that seemed too bright to be the reflection of the nearby low-wattage bulb. He gazed back at her with more hopelessness than passion.

"Molly didn't like you baby-sitting Michael," he said again.

She seemed incredulous. Injured. "Why not? Did she think I was going to harm him?"

"I don't—"

"Whatever the reason, Molly must be going off her rocker chair. She oughta see a doctor, David, really."

His irritation made him want to slap her, hurt and shock her. His voice was tight but level. "Stop saying she's insane."

"Why should I? She's saying things about me. What's good for the goose is good for the rest of the flock."

"Oh, Jesus!"

"I'm serious, David. You don't want to admit it, but the way she's been acting lately, she really does need professional help."

He thought for a second he actually would strike her. Then he knew where it might lead, that it wasn't a solution or even an option.

Without speaking, he reached back and unfastened her hands from behind his neck.

Then he turned away from her abruptly, picked up his duffle bag, and walked into the darkness.

The worst part was, he suspected she might be right about Molly needing help. And it was his fault as well as Deirdre's. He was caught in a terrible, destructive dance with her, and no matter how much he hated himself, he couldn't stop dancing.

At the gym he worked the Nautilus equipment, then the free weights, with a determination and a fierceness that pushed him to surpass his previous limits.

"Aren't we full of piss and vinegar today?" Herb Mindle remarked. "What the hell did you have for breakfast?"

David wiped perspiration from his forehead with a towel and smiled grimly. "You don't want to know."

"Sure, I do," Mindle said. "It's my business."

David paused and nodded. "That's right, I'd forgotten." He chalked his hands, stretched out on his back on the padded bench, and gripped the barbell at the proper width for maximum-weight presses.

He still felt strong, but lying as he was, staring up at the lights on the ceiling, he felt a curious dizziness come over him and erode his confidence. Everyone was human; everyone was weak and broke more easily than they imagined.

"Better spot me on this," he said. "It's ten pounds above my previous high. If I don't make it, the bar might come down and break my neck."

"Then why not try only five extra pounds first?" Mindle asked.

"Because I decided to go for ten," David snapped, tired of Mindle's probing. There was no excuse for it, even considering his profession. He had no right to keep prying, eliciting information, analyzing.

Mindle moved around to be in position to grab the bar in case David lost control. He looked pensive, as if musing over David's answer to his last question.

"Pertinent," he said with a grin. "Pertinent."

28

While David was doing bench presses, Molly was at her desk working on the architectural manuscript, coping with split infinitives and flying buttresses, wondering at the deterioration in the use of language among academics.

A shrill cry of pain made her drop her pencil.

It had come from Michael's room, where he was down for his nap.

She jumped up and ran.

Michael was out of bed, jabbing at a cornered Muffin with a toy rifle equipped with a bayonet. The rifle and bayonet were obviously plastic, but the bayonet was still sharp enough to evoke screeches of pain and rage from the cat, who was trapped in the angle where the bureau met the wall.

Molly was sickened that Michael would do something so blatantly mean and aggressive. She was more sickened by the expression on his face. He was staring intently at the cat, his eyes brightening with each lunge with the bayonet. It was a look she recognized; she's seen it often enough on grown men. At that moment, Michael might have been thirty instead of three.

"Michael! Stop that!"

Immediately he dropped the rifle and looked guiltily at her, three years old and innocent again. Muffin gave a final *Yowl!* and bolted for the propped-open window. Molly watched as he made his getaway via the fire escape, wondering briefly if he'd return after the cruelty he'd suffered.

She was trembling, fighting to control her temper. Temper mingled with fear. Michael's transformation had been so sudden and unexpected; she'd had no idea he could harbor and display such sadism.

"Why were you doing such a thing?" she asked, trying to keep her voice level. "Where did you get that toy gun?"

His lower lip quivered and he began to cry. Molly's anger rushed from her and she went to him and held him close, telling him she loved him, trying to soothe him into silence.

"It's okay . . . Okay, Michael. Mommy isn't mad at you, really . . ."

But she couldn't console him.

"Who gave you the gun?" she asked gently.

"Aunt Deedray," he managed to say between sobs.

Molly stood quietly, bent over slightly and hugging him to her hip and thigh, her anger building hotly deep within her as she felt his warm tears penetrate the thin material of her slacks.

After a few minutes, she picked him up and stalked from the bedroom.

Aunt Deirdre! Jesus! Did the woman think she was a fool?

By the time she'd taken the elevator up to Deirdre's floor and was knocking on her apartment door, Michael had calmed down and was quiet. He lay against her limp and watchful, his head tucked in the curve of her neck and shoulder. He was getting heavy, but she barely noticed.

Deirdre opened the door and smiled out at them. She'd been busy trying to get her new apartment in order and was glamorous even in work clothes. She was wearing tight jeans with a button fly, and a black T-shirt. Though she had a paisley bandanna wrapped around her head, her makeup was flawless and the protruding lock of red hair had to have been calculated. There was a smudge of dirt strategically placed on her nose and she was holding a dust cloth. Molly wondered whom she might have been expecting.

"Hi," she said brightly. "Sorry it took me a while to come to the door. I'm trying to get things organized in here." She reached out and touched the tip of Michael's nose with her forefinger. "Hello, Michael, darling."

Molly tried to rein in her anger as she brought the plastic bayonet-equipped toy rifle out from where she'd been holding it behind her back. "Why did you give him this gun, Deirdre?"

She widened her eyes in surprise. "Why, he's a little boy. Boys like guns." She winked. "You know, it's not like with us. It's some kind of phallic thing."

"I found him trying to stab Muffin with the bayonet."

"Muffin? Oh, the cat." She smiled at Michael. "Well, Michael's not a cruel boy. I'm sure he won't do it again." The red-enameled nail came forward again to touch the tip of his nose. "Isn't that right, Michael?"

Molly knew this confrontation hadn't taken Deirdre by surprise. It was part of a pattern. She was determined not to be sucked into this scenario in a way that fit Deirdre's script. The problem was, she didn't know how this was supposed to play out. Her anger rose.

"Don't you *ever* give him *any* kind of toy without checking with me first!"

Deirdre stepped back, shocked that Molly was so upset over such a trifle. "Hey, I'm sorry. It really isn't a major thing. I found the gun here in the apartment and thought he might enjoy it, that's all."

"An elderly couple rented this apartment before you," Molly said.

"Well, maybe they had a grandson. Or were into some kind of kinky sex with toy guns. Anyway, I certainly wouldn't have given the gun to Michael if I thought it might do him psychological harm, or for some reason he wouldn't enjoy it the way other little boys play with guns without it ruining their lives."

"The cat didn't enjoy it," Molly said.

Deirdre considered that for a second, biting her lower lip somberly. "No, I suppose not. You do have a point there." Then she brightened, smiling again. "Okay, no more guns or knives when I baby-sit you, Michael."

"There won't be any more baby-sitting."

Deirdre looked astounded. "Don't you think you're overacting about this, Molly?"

"You mean 'over*re*acting.' And no, I don't think I am."

"Would David approve of this?"

"That's no concern of yours. My child is no concern of yours. My husband is no concern of yours." Molly tossed the toy rifle past Deirdre into the apartment, harder than she'd intended. It clattered noisily on the wood floor. Probably it had broken.

"Overreacting, then," Deirdre said with maddening composure.

Obviously, on a certain level, she was amused by Molly's rage. Was this how she'd planned their encounter?

Molly stalked to the elevator and slapped at the Down button. The elevator was still at floor level, but it seemed to take forever before the door opened.

Deirdre stood watching as Molly, clutching Michael to her, stepped inside.

"Bye, Michael," she said with a smile, as the door glided shut.

As the elevator descended, Molly swallowed as if to relieve pressure. The entire building was full of pressure since Deirdre had moved in. Molly was holding her breath as if she were dropping toward the ocean floor in a diving bell. She released it and set Michael on the floor, trying to calm herself. But her anger continued coursing through her blood like a disease.

When she'd stepped forward to fling the toy rifle and Deirdre had moved out of the way, Molly had been aware of a scent she'd noticed without realizing it, as soon as Deirdre had opened her apartment door.

Back in her own apartment, Molly got Michael settled in the living room with television and some toys then went into the bedroom. Cartoons were on TV, featuring cavemen and dinosaurs, and probably, Molly admitted with an infuriating thrust of doubt, more violence than Michael had perpetrated on the cat.

There was an argument to be made that violent childhood entertainment—including toy guns—was as much of a catharsis as a cause or predictor of violent behavior. It was a valid argument, Molly knew, but she didn't believe it enough to take a chance with her own child.

She stood at her dresser and examined the neat and glittering row of cosmetics bottles. Then she lifted a slender glass bottle shaped like a candle with a plastic cap made to resemble a flame. Elaborate red vertical lettering on the bottle spelled out *Flaming Fixation*. She removed the cap and sniffed at the bottle's contents.

She knew now without a doubt. It was the perfume Deirdre was wearing.

Molly thought it should have been named *Apropos*.

29

Deirdre threw the dust rag at a lamp hard enough to knock it over. She didn't bother to pick it up from the floor. She paced and fumed, occasionally pausing to kick or punch a piece of furniture.

"You bitch, Molly!" she hissed. "Bitch, bitch, bitch! . . . You don't deserve them!"

Finally she walked over and picked up the lamp, then paused and hurled it back to the floor, bending the shade and causing the brass footing to break loose from the base and lie looped around the cord. She walked to the wall and began slamming her head against the plaster, over and over until she saw bloodstains on the paint and stopped. She staggered to the sofa and fell back on it.

For almost an hour she lay without moving, staring hard and unblinkingly at the ceiling, as if willing it to open like a box lid and free her rage and frustration to the heavens.

Then she remembered Chumley had said he'd be working at the office today. For a moment her hostility hovered around her thoughts of Chumley. She considered calling and having him take her somewhere interesting, cheer her up.

That bitch!

Yes, she needed cheering.

But Chumley wouldn't be capable of giving her what she needed. He hadn't managed it yet. She really didn't want to see him today.

She sat up, reached for the phone, then lay back down with it resting on her stomach. She punched out Chumley's home number.

A woman answered on the third ring.

"Is Craig Chumley there?" Deirdre asked, making her voice a shade husky.

"No. May I take a message?"

Deirdre smiled at the hint of alarm in the woman's voice. Shirley. Mrs. Chumley. Another bitch!

I, uh . . . Is this Mrs. Chumley?" she stammered, as if caught off guard.

"Yes, it is. Who is this?"

"Never mind, there's no message. I called the wrong number. I'm really very sorry I bothered you."

Deirdre lowered the receiver to within an inch of its cradle and held it there. As soon as she heard the inquiring natter of a voice, she gently hung up.

There! Let *that* bitch think about the phone call. Let her wonder who'd called. Maybe it was all an innocent mistake. Or maybe it was precisely what she feared, a threat to her family and home and security, to everything she thought was hers forever. Everything she simply took for granted that she deserved. Let her wonder for a long time. Let her ask Chumley about it. If he ever asked Deirdre if it was she who'd phoned, she'd deny it and he'd believe her.

That was the beautiful part. He would believe her instead of his wife.

Mrs. Fucking Chumley! Another paranormal bitch!

Chumley sat at his desk, working on his notebook computer. Since it was Saturday, he was wearing his Yankee T-shirt, khaki shorts, and thick-soled walking shoes. When he was finished here, he'd take a long walk and work off some of the rich food he'd been consuming lately. It was hard to resist dessert at some of the restaurants where Deirdre wanted to dine. At Tavern on the Green his willpower had crumbled and he'd ordered—

The phone rang, interrupting his caloric ruminations.

"Shirley?" he asked, after he'd said hello and identified himself. "Shirl?"

"That's right, Craig." Her voice was odd, which was why when she'd said his name he hadn't recognized that it was her. Then she hadn't spoken again for several seconds. "I just wondered if you were still at the office."

"Why didn't you speak up? Of course I'm still here. Working on the books like I told you this morning. I'll be here awhile longer. Why did you call?"

"Do I need a particular reason?"

"No, of course not." He sat for a while, a puzzled expression on his long face. "No," he said again. "You don't need a reason to call. Not ever. You know that."

"Are you going to finish there soon?"

"Relatively soon. Depends on how things add up. But I shouldn't be much longer. I'm gonna go for a walk when I'm done here, get rid of some of this spare tire." There was a long pause while he waited for her to reply, this woman he lived and slept with on the other end of the line.

"I still love you, Craig," she said in a flat voice.

He was startled. She hadn't told him that in a long time. "Me too," he said at last. "Love you, I mean."

"Honestly?"

"Of course I do. Always have, always will." He wondered about the monotonal quality in her voice. She'd been taking tranquilizers for a long time, different kinds. He didn't know what she was taking these days. What seemed like dozens of prescription bottles were jammed into the medicine cabinet shelves. "Have you taken one of your pills?" he asked.

"Not today." She was silent for a moment. "You'll be home after your walk?"

"Yes, more or less. This evening, probably after supper. See you then."

More silence.

He hung up and stared thoughtfully at the phone for a few minutes. Something in Shirley's voice had scared him. Not just her flat tone, something else. There was no way she could know about his affair with Deirdre, yet she'd sounded suspicious. He'd told himself he didn't care if she found out, but now he wasn't so sure. He felt sick.

He assured himself he was probably imagining that she suspected. Guilt could do that to a man. He despised guilt; all his life it had prevented him from having so much that he'd wanted. He'd heeded it and done what was expected of him, gotten what other people wanted him to have. He wasn't going to let guilt spoil what he had now.

Trying to put his marital concerns aside, he got back to work. Work to forget, at least for a while.

Suddenly he squinted through his glasses, then leaned forward to study more closely the figures on the glowing computer screen.

He stood up and went to the file cabinets, then stooped and opened a bottom drawer. After leafing through the contents of a file folder without removing it, he slid the drawer closed and opened the bottom drawer of the cabinet next to it.

Again he thumbed quickly through the contents of a folder. When he started to close the drawer, something stopped him, and he reopened it. He removed the folder and looked at its contents more carefully, then carried it to the desk and sat down. From a bottom desk drawer, he dug out a computer disk, fed it into the disk drive, and keyed into it on the computer.

He worked the keyboard until he'd called up the information he wanted. Then he sat almost motionless, staring at the screen, occasionally moving only his middle finger to press the *Pgdn* key to scroll what he was reading.

After a few minutes of study, he said, "Uh-oh! Oh, shit!"

The office suddenly seemed fiercely hot. He made a move to roll up his sleeves, then realized that he had none and wasn't wearing his usual office attire. The building management controlled the thermostat, so there was no way to adjust the air-conditioning. The office was as cool as it was going to be today.

With intermittent worried glances at the computer screen, he began examining and rearranging the papers from the file folder, trying to ignore the perspiration from his hands and arms that was making the desk slick.

Now and then, sweat from his nose or forehead dropped directly on some of the papers.

"Trouble . . ." he kept repeating under his breath. "Always trouble . . ."

David arrived home from the gym, closed the door behind him, and tossed his duffle bag in the chair that usually caught his attaché case.

It wasn't until he'd turned around that he noticed Molly standing in the middle of the living room. She was facing him squarely, her arms crossed and her shoulders raised slightly with tension so that she was slightly hunched.

"You okay, Mol?"

But he knew she wasn't okay. She was obviously angry as hell.

"David, we're going to move!"

He stared at her, perplexed. "We've discussed that one to death."

"Let's discuss it some more."

"Okay, we'll talk to the management company," he said.

"If they won't cooperate, we'll figure out something else. In the meantime, I want to look for another apartment."

He was sure something traumatic had occurred, and probably concerning Deirdre. He hesitated asking about it, but curiosity prodded him the way it prompted people to touch tongue to sore tooth.

"Something happen, Mol?" As soon as he'd asked, he regretted it. Some doors you were a fool to open.

She told him about the incident with Michael and Muffin, then her encounter with Deirdre.

He tried not to show his relief. It might have been so much worse!

"I can understand why you're upset," he told her, "but—"

"We're going to move," she interrupted in her calm voice with steel in it.

He shook his head then grinned at her. "You're kind of determined, aren't you?"

" 'Determined' isn't the word."

" 'Sexy' is the word. You're sexy when you're determined."

"Sexy and transient," she said with finality.

30

David was still asleep in bed, lying on his stomach with his upper body above the sheet and an arm draped down so that the backs of his knuckles rested on the floor. He was snoring lightly.

Molly bent over near the bed and slipped her feet into her jogging shoes. She was already dressed in shorts and a T-shirt, ready for her Sunday morning run. When she sat on the edge of the mattress to tie her shoes, the springs squealed loudly, waking David.

He raised his head like a newborn, turned it, and saw her seated on the foot of the bed.

"Going running?" he asked in a sleep-thickened voice.

"Sure am. Michael's still in bed. He'll probably sleep till I get back."

David yawned and let his head plop back down so his face was mushed sideways into his pillow. "I won't wake him, that's for sure. Wanna pick up a Sunday *Times* on your way home?"

"Sure." She gave the lace on her left shoe an extra tug to be positive it was tight, then stood up. "Coffee's made, if you're interested."

"Definitely am for later."

She walked around to his side of the bed and kissed his forehead. "Bye."

He smiled into his pillow. "Don't wear yourself out. I might have some interesting plans for you when you come back." He rolled onto his back and she saw that beneath the sheet he had an erection.

She had other things on her mind. He reached for her but she sidled out of range of his sweeping, grasping arm and hand, his movements still slowed by sleep.

"Remember," she said, "we have an appointment with a real estate agent this morning."

"Time for everything . . ." he muttered drowsily, then rolled over onto his stomach again and closed his eyes.

She moved to the other side of the room so he wouldn't see her if he did open his eyes; no point in encouraging him. She did a few quick squats and touched her toes several times to loosen her hamstrings, then left him asleep again and beginning to snore.

David had dozed off and wasn't sure how long Molly had been gone when a sudden burst of sound—loud voices from the living room—caused him to wake suddenly.

What the hell?

He lay staring at the wall, trying to figure out what was happening. Then he realized the voices were coming from the television.

Silence then. A loud moan.

He propped himself up on his elbows, then sat on the edge of the mattress. Maybe Michael was up, playing with the remote control. They'd warned him about that, but it hadn't done much good.

David stood up and caught sight of himself in the dresser mirror, a disheveled man in white jockey shorts and undershirt. He looked and felt vulnerable.

With equal parts of curiosity and trepidation, he crept toward the now silent living room.

The TV was on, all right. He stopped, leaning with a hand against the wall, and focused his bleary eyes on the screen. A man and woman were having sex on a bed. The man, who was on top, was thrusting madly into the woman. He planted his palms on the mattress and raised his upper body, pushing his pelvis harder into the soft saddle of the woman's crotch and spread thighs. The woman clutched him with her arms, and her upper body rose with his as she clawed at his back.

David felt his insides go numb as he stared in shock. He was looking at himself and Deirdre.

"You've improved with age, David. Like fine whiskey."

Her voice hadn't come from the TV. He turned and saw her seated in a corner of the sofa with her legs curled beneath her, holding the remote control aimed casually and inaccurately at the TV. She was wearing a T-shirt, shorts, and obviously new red and white jogging shoes. The shoes were exactly like Molly's.

David thought of Michael and an edge of fear knifed through him. "For God's sake, turn that off! Michael's in the—"

But Michael wasn't in the next room. He was toddling into the living room, rubbing sleep from his eyes.

David rushed to him and scooped him up, barely managing to cover his eyes before he could see the TV screen. His breath hissing with anger, he carried Michael back to his bedroom, laid him in his bed, and kissed him and soothingly urged him back to sleep.

When he left the bedroom a few minutes later, he carefully closed the door behind him, wishing there were some way to lock it.

How had this happened? he wondered as he returned furious to the living room. Why was she doing this?

He stopped in the middle of the room as he heard Michael begin to cry.

Deirdre stared at him, used the remote to switch off the TV, then nonchalantly stood up and walked over and ejected a cassette from the VCR.

Michael's muted cries were still coming from the bedroom. Sleepy, urgent wails.

Deirdre seemed not to hear them. "The darndest thing's happened, David. You know that apartment where we made love? The one that belongs to the man who sells electronics? Well, he must be some kind of a pervert. One of us somehow must have accidentally touched something, and everything we did was recorded on videotape."

David wasn't ready yet to try grasping the significance of what she'd said. He glanced nervously toward Michael's bedroom. "You expect me to believe that?"

She put on a surprised expression. "Of course. It's not unheard of. He probably tapes himself and the women he brings there. Or maybe even men."

Michael's cries became softer and less frequent, then ceased.

Relieved, David said, "Give me the tape, Deirdre."

"Sure. That's why I brought it here. I saw Molly leave to go jogging and figured it was a good time."

She came to him and handed him the cassette. When he accepted it, she kissed him on the lips, clinging to him. He broke her hold and pushed her away, but she seemed to have expected that and stayed close.

"Watching it kind of got me in the mood again," she said. "You should see it before you destroy it. We're absolutely terrific together."

David, not only wide awake now but hyperalert, knew why she'd unhesitatingly given him the tape. He stared at the cassette in his hand, then stared at Deirdre. "My God, there are copies, aren't there."

She kissed him again, quickly, while he was still in shock and assimilating what was happening. He didn't respond. He was too stricken by events even to resist.

She cocked her head to the side and flipped her hair as if she were in a shampoo commercial. "Copies? Well, I don't know for sure."

"I do," he said in a voice that betrayed his resignation.

She moved in and kissed him a third time, smiling up at him. "Michael's gone back to sleep," she said, "or he'd be in here again by now."

His mind was still trying to gain equilibrium, to reassess the future. "Molly told me about the incident with Michael and the cat."

She gave him another of her nimble, unexpected kisses, this time on the point of his chin. "She certainly made more of it than there was, David."

"She said you'd been in our bedroom. That you were wearing some of her perfume when she went up to your apartment."

"Anyone can buy any kind of perfume. She's imagining things again, David. She's awfully insecure and she imagines things. I noticed that about her from the beginning, and like I told you, it's getting worse."

She moved up against him. He started to back away. Paused and stood still.

"How did you get in here?" he asked. "I mean now, this morning?"

Smiling, she inserted her hand beneath the elastic waistband of his shorts. He felt her fingers twine around his limp penis and begin their slow and expert pulsing motion, somehow in time with his heartbeat. "Oh, I guess I must have found a key someplace."

He had an erection; he couldn't prevent it. It wasn't his fault!

"Or took an impression and had a key made," he said.

She continued to smile and press her body against his, increasing pressure and backing him toward the bedroom. He was surprised by her strength. She had to have very powerful legs to generate that kind of force.

"No," he said, with some determination, not loudly enough to disturb Michael. "We're not going to do this."

"Of course we are," she persisted.

"No, we're not going to do it here! Especially not in our bed!"

She maintained pressure against him, snaking her free arm around his body to reach the plastic cassette he was holding and tapping it with her long red nails. "Aren't we really?"

"Listen, Deirdre! We have to talk!"

"*Shhh,* David! We don't want to wake Michael!"

"Jesus, Deirdre, we can't do that here!" He was whispering now, pleading. "Not now! Not here!"

They were at the threshold, then past it. He felt Deirdre's body move against him and heard the door shut and latch. She'd adroitly closed it with her foot.

"Damn it, Deirdre!"

Laughing, she shoved hard against him, forcing him backward faster, gaining momentum until they both fell onto the bed.

The springs squealed loudly under the sudden weight of two people.

They continued to squeal.

When Molly returned from her run, she dropped the fat *Times* on the sofa, then noticed the remote on the floor. She picked it up and laid it on top of the VCR.

Then she walked to the bedroom door and opened it.

David was still in bed asleep. He must have gotten up during her absence, though probably only to use the bathroom. The window was wide open and the air conditioner next to it was humming away on high, not the work of a man all the way awake.

She looked down at him lying there with the sheet tucked beneath his chin, and she smiled. She was still perspiring from her run but she looked and felt invigorated. Hurriedly, she removed all her clothes except for her jogging shoes, then climbed into bed.

David sighed and turned his head to the side, not opening his eyes. She drew back the sheet and gripped the waistband of his shorts, then laboriously worked them down over his buttocks, genitals, knees, then feet, and tossed them on the floor. Amazingly, he still hadn't awakened.

She gently prodded his shoulder. He was sweating even though the room was cool. Or maybe she only thought it was cool because she was still warm from her run.

"Hey, you," she said softly, prodding again.

He opened his eyes and stared over at her. "Huh? Hey, I thought I was dreaming."

She grinned. "Want something better than a dream?"

He wiped at his eyes then worked the bridge of his nose between thumb and forefinger. "I don't really feel like it anymore, Mol. Got too much on my mind."

Still grinning, she encircled his limp maleness with her hand and began manipulating, stroking. "It's a mind that can be changed."

It took a few minutes, but he responded to her.

"See," she said. "Grab them there, and their hearts and minds are sure to follow."

Not releasing him, she settled down beside him, her face close to his.

"There's an interesting thing about running," she said. "If you're in the right frame of mind, it can be foreplay. Something to do with endorphins, maybe."

He sighed and rolled toward her. Maybe he was readier than either of them had known.

The bedsprings began their rhythmic squeal.

When Deirdre had returned to her apartment, Darlene was still seated on the sofa, drinking coffee from a cup with a yellow rose design that Deirdre had bought at a shop in the Village. She was wearing a stylish green dress and had her slender legs crossed and twined about each other modestly. The kind of chaste, perfect woman some men liked to muss up, Deirdre thought.

"I told you I wouldn't be gone long," Deirdre said.

Darlene smiled and shook her head. "You are really something else."

Deirdre picked up the other cup on the table and sipped. The coffee was cold. "Want a warm-up?" she asked.

Darlene shook her head again. "Just got one."

Deirdre went into the kitchen, refilled her cup from the glass pot, then returned to the living room.

"You were gone long enough to get into mischief," Darlene said, "considering that you were visiting your ex-husband while his wife was away."

"For crying out loud, Darlene, little Michael was right there in the apartment. Nothing happened."

Darlene's large, dark eyes shifted as her gaze traveled up and down Deirdre. "Your clothes are mussed."

"You're not my mother," Deirdre said.

Darlene sighed. "Sorry. I was being judgmental again."

"You want to listen to some music?" Deirdre asked. She walked over to the stereo, anticipating Darlene's answer.

"Sure. If you don't want to talk about your visit with David."

"Do you like the Beatles?" Deirdre asked, thumbing through her box of audiocassettes.

"Yeah, yeah, yeah."

She looked over at Darlene, surprised that she'd expressed a sense of humor. Usually she was so serious.

"You're frowning," Darlene said. "Put the cassette in and relax."

"Okay, I deserve some relaxation. It's been a hard day's night."

Now it was Darlene who frowned.

By the time the music began, Deirdre was seated next to Darlene on the sofa. They began talking animatedly, sometimes laughing so hard that Darlene's hand would shake and her coffee would spill onto her green skirt.

The Beatles declared that they all lived in a yellow submarine.

Later that day, David exited the apartment, leaving the door unlatched behind him as he strode quickly to the end of the corridor.

Ignoring the white framework of PVC pipes that supported

bags labeled PLASTIC and ALUMINUM, he glanced around to make sure he was alone. Preserving the environment was the last thing on his mind. Self-preservation had brought him here.

He removed Deirdre's videocassette from beneath his shirt and quickly dropped it down a chute whose steel door was lettered IN-CINERATOR.

Then he hurried back to the apartment before Molly realized he was gone.

31

Chumley stood that night in the arched stone doorway of the building across the street from Deirdre's apartment. He was wearing a blue shirt, gray pants, and his clunky walking shoes. In the darkness, he was almost invisible in the shadowed doorway.

He didn't know exactly what to expect from his vigil, but curiosity about Deirdre had driven him there. So far all it had netted him were a few glimpses of her as she passed her living room window, a traversing image that had entered his life and made him alternatingly ecstatic and uneasy.

Maybe he should leave, he thought. The night was warm and the air in the doorway was still. A swarm of gnats had found him and seemed to regard pestering him as the purpose of their brief lives, flitting about his eyes and nostrils, making him itch.

He was vigorously scratching an elbow when a motion across the street caught his eye.

Deirdre emerged not from the street door, but from the narrow walkway alongside the building. Chumley knew from helping her move that it led to a side entrance and the service elevator. She was wearing slacks, and what appeared to be a light sweater despite the heat. And she was pushing something.

Chumley glanced up and saw that her apartment's windows had gone dark. He should have noticed earlier; he'd been distracted by the gnats.

As she moved quickly away from the building and passed beneath a streetlight, he saw that what she was pushing ahead of her on the sidewalk was a baby stroller.

She began rolling the empty stroller at a slower pace. Staying on the opposite side of the street, Chumley followed.

Near Columbus, she stopped in front of a small combination grocery store and deli. She glanced around, collapsed the small, portable stroller, then went inside.

Chumley took up position across the street from the deli and waited.

So she was going shopping, he figured, and used the stroller to carry her groceries. But why had she exited her apartment building from the side door and walked through the narrow, dark gangway? It was a place most women would avoid. And there had been, Chumley was sure, something definitely furtive about her manner.

Ten minutes later she pushed the stroller out onto the sidewalk. In its cloth seat sat a brown paper grocery sack with what appeared to be the leafy end of a cluster of celery stalks jutting up from one side at an angle.

Chumley walked a few steps toward the corner, then turned and began trailing her back along West Eighty-fifth Street toward her apartment. He watched her pause and bend forward from time to time, as if something about the groceries or stroller demanded her attention.

He took a chance and moved closer, to where he could look across the street at an angle that enabled him to see what was happening. She pushed the stroller another fifty feet, paused, then bent forward over it again, her grip still on its handles. Chumley saw with surprise that she was smiling, and she seemed to be talking. Yes, undeniably her lips were moving as if she were talking to whatever was in the paper sack.

His mood plunged. Surely there was an explanation. Maybe she had a reason, a puppy or some other sort of pet in the bag. Possibly a goldfish.

But he doubted that a store specializing in take-out food and groceries would sell any kind of fish not destined for the dinner plate.

Chumley was familiar enough with people who talked to imaginary companions, as was everyone living in New York, and passed them on the sidewalk almost every day. Schizophrenics who carried their own vocal agonies inside their heads, who should be receiving treatment instead of roaming or begging on the streets. But it shook Chumley to think that Deirdre might secretly be one of those people. He preferred to believe that if he asked her about tonight, she'd laugh and offer an easy explanation that hadn't entered his mind.

When she reached her building, she rolled the stroller into the dark walkway without hesitation, as if confident that any waiting predator, and not she, would be in danger. Chumley wouldn't have walked into that black maw with such resolution. He was impressed by her bravery.

He stood for a while waiting for her apartment lights to come back on. Then he saw her walking from the dark gangway. The stroller was gone and she was carrying the sack of groceries.

He watched her push open the glass doors and enter the building's lobby.

The elevator door opened immediately when she pressed the Up button. She stepped inside, punched her floor button, then stood leaning against the elevator's back wall, clutching her groceries to her breast and staring in the direction of the street.

Chumley was sure the bright lobby's reflections on the glass doors would prevent her from seeing him out on the sidewalk, across the street and on the other side of a row of parked cars. He watched as the elevator door smoothly closed, cutting her from his view.

Her actions confused him, and made him even more uneasy about the irregularity in the files.

On the other hand, what had he actually seen? A woman pushing a baby stroller, then buying groceries and using the stroller to convey them to her apartment. It didn't compute that she'd store the stroller someplace in the building's basement, compact and portable as it was, and come and go via the service entrance. But then there was so much in life that didn't compute if you really stopped to think about it.

She'd paused here and there on the sidewalk and done a little talking to herself, but was that a crime? And was talking to yourself even so unusual these days? Maybe what he was doing was technically a crime, stalking her. Only *he* knew his true motives, and they'd be difficult to describe to strangers in an official setting.

Chumley considered dropping in unexpectedly on her for a

visit, perhaps asking her about the walk with the stroller, about the files.

But he'd seen her sudden anger and didn't want to provoke her again.

He stood in the shadows on West Eighty-fifth Street and stared for a while, puzzled. Her apartment lights came on again, but the living room drapes drew closed without him catching sight of her.

He slapped at the gnats, who'd patiently awaited his return, then he shrugged elaborately and walked away.

Molly pushed the empty stroller along West Eighty-fifth Street the next morning, after dropping off Michael at Small Business. Traffic was heavy, and the sidewalks were teeming with people on their way to Monday morning work.

There was a store nearby that had a coupon sale on Healy's Cat Gourmet Meatloaf, the only brand Muffin would eat—in various flavors, of course. Molly needed some other groceries, so she thought this was a good morning to buy them, at the same time stocking up on cat food for the week and hoping Muffin wouldn't suddenly decide to switch brands.

She was waiting for the traffic light to change at Columbus when she noticed a woman in a green dress entering a clothing store across the street.

Molly stiffened behind the stroller.

The woman had looked familiar.

So had the dress.

The light read WALK and the knot of people at the corner began to move. Molly sped up and shot out ahead of most of them, pushing the stroller so fast that the rhythmic squeal of one of its wheels was almost a steady scream.

She crossed to the other side of Columbus and hurried to the clothing shop she'd seen the woman in the green dress enter. The sign in its window boasted that it sold both men's and women's quality irregulars and seconds.

Molly peered through the window at the racks of clothes.

Damn it! Deirdre, or at least the woman Molly had seen enter the shop, was nowhere in sight.

Quickly she collapsed the stroller, lifted it by its light aluminum frame, and went inside. It was possible that the woman had exited the shop unseen while Molly was crossing the intersection, but Molly didn't think so.

The shop's interior was somewhat dim, and crowded with racks of clothing, but it took Molly only a few minutes to look around and conclude that she and an elderly woman in Plus Sizes were the only customers.

"Help you?" a blond sales clerk in her twenties asked.

"I'm looking for a friend I'm sure I saw come in here," Molly said. "But now I don't see her. Is anyone in the changing room?"

The girl shook her head. "No, ma'am."

"Would you look, please?"

The girl stared at her for a few seconds, then walked away toward a curtained doorway at the back of the store.

Less than a minute later she returned. "There's no one in any of the changing rooms, ma'am. Like I told you, no one."

Molly thanked her and returned to the street and the warm morning sun.

No one.

Had she imagined she'd seen the woman? Seen the green dress that was like Molly's dress or *was* Molly's dress, and one of David's favorites on her? Was she hallucinating these days?

She unfolded the stroller, locked its handle into place, and continued rolling it toward the grocery store.

Next I'll be hearing voices, she thought.

A man walking past glanced uneasily at her, and she realized she'd unconsciously spoken.

Talking to myself now, she thought with some alarm.

Maybe *that* was the step before hearing voices.

32

Traci Mack hung up the phone and sat back in her desk chair. Around her in her small office at Link Publishing were stacks of manuscripts, her computer, some shelves of published books she'd edited. A sign behind her desk said IF YOU CAN'T LEAD AND YOU DON'T WANT TO FOLLOW, SIT DOWN AND LET'S TALK.

She'd just been on the phone with Winston Delacort, the author of *Architects of Desire*. He'd called to complain about Molly's breaking up his run-on sentences in the portion of the copyedited manuscript Traci had sent him to work on. He maintained that the prose was more fluent his way and better able to express architectural lines. Traci had been diplomatic, but she felt like sending one of Link's hard-boiled crime writers to bump off Winston Delacort.

But that wasn't the way the game was played. Instead, she would talk to Molly about fixing the run-on sentences by inserting conjunctions whenever possible. A safe, middle-of-the-road solution that should leave everyone only slightly miffed. That kind of philosophy had come to Traci early enough to help her professional life, but she still hadn't gotten around to applying it to her personal affairs.

She leaned forward and used a pencil eraser to peck out Molly's number.

The phone rang six times without an answer.

Traci hung up. She'd try again this afternoon, after lunch. Or maybe she'd talk to Molly about this the next time they met. She was almost finished with the manuscript anyway, and what were a few more revisions, one way or the other? They were slightly ahead of the production schedule now, thanks to Molly's fast and reliable job on the manuscript, and the art department supplying a jacket illustration that had thrilled Winston Delacort.

She slid the manuscript she'd been reading into a drawer then stood up to leave. There was a new restaurant over on Lexington she wanted to try. Well, it was more of a bar, really. But they did serve food.

She told Jock the receptionist she was leaving for lunch, then pushed through the heavy wooden door out into the hall and walked to the elevators.

Plenty of other people in the building must have decided to go to lunch early. The elevator was packed. Everyone edged backward uneasily as Traci wedged her way inside far enough for the door to close.

The elevator stopped again on the fifth floor, but the man and woman standing there wisely decided not to try to board.

When the elevator reached the lobby, Traci was practically propelled out of it.

The lobby was large, with street entrances at each end, and lined with shops. All hard, marble or wood surfaces, it echoed with footsteps and voices. It was crowded not only with the building's occupants on their way to lunch, but with pedestrians cutting through to the next block.

Traci was bumped by a large man in a blue suit. She made sure she still had her purse, then turned to make her way through the mass of people toward the East Fifty-sixth Street exit. A woman walking in the opposite direction, part of the flow of the crowd, caught her eye, but it took a few seconds for recognition to register on Traci.

She stopped and looked in the direction the woman had gone, craning her neck. Almost at once she spotted the woman's green dress only about twenty feet away.

"Molly!" she called. "Mol!"

The woman didn't turn around. Instead she glanced at her wristwatch and began walking faster, elbowing her way through the crowded lobby.

"Molly Jones!" Traci yelled. "Hey! Molly!"

Still she wouldn't turn around.

Traci took a few running steps then stopped, realizing the hopelessness of trying to catch Molly or attract her attention. Actually breaking into a run in this mob was impossible, Traci thought; they were likely to turn on her if she tried. And maybe the woman wasn't actually Molly. Traci really hadn't gotten that good a look at her, and she'd been thinking about Molly because of Winston Delacort's phone call.

Either way, by now the woman would be out on East Fifty-fifth Street, lost in an even larger mass of people.

Someone clutched Traci's elbow.

She jerked away with surprise, then turned and saw it was Beverly Malcolm from the art department.

"Sorry, Trace," Beverly said, dropping her hand from Traci's arm. "Didn't mean to stop your heart. I need to talk to you about that Civil War manuscript when you get back."

"Sure, Bev."

"Who were you shouting at?" Beverly asked.

"I don't know for sure. Somebody I thought I knew. Guess I was wrong."

"Guess so. See you later."

"I'm going to lunch at a new place around Fifty-seventh and Lex," Traci said. "They're rumored to serve food with their drinks. You want to come?"

"I'd like to, but I've got a meeting. Next time."

Traci nodded, then continued on her way toward the exit opposite the one used by the woman in the green dress.

Molly stood before her closet and shuffled through her clothes, first slowly, then so fast that the wire hangers sang on the metal rod.

She withdrew an empty hanger from the end of the closet she only half-jokingly thought of as her dress-up side, where her more stylish and expensive outfits hung.

Feeling anger, puzzlement, and a creepy kind of fear that itself alarmed her, she stood holding the empty hanger and staring at it. She was positive it was where her green dress had hung.

The dress that was definitely missing.

The dress she was sure she'd seen Deirdre wearing earlier that day.

33

That evening, Molly watched David as they ate a dinner of pizza and salad delivered from William's Take-out over on Amsterdam. He seemed preoccupied, worried in a manner he wouldn't share with her. When she tried to enter and understand his concern, he would deflect her with inane conversation about work, or friends they hadn't seen for weeks and sometimes months. It occurred to her that they hadn't seen many people or gone out much with each other since Deirdre had arrived in New York.

Molly waited until they'd had dinner and Michael was asleep before telling David about seeing Deirdre wearing her green dress.

He sat in the chair opposite the sofa and stared at her in a way that angered her. As if she'd become ill and had great bleeding sores on her face and he was too polite to mention them.

He obviously wasn't going to say anything, so she would.

"Dammit! Stop looking at me like that! I'm sure she was wearing my dress."

"But you told me you didn't actually see her face."

"I saw the rest of her. I saw my dress."

Now he furrowed his brow in concern, adding a decade to his face. "Maybe you're imagining things, Mol. You've been under a hell of a strain, you know."

"I also know what I saw."

She realized she was becoming more convinced as she spoke that the woman had been Deirdre; she was digging a foxhole in the face of David's disbelief and patronizing patter. Well, maybe she was being defensive, but that didn't alter what she'd seen this morning.

He smiled and looked curious as well as concerned. Infuriating.

"Why would Deirdre wear one of your dresses?" he asked.

"Why would she wear my perfume?" Molly said in exasperation.

"Anyone can buy any kind of perfume, Mol."

Molly stood up from the sofa. It made her feel better to be looking down at him. "Do *not* treat me as if I'm some kind of mental case. If Deirdre didn't take the dress, then where is it?"

He turned his hands palms up. "I don't know. Maybe you forgot it at the cleaners."

"Come off it, David. I'd know if it was at the cleaners. I always put the receipts from the cleaners in the same place, under a magnet on the side of the refrigerator, so I remember to pick up whatever's there. There are no receipts. Right now we have nothing at the cleaners."

"So maybe you misplaced the receipt. Or it somehow slipped out from under the magnet and fell beneath the refrigerator."

Molly shook her head no. "I had a dress, David. Now I've got a hanger."

He let his hands float up and then dropped them down on the chair arms. "Well, I don't have an explanation, but the dress will turn up."

"Bullshit, David."

Instead of getting angry with her, he stood up from the chair and walked over to her. He hugged her, but she merely stood with her arms at her sides.

After a brief, final squeeze, he released her and stepped back. He was looking straight into her eyes. He'd been doing a lot of that lately, when the situation called for it. Heart-to-heart time.

"I don't believe you're a mental case," he assured her. "But I do have a suggestion. I have a friend named Herb Mindle. A doctor."

It took Molly a second to realize what he meant. She was incredulous that he would suggest such a thing.

"A shrink?"

David pursed his lips in disapproval of her denigrating a noble profession. Looking pained, he drew his glasses from his pocket and put them on, as if to read her more clearly.

"You could talk to him, Mol. Maybe get something to help you through . . . whatever it is you're going through."

"Oh, really?" She almost actually sneered.

He acted as if he hadn't noticed the sarcastic quality in her voice. "I mean, with Bernice's death, everything else that's happened, what could it hurt if you went and saw the man? He's got a reputation as a superb analyst."

Molly had nothing against the art of analysis, but she certainly didn't think she was in need of it. "No, David," she said patiently, "I'm not going to a psychiatrist. It isn't necessary."

"You can't be the best judge of that, Mol."

"But I can be the only judge."

He pursed his lips again, then parted them and blew out air. She knew it was his way of showing disapproval along with his resignation. She was being unreasonable, he was telling her. "Okay, then. No it is."

"We won't talk about it again," she said, driving home the finality of her decision.

She went back to the sofa but didn't sit down. Instead she picked up the folded *Times* then laid it back on the cushion, feigning casualness, putting the subject of Dr. Mindle behind them.

Time to steer the conversation down another road.

"I don't like the way things have been going lately," she said.

"No one does," David replied.

She sat down in a corner of the sofa. "I meant with my work. Traci called about the architectural manuscript. The author's going to make trouble."

"Some of them do," David said. "He's probably relying on the fact that he knows more about architecture than do you or Traci."

"That's the problem. He's an architect and not a writer. Everybody in this goddamned world is trying to be something or someone else." *Like that fucking Deirdre.* "Have you noticed?"

He smiled. "Oh, I've noticed." He walked over and sat down a cushion away from her. "I do have some good news for you, Mol. The company that manages this building says we can move to another apartment it manages a few blocks from here without violating the terms of our lease. We have our choice of two. You can look at them tomorrow while I'm at work."

"That's great," Molly said. And she meant it. Here was a significant first step in the journey away from Deirdre. "But what makes you so hot to move all of a sudden?" she asked. "You were resisting the idea before as if I'd suggested a vasectomy."

"Was I? Well, I thought about it and came to the conclusion you were right. It'd be better for all of us if we got out of this building."

Molly wondered if his "all of us" included Deirdre, but she decided not to ask. Instead she moved over to him and kissed his cheek.

"You said the right thing, David. That does more for me than Doctor whatever-his-name-is could possibly do."

He patted her hand. "I thought you'd feel that way about it. I'm glad."

When he stood up, she reached for the remote control that sat on one of the sofa arms, aimed it at the TV, and pressed the bright red power button.

At the soft electronic pop the TV made when it came on, he turned suddenly. "What are you doing?"

Molly was puzzled by his reaction. And by something in his voice. *Fear?* "I was going to get Channel One," she said. "Catch up on the local news."

"Is Michael asleep yet?"

"Maybe," she said, wondering what this was about.

"Let's take him and go out someplace. Maybe walk down and get some ice cream. He loves to do that."

"But he's in bed."

"So? How much trouble can it be to get him up? Hell, he can go in his pajamas. There are only so many chances in life to get ice cream. You've got to take them."

She wasn't going to argue against that philosophy. She pressed the remote's power button again and the television went silent and dark.

"Are you restless, David?" she asked. "Or is there some reason you don't want me to watch the news?"

"No, no, it's nothing like that. I don't know why, but I don't feel like watching television tonight. *Any* kind of television."

From her window overlooking West Eighty-fifth Street, Deirdre watched David, carrying Michael, walking with Molly toward the lights of shops at the corner.

They paused for Molly to adjust her shoe or sock, and David moved over to walk on the curb side. An unconsciously protective gesture, Deirdre thought with envy. She'd read somewhere that the custom dated back to when gentlemen walked closest to streets of mud to shield against ladies getting their dresses stained from the splashing of passing carriages. She narrowed her eyes and for an instant her lips arced in a tight, grim smile. *Wouldn't want little Molly to get soiled.*

She placed the side of her forehead against the warm glass, leaning forward and staring with fierce attention at them, clenching her teeth so that her jaw muscles danced. Her hands were clenched too, into tight fists that she leaned on against the wooden sill.

When the Jones family was out of sight, Deirdre straightened up and stared down as she unclenched her fists. She'd dug her long fingernails into her flesh so deeply that her hands were bleeding. The blood on her palms reminded her of photos of stigmata, before she'd become a lapsed Catholic.

Leaving the window, she went to a cardboard box and dug out a Bible she'd stolen from a motel room outside Saint Louis. Then she went into the kitchen and got a sharp knife.

She sat down in the living room and began methodically slashing the Bible's pages, tossing them to the floor with abandon when they separated from the binding.

When she was finished, she gathered up the pages and the mutilated fake leather Bible jacket, carried them in to the kitchen sink, then burned them.

The forsaken, the truly lost, obeyed only their own commandments.

It was almost midnight when Molly loomed over David. She'd removed her sleep shirt and panties and stood nude next to the bed, trailing a corner of her silk scarf lightly over his cheek.

She grinned as he swiped at the scarf with his hand, then opened his eyes and saw her in the dim light.

"Mol?" There was surprise in his voice. And, she thought, anticipation.

She bent lower and kissed him then, reached down and felt him between the legs. His penis was flacid now, but she could change that. The really sensual sexual organ was the brain, and she was going to enter David's mind tonight even if he thought it was the other way around.

Standing up straight, she used both hands to twirl the scarf into a taut twist of smooth material. Then she smiled. "How about tying my hands and feet, lover? Would you like that?"

He paused, then surprised her.

"Not tonight, Mol. Not that kind of game."

"You've played that kind of game before."

He almost sat up, as if she'd alarmed him.

"Remember? The lodge in Maine?"

"Ah, yeah." He seemed to relax. "No forgetting that."

Puzzled, she stared at him. "You want me to tie you up?"

"No."

"Something wrong, David?"

"Nothing."

"The way things have gone lately, I thought you might want me to spice up our bedroom time."

He reached up and grabbed the scarf, hurting her finger as the material was wrenched from her grasp, then threw it across the room into shadow.

She was stunned. Confused. "Jesus, David! There's no reason to get mad."

He lay very still for a while, not answering. Then he cupped a hand behind her head and pulled her down to him. She resisted, still unsure and angry. But this was at least some reaction from him. And she needed that, dammit, she needed it! She let the strength drain from her as he kissed her.

He smiled at her with something like regret. She thought he was going to apologize for snatching away the scarf, but he didn't. "Nothing needs spicing up where you're concerned, Mol. I'm just not into that kind of stuff anymore."

She kissed his forehead, then his lips. "You used to be adventuresome in sex. Used to get a little kinky from time to time. I never minded that. I liked it."

"So did I, but I don't feel adventuresome tonight."

She settled back down beside him in the bed.

Within a few minutes, his hand brushed her nipple, then moved lower. As his finger found its familiar spot and began its subtle ro-

THE EX   169

tation, he rolled toward her, craning his neck, and his lips warmly
encircled the nipple that still tingled from his touch.

"Plain vanilla, David," she said, half-jokingly.

Only half-jokingly.

34

A light rain was falling the next morning as Molly delivered Michael to Julia beneath the canopy in front of Small Business.

"Going to rain all day, Michael," Julia said, lifting him from his stroller and hugging him. "But not on us." He seemed to enjoy the irony of that and grinned.

Molly turned up the collar of her yellow raincoat and adjusted Michael's waterproof miniature windbreaker when Julia set him down. She kissed him. "Be a good boy for Julia."

"Michael's always good," Julia said. Her gaze went beyond Molly to a black minivan that had pulled to the curb. A woman climbed out and opened a sliding door in the side of the van to reveal three preschoolers strapped into their seats.

"Two of them are mine," Julia said, possessive about her young charges. "I'll get the littlest one next year."

For a moment Molly and Julia watched the woman lean into the van and begin struggling with safety belts, rattles, and galoshes.

"Family must be a wonderful thing," Julia said, watching the woman and her children.

At first Molly thought she might be kidding, but when she saw the longing on Julia's face, she knew better. Julia actually envied the woman.

"It is wonderful," Molly said. "Someday you'll know, Julia."

"That's what my husband and the doctor tell us. I guess I might as well believe them. And you."

"You'll see that we're right."

"We keep hoping. That's what there is to life—hope and family."

"That sounds about right," Molly said.

She kissed Michael again and went down the steps to where she'd left the stroller.

As she pushed the stroller along the sidewalk, away from Small Business, she felt the light rain work its way beneath her collar. She paused and opened her umbrella, then continued on her way, not looking back.

Behind her, Deirdre, in a yellow raincoat, had approached Small Business from the opposite direction. She patted Michael on the head and chatted for a few minutes with Julia and the woman from the van. Then she lifted Michael, kissed him, and handed him back to Julia.

Later that morning, in Midnight Espresso on Broadway, Molly sat across from Traci at one of the small, round marble tables. The coffee shop was crowded, especially around the counter and displays of gourmet brands, but Traci had managed to get a table in a corner, away from the press of other patrons, where there was elbow room and it was relatively quiet.

Both women had ordered espressos. Molly took a sip of hers and glanced out the window. The rain had stopped and the hot summer street was steaming. Pedestrians streamed past, many of them with folded umbrellas, their raincoats open and flapping, or draped over an arm. Traffic lurched forward a few feet at a time, with intermittent bursts of horn honking. Though it was crowded, the coffee shop was cool and pleasantly filled with the aroma of its product.

Traci rested a hand on the final portion of the *Architects of Desire* manuscript on the table. Its pages were bristling with yellow Post-it flags, revisions of revisions.

After a few minutes, Molly and Traci had forgotten about the manuscript as Molly filled Traci in on some of the agonies of the last few weeks.

Now Traci slipped the manuscript into her attaché case, then placed the case on the floor and said, "So, it turns out you're not all happy under one roof."

"We're not going to be under one roof much longer," Molly

said. "David and I are searching around for another apartment. In fact, the management company gave me the keys to two that I'm going to look at when I leave here. Want to come along? Help me figure where the furniture's going to go?"

Traci laughed. "No, thanks. I'm not very domestic and wouldn't be much help. My idea of good furniture is something you can hose down."

Molly rotated her clear glass cup on its coaster. "How's it going with the novel?"

"Novel? Oh, the one where the ex-wife enters the picture and the wife becomes dog food or compacted trash." She smiled sadly. "I'm afraid it ends the same way, Mol. Bad news for the wife. But like you said, life doesn't always imitate art. Or vice versa. In fact, I think I can guarantee you that certain reviewers probably won't even regard this novel as art."

"But you do?"

"Yes, it's very good. It just happens to be about a subject that's sticky with a lot of people."

"Do you know much about the author?"

"Sure. He's a kind and simple man who's been married to the same woman for thirty-five years." She finished her espresso and smiled. "Case in point. This guy doesn't even have an ex-wife to conspire with, and probably the thought of murdering his own wife never seriously entered his mind." She reached for her attaché case and grinned. " 'Probably,' I said."

Molly laughed and shook her head. "I always feel better after talking with you. Once I get over my terror."

Traci gripped her attaché case and stood up. "We all know life's a dangerous road," she said. "And if it weren't, the safe, smooth stretches wouldn't be nearly so enjoyable."

"Well, that's a comforting thought to hold on to while the potholes are jarring the fillings out of my teeth."

"Anyway," Traci said, "I've gotta get back to the office and meet one of my ego-inflated writers." She shifted her attaché case, heavy now with the manuscript pages, to her other hand. "By the way, were you at Link looking for me yesterday?"

"No, why?"

"I thought I might have seen you down in the lobby a little before noon."

"Not me," Molly said.

Traci reached into her purse with her free hand, fished out some bills, and dropped them on the table.

"This one's on the publisher, Mol. You look like you need a break."

Molly smiled. "Thanks, I do."

She watched Traci push through the crowd near the door, leave the coffee shop, and join the throng of pedestrians on the other side of the window. Within seconds she'd passed out of sight.

Molly drew a slip of paper from her purse, unfolded it, and reread the addresses of the two apartments she was going to inspect in the West Eighties.

They were a short cab ride away, but since the rain had stopped, she decided to walk life's dangerous road and save the fare.

35

Molly stood across the street and stared at the six-story prewar brick building that was the first address on the slip of paper she carried. It wasn't unlike the building she and David lived in now, or most of the others that lined the avenue, stone or brick structures with ironwork at the windows and balconies, many of them with stone steps leading to stoops and tall doors. Here and there were canvas awnings, and flower boxes dotted with colorful and fresh-looking blossoms thriving after the recent rain.

She crossed the street and entered the building, finding the vestibule small but clean, with blue-tiled walls free of graffiti. She rode the elevator, also small, with wood paneling that seemed to be closing in on her, to the third floor, then walked down a narrow corridor to 3E and used the management company's keys to unlock the paint-checked door. There was a lock near the doorknob, and above that a heavy deadbolt lock.

She pushed the door open, then tentatively stepped inside and looked around. It made her uneasy, examining these apartments by herself. She wished David were there, in case . . . Well, she didn't know specifically in case of what, but in this city there were plenty of dreadful possibilities.

But she soon forgot her fear as she concentrated on the apartment. The living room was freshly painted an off-white except for one wall, which the painters hadn't gotten to with a main coat but had prepared with plaster-patch and primer. A white plastic paint bucket and a paint-speckled, folded drop cloth sat in a corner. The smell of fresh paint made the place seem clean and acceptable.

From overhead came the rapid, muted thuds of a child's footfalls. Molly smiled. That kind of noise wouldn't bother her. Besides, the apartment above was apparently carpeted.

She examined the bathroom and found it old but in good repair, with adequate water pressure. The kitchen was in the same condition, but it had a new dishwasher and plenty of cabinet space. It was smaller than the kitchen Molly had now, and the cabinets had multiple coats of white enamel on them, but there was room for a table and chairs. She went to the sink, turned the spigot handles on and off, and nodded with approval.

"This will do," she said under her breath. "This will definitely do so far."

The bedrooms hadn't yet been painted, but they were both slightly larger than those in the present Jones apartment, and there was enough closet space. A large air conditioner with a round plastic grill was mounted in one of the master bedroom's windows. It looked powerful enough to cope with summer, but it wasn't running, and Molly suddenly realized the apartment was uncomfortably warm.

Satisfied, she took a last look around and then left, locking the door behind her.

In the elevator she paused, then decided to check the laundry facilities in the basement. She pressed the button marked B, and the stifling little elevator descended with a speed that made her stomach queasy.

When the door glided open, she stepped out into a gloomy, stone-foundation basement. Faint light was making its way through dirty, iron-grilled windows, revealing a rats' maze of wooden partitions for tenants' storage.

Something brushed Molly's forehead and she jumped. Then she saw that it was a pull cord for an overhead light fixture. She gave the cord a firm yank, but the light didn't come on. Then her eyes adjusted and she noticed a sign: LAUNDRY ROOM—SUBBASEMENT. An arrow pointed through the dim, partitioned basement to a door with what looked like a handmade sign nailed to it.

Molly walked across the hard concrete floor and saw that the sign on the door indeed marked the entrance to the subbasement and laundry room. She opened the door and found herself at the top of a flight of stairs leading down into blackness. Leaning slightly forward, she ran her hand over the rough wall, feeling for a light switch.

A slight scuffing sound alarmed her, and she started to turn around. But she'd barely moved when something smashed into the small of her back and butted her out over the stairs into darkness.

She came down on the wooden steps on her side and slid to the bottom, bruising her hip and ribs and banging her right elbow.

Only when she was sprawled on the floor at the base of the stairs did she comprehend what had happened. *Someone had shoved her! Tried to injure or kill her!*

Even as she painfully scrambled to her feet in the darkness, she heard the shuffle and creak of someone coming down the stairs.

She panicked.

Her heart racing with terror, she saw a dim light at the far end of the basement and ran toward it. She struck an ankle on something in the dark and almost tripped, but somehow remained on her feet and lurched forward, her hands outstretched to feel for unseen obstacles.

When she reached the source of the light, she saw that it was a high, narrow window that had been filled in with opaque glass blocks.

No escape that way!

She could hear the unmistakable sound of leather soles scuffing on the gritty concrete floor, closing in on her!

She fled at an angle and made out the outline of a half-opened door. As she bumped her aching hip on something—a wheelbarrow hanging on a wall—she almost cried out in pain. But she swallowed the sound. If whoever was pursuing her in the dim basement didn't know exactly where she was, she didn't want to make her location known.

When she reached the door and opened it wider, she saw that it led to a short flight of wooden stairs leading back up to the basement. She climbed the creaking steps, briefly on all fours like an animal, then straightened up and closed the door at the top of the stairs behind her and leaned with her back against it.

There was more light here, revealing the maze of partitions from another perspective. She was totally disoriented. The only sounds were her rasping struggle for breath, her hammering heart.

She felt the doorknob rotate like a drill bit against her back and gasped.

In a panic, she fled through the labyrinth of wooden partitions, bouncing off them. She couldn't help it—she screamed. Though the sound was deadened in the thick-walled and cluttered basement, she knew she'd revealed her position to whoever was after her.

Finally she reached a crude, unpainted wooden door, another barrier between herself and her stalker. She yanked the door open, stepped to the other side of it, then slammed it behind her and fumbled for a lock.

There was none.

She looked around and found herself trapped in a small storage room. There was somewhat more light there, filtering in through a narrow, iron-grilled window and illuminating a swirl of dust motes.

Frantically she threw herself against a wooden storage crate and shoved it against the wall beneath the window. When she climbed up on the box and peered through the dirty glass, she was looking at a narrow alley littered with trash. There was no one to signal or call to for help.

She was trapped and alone.

Think! she urged herself. *Stay calm and goddamn think!*

She scampered down from the box, found a thick wooden plank, and wedged it between the door and a support post so tightly that the board had a slight bow in it.

Within seconds something or someone crashed loudly against the door, making the bend in the board even more pronounced.

Another crash!

Another!

The board bowed even more, the door shivered, and Molly saw one of its upper panels crack.

The crack widened with the next crash, and the dry old wood splintered and sagged inward. But brittle as it was, the door had just enough flexibility to hold and spring back.

Molly knew it wouldn't hold indefinitely. She climbed back onto the crate and tried to work the lever that unlocked the window. It was ancient and rust-fused and broke off in her hand.

Something crashed against the door again, causing the plank wedged against it to jump a fraction of an inch to the side.

Molly struggled with the jagged metal stump of remaining lever and managed to force it sideways, slicing her palm in the process. The old wood-framed window was the sort that opened inward, with hinges at the top. She gripped the tarnished brass handle and yanked the window in and up, ducking her head so it wouldn't brain her.

She got a mouth full of cobwebs for her effort, but the window rose.

Coughing, spitting, she clasped her hands over the iron grill and pulled and pushed. There wasn't the slightest give in the ancient grill.

Then she placed both hands on an end bar, bringing to bear more strength than she would have thought possible, and a corner of the grill gave slightly where it was anchored to stone. She began frantically working the old iron structure back and forth against its mooring, each time causing a raucous squeak she only hoped someone outside might hear. She didn't think there was enough play in the grill to allow her to weaken it enough so she could escape, but there seemed nothing else to try.

The crashing against the door stopped, as if whoever was out there was getting tired and needed a second wind.

Molly continued working on the grill.

Finally, its lower right corner broke free.

She almost couldn't believe it.

Whimpering, determined, she leaned her weight against the grill and pushed with her weary arms, trying to bend it outward.

It wouldn't budge.

Deirdre stood outside the unyielding door, glaring angrily at it and gasping for breath. She'd explored the basement and knew the bitch was trapped on the other side of the door. No way out. There might be plenty of time, but Deirdre wanted to get this over with, to get to her prey before some joke of fate interrupted what was about to happen.

She dragged a forearm across her perspiring forehead, looked around, and smiled.

Leaning against a wall were some old, rusty tools. One of them was a long-handled pickax.

Deirdre rubbed the shoulder she'd been smashing against the

door, then walked over and grabbed the pickax, hoisted it, and gave a few practice swings.

Then she returned to the storage room door, drew the pickax well back, and with all her might swung the pointed end at what she knew was a weak spot on the door.

The satisfaction she felt as the old wood split was almost like sex.

Molly continued to work frenziedly on the iron grill, glancing behind her as the rusty point of the pick repeatedly punctured the brittle old door.

She was sobbing now, trembling, working her arms and hands with difficulty. Her palms were bleeding but she didn't feel the pain, only her terror.

Deirdre knew she was close.

She could sense it!

Over and over she smashed the pointed end of the pickax into the door, seeing the gaps in the wood widen, the cracks turn into fissures that had to fly wide apart soon. Whatever Molly had wedged against the door was squealing with each blow as it jumped and vibrated and slid to the side.

Her mouth gaping wide to suck in air, Deirdre went into a mad fury of motion. The old door bucked on its hinges. Chips and splinters flew. Ancient nails bounced and pinged off the concrete floor.

She grinned wildly as she heard the wooden prop on the other side of the door clatter to the floor.

Wielding the pickax like a weapon, Deirdre kicked what was left of the door open and rushed into the storage room.

Immediately she saw the iron grill bent wide away from the window.

The crate directly beneath the window.

She wheeled insanely in a wide circle, grunting and swinging the pickax like a baseball bat with all her might until it contacted a wooden support beam and stuck, its long wooden handle leaping from her grasp.

She was alone.

A hand touched her shoulder. She jumped and spun around.

"You've got to get out of here," Darlene said.

Deirdre was amazed and outraged. "You followed me!"

"Of course I did. Because I'm worried about you. You've been acting more and more strangely, and now this. Were you chasing someone?"

"Don't you know?"

"Of course not. I just got here."

"I'm not chasing anyone. I came in here because . . . well, it was an impulse. I like basements."

"That's absurd, Deirdre."

"How would you know?"

"Anyone would say there was something seriously wrong with a person who suddenly entered an apartment building basement on impulse and began beating at things with . . . what is that thing?"

"I don't know. A tool. Some kind of pick. When I saw it, I liked it. So I took it."

Darlene glanced around in the dim light. "We can talk about this later. Let's get out of here now!"

Deirdre humored her and trailed along behind, but she was still furious.

With Molly and with Darlene.

36

After the terror of her encounter in the apartment building basement, Molly had been in no condition to resist David's insistence that she see Dr. Mindle.

She sat now in his spacious office on Lexington near Thirty-eighth Street. It was a restful room with green carpet and drapes, dark woods and black leather furniture, no noise and no sharp corners. All colors seemed to be in the same spectrum. Nothing in the decor jarred.

According to the lobby directory, there were several psychoanalysts in the building. Maybe it was a co-op and they owned it. Even the elevator had provided a relaxing interlude, plush carpet, soft music, no mirrors to reflect anyone's interior horror. An "up" experience and a prelude to therapy.

Molly was seated in a comfortable chair at an angle to Dr. Herbert Mindle's desk. He was much as she'd imagined from David's brief description, middle-aged, balding. But unlike her imaginary Dr. Mindle, he had a deep tan and an athletic build beneath his well-cut suit. The tan reminded her of those acquired at tanning salons then augmented by shopping and drinking expeditions during Caribbean cruises.

He leaned back in his padded desk chair and smiled reassuringly at her. It was the sort of smile shaped by practice at a mirror.

Molly smiled back at him, but only slightly. There was a faint scent of lemon mingled with something less acrid—Dr. Mindle's shaving lotion or cologne—in the room, and she noticed now that from time to time the traffic out on Lexington was barely audible.

He said nothing, so she said, "It was my husband's idea for me to come here." Great! she thought. She'd sounded like some sort of codependent, Babsie Doll wimp.

"I know," Dr. Mindle said in his easy, conversational tone. "He's the one who called and made the appointment. He said you finally agreed to talk to me as a favor to him." He made a steeple with his fingers. Molly was surprised that a real psychiatrist would actually do that. "Despite what's been happening," Dr. Mindle said, "and your ordeal in the apartment basement yesterday, you told him again that you didn't need a shrink."

Molly stared at him. "Are you trying to make me feel guilty for insulting your profession?"

Dr. Mindle smiled tolerantly. "No. It happens all the time. I'm used to it. Besides, maybe you really don't need a shrink."

Molly drummed her fingertips silently on the padded chair arm. "David said you and he worked out at the same gym."

"That's right, we do."

"Friends? Weightlifting buddies?"

"You could say that." Dr. Mindle's smile changed to one of amused understanding. "I'm charging you for this visit, Mrs. Jones."

Molly let herself relax and settle back in the chair. "Good. I feel better now."

"That's the idea, Molly, making you feel better. I can't solve your problem in a short time. That is, if I can solve it at all." Another soothing smile. "If you have a problem."

"David thinks I do."

"Well, he *might* be right."

"He told you everything?"

"Yes."

"Then he told you more than he told me."

Without changing expression, Dr. Mindle stood up and walked out from behind his desk. He went to the window and faced the view of office buildings and searing blue sky. His voice was so soft she had to strain to understand his words. A stratagem, no doubt.

"This city, Molly, is a monster. It doesn't eat people alive all at once, but it eats them. Some of them from the inside."

Molly quietly watched him, a classic, inverted-triangle male figure silhouetted against the light. Pigeons cooed softly on a nearby ledge. Traffic hummed.

"You agreed to come here to see me," Dr. Mindle continued, "so it must be that you admit to yourself at least the possibility that none of this is true. That no one is stealing your clothes. That no one tried to kill you." His padded Armani shoulders rose in a subtle shrug. "Just the possibility, mind you."

Molly felt anger rise in her. She held up her hands, scraped and blistered from frantically bending and twisting the iron grill over the storage room window. "Exhibit A, as they say in court."

He turned around to face her. His expression was mild, composed. He barely glanced at her hands; the mind was his province. "We're not in court, Molly. But if we were, the prosecution would say that you acted out and deliberately splintered that storage room door then injured yourself escaping from someone who thought you were a prowler. That apartment building isn't in a crime-free neighborhood. Nowhere in New York is crime-free."

"But suppose Deirdre *was* really there. And trying to kill me."

Dr. Mindle faced the window again, slipping his hands into the pockets of his suit's pleated slacks. "What would be her motive?"

"What if she's trying to steal my life?" Molly said. "To take my place with my husband and son? To become me?"

"Then I'd say *she* should be here and not you. But you're the one whose husband is concerned with your actions lately. And they've disturbed him enough to talk you into coming here."

"Well, don't we usually put away the people who disturb us, rather than the people who are disturbed?"

"Sometimes," Dr. Mindle said. "Though not nearly as often as we used to, I assure you. And it seems to be you and no one else who sees yourself as a candidate for confinement. I see before me a badly frightened young woman, but not one who's necessarily mentally ill. Fear can exist in perfectly normal people and still have no basis in reality. Sometimes when we remove the fear, reality again becomes clear."

Molly sighed and stood up. Slick word games she didn't need. "You're trying to bullshit me, Doctor."

He turned toward her and smiled. "That's my job, bullshitting you. It's also my job to be honest with you. It's a balancing act.

And you have to be honest with me at least some of the time. We might get somewhere that way."

Molly knew the hopelessness of what he was saying and felt the familiar desperation and fear take control of her. "We might," she told him. "But like you said, Dr. Mindle, it would take time."

Her right knee and hip still ached from her ordeal in the apartment building basement. She tried not to let her pain show.

Limping slightly, she strode from the office.

The receptionist in the anteroom glanced up at her and smiled. "A man just poked his head in here and looked around to see if anyone was waiting to see the doctor. Might he be with you?"

"No," Molly said. "No one is with me."

37

It was dark when Lisa Emmons left the movie and made her way along East Fifty-seventh Street toward the subway stop. Beside her in the street, light traffic hissed along in the dampness of a recent drizzle. The remnants of the audience that had left the theater with her and walked in the same direction were thinning out, going down side streets or getting into cabs. Lisa's mind was still on the movie—a satisfying drama about three independent women who got even with the abusive men in their lives then formed an investment company and became millionaires—when she was aware of someone walking behind her, whistling the theme song from the movie.

Lisa slowed her pace and glanced back, then stopped and turned all the way around. The sidewalk wasn't crowded. There was no one within fifty feet of her. A panhandler who'd appeared from somewhere was standing half a block away with a cup and a cardboard sign. A short man with puffy dark hair was bustling away in the opposite direction. It was possible that he was the whistler. Even the beggar might have followed and whistled the tune. He didn't necessarily have to have seen the movie; he might have picked up the melody from some other member of the audience who'd walked past him.

Or the whistler might have ducked into a nearby all-night deli or entered the shop Lisa had just passed that had an assortment of jade figurines displayed in its lighted window.

There was no way for her to know for sure. That was one of the problems with a city like New York that lived late into the night; there were too many possibilities.

Her heart beating faster, Lisa continued on her way. She thought, for only a few fleeting seconds, that she heard the whistling again. A sound of the night that might have been the trailing notes of a faraway emergency siren, or an echo from blocks away. Sound carried that way sometimes in the nighttime canyons of tall buildings, the way images sometimes appeared out of their proper place in the desert.

She began walking faster. There had been a monotonal quality to the whistling that was oddly threatening and made her afraid to look behind her again. Yet without looking, she was sure she was being followed.

A cab turned the corner and drove toward her. She ran a few steps, her arm raised.

But despite the fact that the cab's rooflight showed it to be available, Lisa saw a passenger slumped in back, and the cab accelerated and spattered droplets of rainwater on her as it sped past.

A horn blared at her, and she realized she was standing off the curb, almost a yard into the street. She hurriedly moved back up onto the sidewalk just as a string of cars roared past.

The blare of the horn and her sudden action had jolted her mind. She was angry with herself now. This was absurd. She wasn't exactly alone—this was midtown Manhattan and there were other people on the streets. She had done nothing and had no reason to be afraid of anyone.

Holding her breath, she stood and stared back in the direction she'd come from along the wide, shadowed sidewalk. There were two women walking away from her, holding hands. Lovers? Mother and daughter? Merely fast friends?

A tall man in baggy pants and a shirt with the sleeves rolled up emerged from the shop that sold jade. He glanced her way, then drew something from his pocket and appeared to be studying it. Two business types in suits and ties walked past the man toward Lisa. She stood and waited while they passed. ". . . should never have traded so much to get him," the man on the left was saying, gesticulating with his right arm.

Lisa didn't move. She continued staring boldly at the man still standing in front of the shop with the jade.

He glanced at her again, slipped whatever he'd been holding

and looking at back into his pocket, then walked away in the other direction.

Lisa walked on, feeling better.

But she decided she didn't want to go down into a subway station. The subways were better these days, safer and more brightly lighted, but still they gave her the creeps. Though she regretted spending the extra money, she'd take a cab.

Even as she made the decision, the traffic light at the next intersection changed and several cabs turned and drove down the street toward her.

She moved back into the street and waved an arm to hail all of them. It was the first one that veered in her direction and came to rocking stop before her. She climbed in and gave the cabby her address, then settled back into the soft seat and closed her eyes. She knew that if she wanted to, she could keep them closed until she felt the cab stop in front of her apartment, where she'd be safe.

She'd been home for fifteen minutes and was sitting on the sofa, sipping a cup of orange-flavored tea, when the phone rang.

When she picked it up and said hello, a woman's voice said, "You were followed from the movie."

Lisa felt the night's earlier fear come alive and leap into her throat. "Who are you?" she asked in a choked voice.

"I'm somebody who saw you followed from the time you left the theater until you got into a cab. It's okay, though. No one followed you home."

Lisa was angry now, but still afraid. She looked down and saw goose bumps on the backs of her pale hands. "Why are you telling me this?"

The woman gave a short laugh, as if the answer to Lisa's question should be obvious. "To you, of course."

"Then tell me more. Say who was following me. If you know."

"That really wouldn't change anything."

"Then *why* are they following me?"

"You're perceived as a threat to this person."

Lisa's mind worked furiously but came up empty. "No. I'm not a threat to anyone!"

"I said it was a perceived threat."

"How do you know all this?"

"An acquaintance of mine has talked to me about you. This person is dangerous."

"Is it a man or a woman?"

"I can't tell you. I don't want anyone to find out we've talked."

"How could anyone find out?"

"You might tell them."

"Don't be absurd. If you help me, why should I do anything that would hurt you?"

"It would be an accident."

"What's your name?"

"You don't need to know."

"You might call again," Lisa said. "If you do, how will I know it's the same woman?"

There was silence for such a long time that Lisa thought the woman might have hung up without her hearing the distinctive double click of the connection breaking. Then the voice said, "My name's Darlene, Lisa."

"What about a last name?"

"No. I've warned you because I saw it as my duty. I've fulfilled my obligation. That's enough."

"I promise I won't—"

But now Lisa did hear a sharp double click that might have been a hang-up, then only a thrumming silence.

"Hello," Lisa said tentatively into the void.

The phone company took her voice and didn't give it back.

38

They'd argued much of last night about her visit with Dr. Mindle. Perhaps that was why David had phoned this morning and suggested in an apologetic tone that they meet for lunch.

Molly had left Michael with Julia and was caught up on her work, waiting for another assignment from Traci, so she left the apartment at eleven-thirty and walked toward the subway.

She first noticed the man watching her while she was walking along Eighty-sixth Street toward the station at Central Park West. He was well over six feet tall and very thin, with a narrow face, sad eyes, and straight red hair that hung lank almost to his shoulders. He was wearing jeans and a baggy black T-shirt lettered GREAT GOTHAM below an outline of the city skyline in yellow. Molly had sensed that someone was staring at her, glanced to the side and saw the man, and he quickly and somewhat guiltily averted his eyes.

She figured she knew what he'd been thinking; he was sizing her up, gauging her sexuality. That wasn't unusual in New York. It was as much a part of subway travel as tokens and turnstiles.

She noticed, though it didn't greatly concern her, that he'd descended the subway station stairs behind her. Now he was standing well away from her on the platform. She might not have seen him if it weren't for his height. He was looking away from her, in the direction from which the train would make its approach.

Within five minutes Molly felt the cool breeze that meant a train was bearing down on the station, pushing the air before it. A single white light became visible down the tunnel, and with a thunderous roar the train flashed in a blur along the tracks and appeared to be an express speeding past this station. But it slowed and squealed and clattered to a stop.

Molly was standing within a few feet of the train, and she boarded the sleek steel car as soon as the doors hissed open. She sat down on one of the plastic seats on the opposite side of the car, near the end, across from an old woman with a large shopping bag resting on the floor between her legs, and a man who appeared to be sleeping despite the open magazine spread out on his lap. The glossy cover of the magazine featured a blond woman wearing a skimpy red outfit and wielding a whip. Above the woman with the shopping bag was an ad with a phone number to call if you needed repair of a torn earlobe.

There was a nasal, indecipherable public announcement concerning the route and the next stop, then the train jerked and accelerated away from the station, and Molly settled back to ride.

As they were running through darkness, the door at the opposite end of the car opened, the one that allowed access from the following car. There was a momentary burst of sound—steel wheels thundering along the tracks—then the redheaded man stepped inside and slid the door shut.

Molly stared at him, but he merely glanced at her as he gripped a pole to keep his balance and sat down.

She remembered him standing far away from her on the platform. Which meant he must have made his way through at least two or three cars to get to this one. And apparently he was going no farther.

When she got off at the Seventh Avenue stop and transferred to an E train that would take her to the Lexington station, she lost sight of the man.

But when she surfaced to the street near the Citicorp Building, there he was, standing on the opposite sidewalk.

She ignored him, tried not to think of him, as she walked down Fifty-third toward Second Avenue, where she was going to meet David.

Near Third Avenue she paused to pretend to look in a shop window, and there was the man's reflection, along with a cluster of people waiting to cross the intersection. He was staring at her, but when he realized she was watching his reflection, he looked away and moved out of sight.

She was scared now. And angry. But at least she knew the man appeared in reflection, unlike vampires and imaginary figures of the mentally unbalanced. And he was certainly following her.

What would Dr. Mindle say if she told him about this? Paranoic delusion, he'd probably say.

Deirdre would undoubtedly say the same.

David might agree.

Though she was on the lookout, she didn't see the redheaded man again as she made her way to the diner where she was to meet David.

As she walked across Second Avenue, she saw David through a diner window, seated in a booth. She waved to him, but he didn't see her among the still tightly knotted crowd of people who'd just crossed the intersection.

Molly felt better as soon as she entered the Apple Blossom Diner. It was a sunlit, hamburger kind of place, with Formica-topped tables and a stainless steel counter with red vinyl stools. A few dozen customers sat in booths or at tables, another half dozen at the counter. As she walked toward David, she heard the sizzle of something cold being placed on the hot grill.

She slid into the booth to sit opposite him.

"You're late," he said, looking up from a brightly colored pamphlet he'd been reading—something about a medical plan. He didn't seem irritated by her tardiness; it was merely an observation.

"Sorry, had to wait awhile for a subway." In truth she'd simply lost track of time and left the apartment ten minutes later than she'd planned. Another symptom of her slipping mental faculties?

A waiter came over and set two glasses of water and menus on the table. Molly and David had been to the diner often and knew what they wanted, so David handed back the menus, and the waiter took their order without having to leave while they made up their minds. They both ordered hamburgers and Beck's dark beer.

When the waiter had jotted kitchen code on his order pad and left, David stuck the medical plan pamphlet into his suit coat pocket. "How late can Julia keep Michael?"

"Two o'clock. We've got plenty of time. Is there a reason why you invited me to lunch today, David?"

"Does there have to be?"

"Yes. And I think I can guess what it is. We both feel bad about arguing last night over my visit with Dr. Mindle. And you still don't like the way it turned out."

"The visit or the argument?"

"Both, maybe." She hoped he wasn't still angry, determined to play diversionary word games. Like Dr. Mindle's games.

He took a sip of water then set the glass back down carefully in its ring of condensation, as if that were required by Miss Manners. He shrugged and smiled. "You're right, I guess, but at least you went to see him. I can't ask you to do more than that."

"And you still don't agree that Deirdre tried to kill me."

"No," he said thoughtfully, and no doubt honestly, "I can't agree with you on that. And you said yourself you didn't see whoever was in the basement. Whatever happened, Mol, I'm thankful you weren't seriously hurt."

Molly smiled resignedly. Changing the way he thought was like trying to claw through a stone wall. "You think she was just trying to scare me?"

"I don't think she was there, Mol." He reached across the table and held her hand. "Do you realize you're accusing someone of attempted murder?"

"I realize more than that. She did try to kill me, David. And I think she might have succeeded in killing Bernice so she could get closer to us through Michael. If she's the woman I saw in the park, she's in great physical shape, an athlete. She'd have the lung capacity to hold Bernice underwater until she drowned. Bernice would have been struggling, panicking, using up oxygen fast."

He stared at her in astonishment. "My God, Mol! That's wild speculation. You shouldn't be saying it."

"I've smelled my scent on Deirdre, seen her on the street in a dress that's missing from my closet. Seen how she looks at you. She wants you again. She wants Michael. She wants my life and I'm in the way."

David shook his head, gazed out the window for a moment as if gathering his thoughts, then looked at her. He still had on his glasses from when he was reading the pamphlet, and he seemed to be focusing on her with an effort spurred by intense curiosity. "Do you really think she's sneaking into our apartment and pilfering your cosmetics and clothes?"

"Yes, I think so." She sipped from her water tumbler, then put it down and stared into it. The water was trembling gently, its ice-cluttered surface tilting this way and that against the sides of the glass. But she could see all the way to the bottom and pick up the cream color of the table. She wished her future were as clear. "If she wants to steal my life, why wouldn't she steal my green dress?"

David apparently considered her question rhetorical, because he didn't attempt an answer. "The only way she could be getting in is from the fire escape," he said, "through the window we keep propped open for Muffin. If it will make you feel more secure, I'll nail it so it can't be raised any farther than six inches."

Molly continued staring into her glass. "David, when I came here to meet you, I was followed."

He sat back and said nothing. She knew what he must be thinking: *Here's something new.* How would he cope with it?

"How can you be sure?" he finally asked, his voice wary.

"He was on Central Park West, then on the subway, then behind me as I was walking here. I sneaked looks and saw him several times, saw his reflection in a shop window."

"Him?"

"Yes. A man. Tall, with red hair. Sometimes he'd be behind me, sometimes on the other side of the street."

She could hear him breathing hard, trying to assess this latest development.

"You joking, Mol?"

"I wish I were," she said to her ice water. "I know how this sounds. Don't you think I know how this sounds? Well, I know exactly. You'd like to send me back to Dr. Mindle."

"Do you know who this man is?" He was clearly frightened and puzzled by her state of mind. "I mean, have you ever seen him before?"

"No and no, but that doesn't mean he wasn't there. Doesn't mean he wasn't real." She looked up at him abruptly, which seemed to startle him. "I know what you think—that I'm going crazy."

He squirmed in his seat. "No, no, Mol! I think you're a case of nerves, and I don't blame you. Hell, everything that's been happening lately, I'm not the calmest guy in town myself."

Molly had his support, she knew. He was on her side. Yet he couldn't seem to believe any real ill of Deirdre, couldn't believe his wife entirely. The tug of war he must be feeling, that he was helping to instill in her, was confusing. There were moments when she sometimes took *his* side, when she thought this whole period of discontent and fear might really be her fault. She absently inserted a finger in the cold water and trailed it in a circle, creating ripples that sometimes overran the glass's rim.

"Lately I wonder about myself," she said. "I can't help it. I know that's what she wants, but I can't help it."

David stared at her in such obvious sympathy and pain that her heart ached. "Maybe you *should* go back to Dr. Mindle, Mol."

Her anger stirred. "Don't be absurd. I don't need an analyst."

"Half the people in this city are in some kind of therapy," David said with a glance out the window.

"The other half roam the streets talking to imaginary companions."

He squeezed her hand and gave her a strained smile. "I'd like for us to stay in the first half, Mol."

The waiter brought their burgers and beer and laid everything out on the table. There were heaped french fries, almost burying those tiny containers of slaw that looked like the miniature paper cups dentists gave you when they instructed you to rinse. The food's pungent aroma stirred Molly's appetite then almost simultaneously made her nauseated.

"I love you, Mol," David said, when the waiter was out of earshot. "I really do love you."

He didn't add that he was concerned for her sanity. That was kind of him, she thought. He was a genuinely kind man and in so many ways a good husband. But something was wrong between them, something was secret and festering.

She smiled sadly at him.

"Possibly you do, David. Yet you ordered onions on your hamburger."

39

Deirdre had told Chumley she wasn't feeling well. As she expected, he urged her to take the afternoon off. He'd been trying to coach her to increase her skill in double-entry book-keeping. She'd become bored within minutes.

After buying a knish and a can of Diet Coke from a street vendor, she sat on a stone wall and ate lunch, then took a cab home. She didn't like riding the subway. It was too crowded, not to mention the way those assholes stared at a woman. She almost wanted one of them to try something.

Besides, it hadn't been that long ago when one of them had set off a fire bomb in a subway car. The bomb had detonated in a station, but it might have gone off when the train was in a tunnel and caused even more death and injury. The idea of being trapped in a tunnel to die of smoke inhalation or burn to death made Deirdre shudder. There would be nothing she could do about it other than to suck in the smoke or flames and make death as quick as possible. She didn't want that to be her final and uncontrollable destiny.

She entered her apartment and changed to jeans and a blouse, leaving her shoes off. After settling down in front of the TV to watch CNN, she became restless. Wolf Blitzer appeared on screen, talking about impending legislation that had to do with foreign aid. Maybe it was his name, but with his beard that never looked as if it had quite grown all the way out, he always seemed to Deirdre like a man in the early stages of transforming into a werewolf. Not that she believed in such things. Or needed to, like some people. There were plenty of very real threats and injustices in the world without worrying about the inventions of writers.

Blitzer was pointing to a bar chart with a pen or pencil. She found that she couldn't sit still; a wild animal seemed to pace inside her chest.

When Newt Gingrich appeared on camera to be interviewed in front of a bookshelf lined with obviously phony books, she switched off the TV, stood up, and stretched to loosen stiff limbs and eager muscles. Standing tall with her head back, her arms extended straight up, she could almost feel the rough-textured ceiling with her eyes as she peered at it between the widely spread fingers of each hand.

She lowered her arms and her body shivered almost in the manner of a dog shaking off water. Then she went to the phone on the desk and used the blunt end of a ball-point pen to peck out Molly's number. With the receiver pressed to her ear, she listened to the muffled ring and could imagine it much louder in the apartment two floors below. If she was home, Molly would probably be working. She would already have picked up Michael from Small Business. Maybe he'd be taking his nap. Molly would be interrupted at work, and Michael might awaken and cry and receive some of the attention he craved and was denied.

But when the phone stopped ringing, it was Molly's voice on the answering machine that came on the line, explaining that the caller had reached the Jones residence but no one could come to the phone right now.

So the bitch wasn't home.

". . . but leave a message after the tone," Molly's voice was saying. The voice that whispered in David's ear, that praised and reprimanded Michael, that uttered words that passed the wrong lips.

The answering machine tone screamed then was silent.

Deirdre knew what she wanted to do. She couldn't hang up. She smiled.

"Fuck you, Molly!" she said. Was the bitch screening her calls? Sitting by the machine listening? Deirdre doubted it, yet maybe it was so.

She ran her tongue over her lips as if tasting them. Sometimes you had to take a chance, leave things up to destiny. Sometimes it was *fun* to take a chance.

"This is Deirdre, Molly. The woman who fucks your husband!"

She tried to say more, but laughter almost strangled her and she had to hang up the phone.

Her blood was roaring in her ears like wild music, singing to her that now she *had* to do what she'd been considering. Otherwise, how could her message be erased before Molly returned home?

She started to slip her feet into her shoes, then stopped. Maybe what she planned would be better barefoot. More contact with the flesh and more intimate. Definitely it would be quieter. That might be important if Molly happened to be home and not answering her phone.

Deirdre padded barefoot to a small vase shaped like a star that she'd bought at the flea market at Sixth and Twenty-sixth. She turned the vase upside down and the key she'd had made for Molly's apartment fell out into her waiting palm. She squeezed it hard until it was as warm as her own body.

She went to the door and opened it, peeked out to make sure the hall was empty, then crept to the stairs.

It took her only a few minutes to descend the stairs and let herself quietly into the Jones apartment.

She stood inside the door and knew immediately that no one was home. She could always tell about that when entering a house or apartment; she had a sense about such things.

But just to confirm what she already knew, she walked about the apartment, glancing into the bedrooms and bathroom.

Then she went to Molly's desk and saw by the digital counter on the answering machine that there were three messages. She sat down in Molly's desk chair and pressed Play, then got a pencil out of the mug on the desk and sat bouncing its point on the flat wood surface while she listened.

Beep.

"David, Mol. Just wanted to remind you of lunch, but I guess you've already left. Hope so, anyway."

Beep.

"Traci here, Molly. The architectural manuscript is fine. Reads beautifully. Even the author is orgasmic over it, and he's an architect who hasn't been responsible for an erection in years. Got another assignment for you if you're interested. A mystery. Not like the wife-in-the-trash-compactor book, but almost as juicy. Was that a joke? Call you later. Bye."

Beep.

"Fuck you, Molly! This is—"

Deirdre pressed Fast Forward, then Erase.

So they were at lunch, together, and Michael was probably being watched by Julia after hours at Small Business.

When the machine was silent, Deirdre put down the pencil and walked into Molly and David's bedroom. She went to the closet and opened the door, then stood looking at the now familiar array of clothes. Molly should certainly dress better for David. More the way Deirdre dressed. She smiled. Didn't Molly know clothes could make the man?

She shut the closet door and walked to the dresser. In the mirror she saw Molly's SLEEP OR SEX T-shirt lying on the bed. She went to the bed and picked up the T-shirt, then noticed the toes of a pair of women's terrycloth house slippers protruding from beneath the spread where it draped to the floor. So this was Molly's side of the bed.

Deirdre walked over and stood in front of the dresser mirror. She was visible from mid-thigh to the top of her head.

Staring at her reflection, she slowly and sensuously undressed, doing a striptease for the woman watching in the mirror, dropping her clothes on the floor.

Naked, she flipped her hair back from her pale shoulders then struck some poses in the mirror, some attitudes. The woman she was observing still had a superb body and no doubt about it. Breasts with gravity-taunting lift and lush, erect nipples. Her hips were still trim and there weren't any stretch marks—none that she could see from where she stood, anyway. Her stomach was smooth and flat, her thighs muscular but not too thick.

Moving closer to the dresser, she selected one of Molly's perfumes, unscrewed the cap, and cautiously sniffed as she waved the neck of the bottle beneath her nose.

Rose-scented, she thought. She liked it. She applied some of the perfume to the insides of her wrists, then dabbed some in the cleavage between her breasts, so much larger and riper and more appealing than Molly's breasts. Finally she used her fingers to work perfume into the dark mass of her pubic hair.

She returned the bottle to where she'd found it, then went to David's dresser. Familiar with the contents of the drawers, she slid open the top one. There in the left front corner were the ribbed condoms and the tube of K-Y lubricant.

She took the K-Y tube to the bed, slipped into Molly's SLEEP OR SEX T-shirt, then threw back the spread and top sheet. Wearing only the T-shirt, she lay down on her back on Molly's side of the bed. She worked the back of her head powerfully into Molly's pillow, leaving a deep impression, letting her long red hair fan out on the white linen. More lustrous, more beautiful than Molly's hair. She uncapped the K-Y tube and squeezed a bead of the slick substance onto the middle finger of her right hand.

Closing her eyes, letting her mind soar where it might, she lowered her hand and touched her finger to the precise spot she sought and began to masturbate.

When she was finished, she replaced the K-Y tube, then wiped her hands on the T-shirt, and laid it on top of the sheet.

Standing at the foot of the bed, dressed in her own clothes again, she drew a deep, triumphant breath, taking in the rose perfume mingled with the scent of her sex still on her hand. Surely destiny was her ally. Any threat or obstacle would be destroyed. Nothing could stop her from claiming what was hers, from being who she was.

Nothing.

No one.

Silently, she padded barefoot from the quiet apartment and locked the door behind her.

She did not make the bed.

40

David had a difficult time concentrating on work after his lunch with Molly. He left Sterling Morganson at four forty-five, missing most of the evening subway rush, and was home before five-thirty.

As he closed the apartment door and hung up his suit coat, he saw that Molly was seated at her desk working at her notebook computer.

"Another job for Link?" he asked.

"No," she said without looking around at him, "it's the article for *Author.*"

She was trying to sell an article on editing from the editor's point of view to *Author* magazine. It would be her second article for the publication whose readership was largely amateur writers. David was glad to see her working instead of worrying.

He kissed the back of her neck as he walked past her—without response—then went into the bedroom to put on jeans and a casual shirt.

Inside the bedroom door he paused.

The bed was unmade, the sheet rumpled. Molly always made the bed, even on the mornings when she was rushed. And there was the T-shirt she slept in, wadded up instead of folded as usual, lying on the bed.

As he moved closer, David saw the depression in Molly's pillow, as if she'd been resting and had just gotten up. But he doubted that she'd taken a nap in the middle of the afternoon. In fact, he doubted that she'd returned directly home after having lunch with him.

Yet there was her bizarre story about having been followed. How might that have affected her behavior this afternoon.

He bent to straighten the T-shirt and saw that it had been smeared with something clear and oily, as if the substance had been deliberately wiped there.

Then he saw the single, long red hair on the pillow.

His grip tightened on the T-shirt as he figured out what must have happened. Deirdre had been here. Apparently Molly had set to work whenever she arrived home after meeting him, and hadn't yet gone into the bedroom. Hadn't yet seen this.

Deirdre again!

"Bitch!" David whispered.

Quickly he used a tissue to rub most of the slick substance from the T-shirt, then folded the shirt as Molly usually did and set it aside. He made the bed, straightening the wrinkled sheet and plumping the pillow. Then he laid the T-shirt on the bed where Molly kept it when it wasn't in the wash, making sure the faint stains were facing down.

After changing into jeans and a faded Lands' End shirt, he took a last look around the bedroom, then returned to the living room.

Molly was still working at her desk. She didn't seem to have moved.

"I'm going out to get a *Post*," he said. "Want anything?"

"Supper," she said, without turning around.

"I'll bring something back. Chinese? Pizza?"

"Anything," she told him, working her fingers over the small, silent keyboard delicately, as if she were weaving.

He said nothing else as he went out the door.

He didn't leave the building. As he climbed the stairs to the fourth floor, he became angrier with every step. And more frightened.

Deirdre answered the door immediately after he knocked, almost as if she'd been expecting him. She was wearing a robe fastened tightly at the waist with a sash and was barefoot.

"David," she said simply, not in any surprise.

"We need to talk."

"Of course. Anytime."

She stepped back and he entered and closed the door.

"You look upset," she told him.

"You were in our apartment, weren't you? In our bedroom?"

"Why, you know I've been there. With you."

"I mean today, while we were both gone. You were there today."

"Heavens no." She smiled.

"You wanted her to find it, didn't you?"

"Find what?"

"The unmade bed. The shirt she sleeps in. Maybe even the red hair on her pillow. But I found the mess you left. Molly hadn't been home long and didn't go into the bedroom, never saw any of it."

"Then even if what I think you're implying is true, no harm was done."

"Listen, Deirdre—"

"I just got home from work, David, and I was about to shower. The water's running, if you'll excuse me."

"I won't excuse you. Myself, either."

"Martyrdom doesn't become you. Guilt's like acid, David. It's a stupid thing to carry around inside you." She walked away from him, toward the hall.

As he followed her, he became aware of the roar of water thundering into the old claw-footed tub. At least she hadn't lied to him about that.

"I want your key to our apartment," he said.

Still walking, she untied the sash of her robe and let it fall from her body as she made a right turn into the bathroom and left the door open.

He stepped over the robe and trailed after her, saw her part the shower curtain and step into the tub.

"Deirdre!"

She didn't answer him from behind the curtain.

He moved toward the shower, knowing he shouldn't. Her form was barely visible behind the opaque plastic.

Suddenly she opened the curtain and smiled out at him. Her hair was wet and plastered to her skull. A layer of soapy bubbles was just disappearing beneath the hot needles of water, flowing in milky streams along her smooth stomach, down between her thighs, to swirl down the drain.

"Come in here with me if you want to talk, David."

Standing there staring at her, he wanted to, but he didn't move. Heat rolled out at him. The shower continued to roar.

"Then you'll just have to wait until I'm finished," she said, and closed the curtain.

He knew his time was limited here. He *had* to talk to her. And what more could he be guilty of than he was already?

He hurriedly unbuckled his belt and peeled off his shirt, removed shoes and socks and stepped out of his clothes.

"Well, hello!" Deirdre said with a grin when he opened the curtain and stepped into the tub. "This is where you belong, David, with me. Birds of a feather fly together."

He kissed her hard on the mouth, held the length of her wet body to him. The bar of soap thumped hard on the bottom of the tub, something to avoid. His hands moved over the small of her back, down the smooth soapy mounds of her buttocks.

"Isn't this rape?" she asked, still smiling.

"Hardly," he said, and kissed her again.

Her tongue slid into his mouth, then out. "No, don't do this," she said without conviction. "No means no, David. That's the law. This is definitely rape." She bit his earlobe, then inserted her tongue in his ear, flicked it around. "No is easy to understand." Her words were distorted, her breath hot. He felt her fingers gently grip his erect penis and stroke it vertically. "No, no, no, please!" She laughed.

He gripped her slippery body with both arms, lifted her, then brought her down on him and was inside her, turning her sideways and pinning her against the wet tile wall. He felt the bar of soap with the edge of his foot and kicked it away, struggled and found purchase on the slippery porcelain and drove himself into her. She groaned and laughed again, breathlessly. "No, no, no! . . ."

He grabbed a handful of her wet hair and yanked her head back so she was looking up at him as he slammed into her, bouncing her off the wall.

She never blinked but her eyes narrowed beneath the stream of warm water from the shower head. "That's right, David. You're angry. Take it out on me. Get it all out. Harder! Harder!"

Gripping her hair tighter, he braced a foot against the side of the tub and hurried his thrusts into her, felt her body stiffen and her stomach press hard into his, heard the wet slap of flesh as his rhythm drummed her against the tiles.

He climaxed and pressed against her hard, then realized her eyes were bulging. He was squeezing the wet clump of her hair harder than he'd realized, straining her head back so that she was staring up at the ceiling. Her pupils were glazing over as if she were strangling, but she was grinning.

Alarmed at the violence within him, he released her, pulled out of her, and stepped back.

She stood gasping and hunched over, still leaning against the tiles, one trembling arm outstretched as if for balance.

When she caught her breath, she said, "So how do you feel now, David?"

"Brimming over with that acid you talked about."

He threw the plastic curtain aside and stepped out of the tub, then began drying himself with one of the towels from a porcelain rack.

She remained in the tub with the shower running and the curtain open, languidly soaping herself and gazing lovingly at him as he began to get dressed.

"Where are you going?" She asked as he sat on the commode and put on his shoes and socks. "Look out the window. It's starting to rain."

"Only to your phone to order some Chinese carry-out, so it's ready for me when I walk into the restaurant. That's where I am now, out buying dinner to bring back to the apartment for Molly. I'm sitting at the bar and waiting patiently while it's being prepared."

"You'll still be away longer than if you'd gone straight to the restaurant."

"They were busy, so the kitchen was backed up. A rowdy group from a convention of some kind, all of them drinking too much and making unreasonable demands on the waiters. They were feeling good and singing songs. You had to wait a long time for the food."

"That's imaginative. Won't Molly think it might be a lie?"

"No. She won't want to think that."

"Do you tell a lot of lies, David?"

"Lately I do. I have to. But it's to be kind, to avoid trouble and pain for other people."

"That's what all liars say."

"The ones who tell mostly defensive lies." He'd tied his shoes and knew he should finish dressing, then make the phone call to the restaurant and leave, but he couldn't take his eyes off Deirdre.

She glided the smooth bar of soap through the cleavage between her breasts, then over her erect nipples. "You certainly are deceptive, David the rapist."

"Aren't I, though?" he said, standing at last and buttoning his shirt.

Whatever she wanted, he always gave her, even over his own protestations and denial. Even rape. Not really David the rapist, though. David the liar. David the rationalizer.

He smoothed back his hair and checked his image in the fogging medicine chest mirror, looking away as quickly as possible.

41

Later that night, after David had fallen asleep watching television and Michael was in bed, the phone rang.

Molly was standing next to the phone in the kitchen, pouring Diet Pepsi into a glass with ice in it, and she grabbed the receiver after the first ring so Michael wouldn't be awakened.

She expected the call to be for David; he'd mentioned something concerning Josh phoning about work. But the caller, a woman, asked for her.

"You're David Jones's wife?" the woman said in a clipped, educated voice.

Molly said that she was.

"You don't know me, Molly. My name's Darlene."

Molly remembered Traci mentioning a woman who'd called Link Publishing looking for her. Darlene. Molly was pretty sure that had been the name. Maybe this was about a copyediting job. But at this hour?

"I feel I should warn you about someone," Darlene said. "There's a woman named Deirdre."

"I know her," Molly said in a choked voice, speaking softly. She didn't want David to wake up and hear.

"She means you harm," Darlene said.

Molly didn't want to think about Deirdre, didn't want any more trouble or even to talk about trouble. She wished fervently that she could hang up the phone and pretend it had never rung.

But she knew she couldn't. She had to talk with Darlene.

"You're warning's a little late," she said. She could feel a muscle in the right side of her neck twitching. "Deirdre's already tried to kill me."

"Are you *sure?*" Darlene sounded aghast.

"I'm sure. There are some who don't believe it, but I'm sure."

"I believe you," Darlene said, "though I didn't think she'd go that far this soon. I mean, she's a little weird. Well . . . more than a little. And I know something's building in her."

"Where do you know her from?" Molly asked.

"From the time she came to New York, not long ago. At first she seemed okay, I liked her. Then I noticed some things about her. I didn't mind. Okay, so she was eccentric. Lots of my friends are oddballs. It didn't bother me that she had a strange view of the world. Then she started talking like she was crazy, telling me about things she thought, things she'd done. After a while your name came up. And your husband's."

Molly squeezed the receiver. "David's?"

"Deirdre has some . . . well, kind of possessive ideas about him. I guess you know they were married a long time ago."

"David's told me. That's no secret."

"Deirdre thinks she can steal him from you. I mean, seriously."

"How do you know this?"

"She trusts me and talks to me. I might be the only person she can trust in New York, so she tells me things in confidentiality. And I'd keep them confidential, only they're so . . . weird. You should watch out for Deirdre."

"What's she told you about David?"

"I don't want to repeat it, because I don't know how much of it's true. But I'm sure some of it is. Sure enough that I figured I had to call you."

Molly was still trying to figure out what the phone call meant. For some reason, she believed this woman, and she had no idea why. "How much does Deirdre tell you?" she asked.

"Not everything. She's basically untrusting and manipulative. People like that always keep some things to themselves."

"What has she said about me?"

"She doesn't like you, Molly. It isn't just that you're in her way, that you have something she wants. She *really* doesn't like you. She thinks you stole her life."

"You mean because I'm married to David?"

"I guess so. Even though a lot of time has passed since they were together, she wants him and won't let go of the idea. Sometimes she talks almost like she's lost her mind."

"Darlene, did you phone Link Publishing and ask for me?"

"No, it must have been someone else. Some other Darlene."

"What's your last name? Who *are* you?"

"I can't tell you that. I don't want to get involved. I only called you because it was my duty. Something terrible is going to happen. I can sense it. You're not the only one I've had to warn."

"Can I have your phone number?" Molly asked.

"No. I said I didn't want to get involved."

"But you *are* involved!"

"Only to the extent that I felt I should warn you about Deirdre. If she's already tried to kill you, you need to make sure she won't try again."

"Can we meet someplace, talk some more?"

"No. I cautioned you, and that's enough. I had a responsibility to do that."

"Are you afraid of Deirdre?"

"Sometimes, yes. You should be, too. Goodbye, Molly."

"Wait! Please! Will you call if you learn anything else I should know?"

"I don't think so. I've done what I decided was necessary. Be on your guard, Molly. Deirdre wants what's yours. And there's something about her. I think she always gets what she wants."

"Darlene—"

"Listen, I'm sorry. We've talked long enough. And don't mention to anyone that I called. Especially David. I wouldn't want Deirdre to find out."

"Why don't you tell me some way I can get in touch with you?"

There was only soft silence on the line. Darlene had hung up, but not before uttering, "She's dangerous."

42

Lisa Emmons had stopped for groceries that evening on her way home from Sterling Morganson. She bought food often, a little at a time, since the nearest place to buy groceries was three blocks from where she lived. That way she never had to carry several heavy bags and then lug them up the three flights of stairs to her walk-up apartment.

She entered her apartment and, still gripping the plastic bag of groceries, backed into the door and gave it a final shove with her rump to close it.

After fastening the chain lock, she carried the bag into the small but neat kitchen and laid it on the breakfast counter. She draped her purse by its strap over the back of a chair then began unloading the bag and putting away the perishables she'd bought—a pint of milk, half a dozen eggs, frozen yogurt, a tomato; small amounts, recipe portions for one.

When she was finished, she got a bottle of Evian from the refrigerator, opened it, and carried it into the living room.

That room was small, like the kitchen, and also neat, with a gray area rug, blue upholstered chair and sofa, and bookcases that a onetime boyfriend named Chuck had built for her lining one wall. On another wall were two original oils by unknown artists, which she'd bought in the Village on the recommendation of a friend who painted. Alongside a combination secretary desk, bookshelf, and TV stand hung an old-fashioned, schoolhouse wall clock that had a modern quartz movement and ran on tiny AA batteries.

Lisa sat down on the sofa, slipped her feet out of her high-heeled shoes, and relaxed. Sterling Morganson had briefed everyone on the necessity of the fee reading department to generate more income. Lisa would be given additional duties. There would not be a commensurate increase in salary. It had been a long day at work.

She sipped water from the clear plastic Evian bottle and again considered seeking another job. She lived alone in her one-bedroom apartment and had few bills, but in New York even a modest lifestyle was expensive. She had excellent qualifications and could possibly find a higher-paying position, but there were other considerations: security, the new health care plan the company might make available . . . other considerations.

Maybe tomorrow she would check the classified ads and see how the job market looked, she told herself. She might even call a few people she knew who could furnish leads. It wouldn't hurt to inquire.

She smiled. She'd had this conversation with herself a hundred times but hadn't acted on it with any real resolution. Circling want ads with a pen and calling some of their phone numbers was as far as it usually went. Once she'd gone to interview for an associate editorial position with a large publisher, but at the last moment she'd decided she couldn't accept the job even if it were offered to her. Which, to her relief, it wasn't.

Well, maybe someday she'd listen to herself and take her own advice.

When the Evian bottle was empty, she took it into the kitchen and dropped it in the container for plastics. Then she went back into the living room, picked up her shoes, and carried them into the bedroom.

The window looking out on the air shaft was open, letting in warm air and the peculiar musty odor she suspected came from the pigeon droppings on the outside sill. The pigeons used to keep her awake at night, with their periodic cooing and flapping, but finally she'd gotten used to them and even found their presence oddly soothing. Lisa lowered the window and locked it.

The bedroom was the size of the living room, with a tall walnut wardrobe as well as a closet. The bed had a brass headboard with white porcelain knobs, a gift from her father when she'd moved into the city. A framed blowup of a Gothic romance paperback cover illustration given to her by a writer was on the wall opposite the bed, a young woman with windblown hair and a long, flowing dress standing on a cliff looking out at a sweeping view of sea and clouds. The woman had her hand raised to her forehead, as if straining to see something far out from shore. Something in her stance and expression suggested that she yearned to sail on that sea. It was a corny illustration, Lisa knew, yet some nights in bed it comforted her to lie and stare at it until she fell asleep with the light on. She didn't like to admit that her life was lonely.

Still with her shoes in her right hand, she walked to the closet, opened the door, and was face to face with the woman from the office, David's woman Deirdre.

Lisa was shocked into paralysis. The shoes slipped from her hand and *thunked* on the floor.

This couldn't be happening!

Deirdre was smiling and holding some sort of long-handled tool close alongside her body. A shovel, maybe. She moved it slightly and a rusty implement came into view from between two dresses—a mining tool, Lisa thought. A pick.

This wasn't real!

Deirdre took a quick step forward.

"Wha—" Lisa managed to say, before the pick struck her in the chest, knocking the wind from her.

She was lying on her back on the floor with no sensation of having fallen, and she was having great difficulty breathing.

She tried to roll over and found she couldn't move. It was then that she saw the wooden pick handle extended upward at an angle from her body. She glanced down and there was the rusty pick itself protruding from her chest just below her heart.

. . . couldn't be real!

When she inhaled, a terrible pain jolted through her body.

She lay back and was very still, as if her life depended on an intricate balance she didn't understand.

"Hurts . . ." she heard herself moan.

Above her, Deirdre grinned wildly and shook her head in mild disapproval. "Picky, picky!"

Lisa saw her bend slightly and grip the wooden handle firmly with both hands. She planted her foot on Lisa's stomach and grunted with effort as she withdrew the pick. As its long, rusty point pulled from the gaping wound, pain too severe to allow breathing or thought raged through Lisa like fire.

Through blurred, agony-slitted eyes, she saw Deirdre raise the pick high, saw its bloody point descend in a rush toward her head.

She tried to turn her head to get it away from the deadly arc of the pick. Pain exploded in her temple—and was gone in a burst of brilliant red.

Then she was falling, plunging faster and faster, and everything was white.

Then black.

43

Deirdre lowered the pickax and listened to her own breathing in the quiet bedroom.

"My God!" a breathless voice said.

When she raised her head, Deirdre saw Darlene's reflection in the dresser mirror.

"She wanted David," Deirdre said to the reflection.

"She wanted what you wanted, so you killed her."

"Exactly. I have the right. David was always mine, and always will be mine."

"You're evil, Deirdre. You were always evil."

"That isn't true! Evil was done *to* me."

"That's not an excuse."

"You were lucky. You died when you were five. You stayed good. Father never had a chance to—"

"To what?"

"You know. Mother knew too, but then she didn't know. So I was never good enough, never bright or pretty enough. I was never *you*. I couldn't live up to you because you weren't there to live up to. It wasn't fair!"

"Scarlet fever wasn't fair to me."

"I would have been better off dead too. Almost every night I wished I was dead. Someplace where I couldn't be touched. At peace like you. You could never have been what they pretended. You would have been just like me if you hadn't gotten sick and died, not some pure and perfect angel that belonged in heaven. That's where they always said you were. When you died, I was condemned to hell. I wish it had been you in the bedroom when the door opened, and you who was forced—"

"Forced?" Darlene smiled. "You know that isn't true."

"Not after a while, maybe." Pressure built in Deirdre's throat and she swallowed. "You never knew what it was, never saw the blood on the sheets. I have scars, inside and outside. I look different from what I am. Sometimes people think a sexy woman is dumb."

"Not you, Deirdre. Nobody ever took you for stupid after they knew you for a while."

"But when they did think I was stupid, I made them sorry."

"It's time to be honest with me. Honest all the way."

"I learned to do to men what was done to me. To control them."

"That must have proved useful."

"It's still useful."

"What about the fire?" Darlene asked. "Remember that night? Mother and Father? It was like our house was screaming, only it was—"

"Shut up! Now!" Deirdre stood very straight and glared.

"You don't like thinking about it, do you?"

"You don't know about the fire!"

"Oh, sure I do. And I know about that place you ran away from."

"I'm not surprised by that," Deirdre said bitterly. "You're nosy, a spy. You've spied on me for a long time, haven't you?"

In the mirror, Darlene smiled. "You sound just like a little girl I used to know."

"I didn't do what they said I did," Deirdre told her.

"Sure you did. But you don't remember."

"Hah! Like you were there!"

"I'm *here*, aren't I?"

"Yes. Still spying, sneaking, working against me. You'll tell the police what I did here, won't you."

"Of course I won't. We're sisters. You more than anyone know how certain things must stay within families."

"Mother and Father! You'll tell them!"

"They know all about you, anyway. Everybody who's dead knows all about you. I won't tell anyone who's alive."

"I don't trust you."

"You shouldn't," Darlene's reflection said smugly. "You can't trust me any farther than you can know me."

Deirdre drew a deep breath, then turned away from the mirror and faced Darlene.

She raised the pickax.

Darlene didn't move.

Only closed her eyes and smiled.

44

David took care of the matter the next morning, as promised.

He was aware of Molly watching him closely, standing in the center of the room with her arms crossed, her shoulders slightly hunched in a manner that was becoming habitual.

"This will solve the problem," he said, looking down at the red-handled hammer and the small box of nails he'd bought at a hardware store on Second Avenue. Hammer and nails were lying on Michael's bed, within easy reach of Muffin's permanently propped-open window.

"Of course," he said, "this is breaking the city code, interfering with access to a fire escape."

"We don't have fires in this building," Molly said flatly, "only fire alarms."

"Nevertheless, I bought long nails so we can leave them sticking out half an inch and I can easily pry them out with the hammer. We'll keep the hammer on the top shelf of Michael's bookcase, where he can't reach it and we can get to it fast if it becomes necessary."

She said nothing, and he was aware of her in the corner of his vision as he wielded the hammer and drove a long nail into each side of the wooden window frame.

"It's always possible the faulty wiring that causes the alarm to sound might also cause a fire," he said.

She remained silent and solemn, ignoring his pass at irony.

He tucked the hammer in his belt then, with effort, worked the paperback books loose that had been propping open the window.

The rending action ripped the cover from the top book, a best-selling British mystery novel of a decade ago, and caused the pages of another to come loose from the binding.

"Do you want to keep any of these?" They were used paperbacks they'd bought years ago at the Strand, and he knew they wouldn't have been used to prop open the window if they'd had any lasting value in the first place. But he thought he'd better ask the question anyway before he condemned the books to the incinerator.

"They're out-of-date reference books and a couple of cozies," Molly said. "Go ahead and pitch them."

He dropped the books into Michael's painted wicker waste-basket then returned to the window. It was frozen open six inches now. Spreading his feet wide for leverage, he yanked and pulled on the sash to demonstrate to Molly that the window was immovable.

"See, Mol," he said, turning to her and smiling, "problem solved."

She simply walked from the room, saying nothing.

He wondered if Molly knew or merely suspected that nailing the window frame had been a show for her benefit; that not even changing the locks would help. He had to find some way to stop Deirdre.

He propped his fists on his hips and stared at the window. At least his handiwork should be good for Molly's peace of mind.

And they owed her some peace of mind, he thought guiltily as he laid the hammer and remaining nails on the bookshelf and left the room.

He walked into the living room and got his sport jacket from the coat closet, then picked up his attaché case from the chair. Molly was nowhere in sight. She'd already dropped Michael off at Small Business. Maybe she was in the bathroom, or had decided to jog and was changing clothes in the bedroom.

"I'm going, Mol!"

There was no answer.

More concerned than angry, David draped his jacket over his shoulder and went out the door.

The business with the window had made him late leaving the apartment. Then someone had fallen ill on the subway, necessitating an unscheduled stop and emergency treatment, and causing all the trains on the line to grind to a halt and not move for more than an hour. It was almost eleven o'clock when he finally arrived at Sterling Morganson.

He'd barely gotten settled in his office when Josh, carrying a tall stack of manuscripts, stopped at his door and stuck his head in.

"Heard from Lisa, David?"

David looked away from his flickering computer monitor. "No. Should I have?"

"She didn't come in this morning, and she doesn't answer her phone." Josh was obviously worried.

David didn't see any big problem here. "Call her father's number. It's in her file. He might know where she is."

"I called him. That's what seems odd about this. He says she was supposed to meet him for dinner last night but didn't show or call, and she didn't answer her phone. He hasn't heard from her this morning. He phoned back a few minutes ago and said he'd gone to her apartment but she wasn't home, and there was no indication of where she might have gone."

"It's only ten minutes past eleven," David said. "I don't see why you're concerned."

"Her father noticed a throw rug in her bedroom where there hadn't been one before. When he lifted it, there was a damp, dark stain underneath."

David looked at him more closely. "Are you saying you suspect foul play?" God, he'd sounded like one of the characters in the manuscripts that poured into Sterling Morganson.

Josh seemed puzzled. "Well, I don't know. But her being so late and not calling in, and standing up her father last night . . . it doesn't seem like Lisa."

"Maybe she would have called her father this morning, but she got sick and went to see a doctor. That would explain the stain on the carpet. Also explain why she hasn't called in yet."

"Waiting rooms have phones," Josh pointed out.

David suspected that Lisa might have gone to an early job interview somewhere and had been taken seriously enough to be asked to stay for further consideration. She was overqualified for her work at the agency and had gone job hunting before, and now she was scheduled to do more work for the same salary. He wouldn't blame her for switching jobs.

Josh smiled suddenly and shook his head at his own concern. "I guess it's too early to bring in the police," he said.

Another line from the amateur manuscripts piling up at the agency. It was affecting them all.

"When the time comes," David said, "they'll round up the usual suspects."

Perceptive Josh knew what he was thinking. "Maybe I've been reading too many unsalable mystery novels and it's gotten to me," he said. "Still, it's after eleven o'clock, David. You'd think she'd have called by now. Or that she'd be home and answer her phone. I don't know why, but I've got an uneasy feeling about her. It really is possible something's happened to her and she needs help."

David imagined Lisa dressed in a business suit, sitting for an interview at one of the major publishing houses. "Anything's possible. Maybe she fell in love and eloped."

Josh looked at him curiously, then smiled wryly and shook his head. "I doubt if that's what happened, boss."

David had so many other problems that he couldn't work up much worry over Lisa not coming in for work. "If she doesn't turn up tomorrow," he said, "we'll call the morgue and all the hospitals." Another deliberate cliché.

"Bad joke," Josh said. "Anyway, tomorrow's Saturday. But if nobody makes contact with her and she isn't here Monday, I think we'd better bring in the police."

"That would be Morganson's decision."

"No," Josh said, "my decision." He went on his way, as serious as David had ever seen him.

David got to work and didn't think any more about Lisa except to wish her luck job hunting.

Lisa didn't report for work that day, nor did she phone in sick.

Her father, worried now, went back to her apartment to see if she'd returned there. He rang the doorbell, knocked, then used his key to enter.

The apartment was still and silent. There was a faint, peculiar odor in the air. He couldn't quite place it, but it disturbed him though he couldn't say why. He did know that for some reason it carried him back more than thirty years to the early days of the Vietnam War, when he'd been an Army infantryman. He might have guessed it to be the coppery scent of blood, but thirty years was a long time.

"Lisa!" he called.

"Lisa!" More worried. Afraid. Maybe with the same premonition as Josh's.

Before leaving the apartment, he walked around to make sure she wasn't there ill and unable to speak, perhaps unconscious. He looked in the kitchen, the bathroom, the bedroom.

Everywhere but under the bed.

Josh called Lisa's apartment three times that weekend, then Sterling Morganson called him with bad news of a lesser nature than Josh had feared. There was a glitch in the software program that had to be dealt with before Monday, when the agency's new system was going into effect. Everyone was instructed to come in to work Sunday afternoon to solve the problem.

Josh wondered if "everyone" would include Lisa.

45

After achieving the proper mix from the faucet so the spiraling stream of water was lukewarm, Molly poured bubble bath powder directly into the tumult of swirling crosscurrents at the bathtub's rubber drain plug.

She sat on the curved edge of the claw-footed tub and watched the water level rise, then disappear beneath the spreading, foamy layer of bubbles. It was nine o'clock Sunday evening. David had gone into Sterling Morganson to help program the computers for the new system they were to begin using the next day. He'd phoned at five to say he'd be late. Nine o'clock was late, all right. But Molly wasn't surprised. His behavior hadn't adhered to any sort of schedule or structure for weeks now.

She'd called him at work at seven to see if he'd left, and he'd answered the phone, complaining about the unreasonableness of the tyrannical Morganson in having his employees work so late on a Sunday. At least he hadn't lied to her; he was actually at Sterling Morganson. And she knew it was true that the agency was instituting changes to make the operation more cost-effective.

There was actually no reason for her to have thought David wasn't really in his office. Yet she'd suspected his phone wouldn't be picked up. In fact, she knew her phone call might have been an effort to confirm her suspicion that he'd lied to her. Dr. Mindle would no doubt have a medical term for that sort of behavior.

The bubbles were almost at the halfway point of the tub. Molly stood up and slipped out of her jeans and panties, her T-shirt and bra. She left them in a pile on the tile floor. Catching sight of herself unexpectedly in the medicine cabinet mirror, she noticed how she'd begun to carry herself, with her shoulders slightly hunched. Was twenty-seven too early to begin worrying about developing dowager's hump?

Leaning over the bathtub, she twisted both large white porcelain handles to the off position. Then she submerged a hand to make sure the water temperature was right. It was a bit too warm, but it would do.

After testing the temperature again with her big toe, she started to climb into the tub.

She stopped when she noticed that Muffin had entered the bathroom through the half-open door and was lying curled cozily on the clothes she'd just taken off.

No sense loading the washer with cat hair, she thought.

She withdrew her foot from the tub, shooed the reluctant Muffin from the clothes, and put them in the wicker hamper alongside the washbasin.

Finally she was able to settle into the old, deep bathtub. The warm water was well up on her breasts, the lush layer of bubbles almost to her chin. She began to perspire almost immediately, but she knew the water would soon cool enough to be comfortable.

Luxuriating in the warm bath, she rested the back of her head on the gentle curve of porcelain and let herself relax. She took the brown washcloth from where it was draped over the side of the tub, submerged it, then raised it and wrung it out so trickles of warm water played over her shoulders and upper arms. Muffin had returned and was curled on the hamper lid, watching her as if mildly amused and contemptuous of such bizarre human behavior.

This was as secure and sane as Molly had felt in days. For the moment, anyway, her life seemed under control. She knew where her husband was, and Michael had just gone to sleep in his bedroom.

In a way she was glad David was working so late. The strain of recent events was creating a barrier between them; at times they were uncomfortable in each other's presence. Silences had begun to weigh.

She raised the washcloth again, let water trickle over her, then closed her eyes and spread the wet cloth over her face, breathing through its soapy warmth.

A shrill clanging sound, like a school bell, shattered her peace and relaxation.

Muffin looked startled and leaped down from the hamper and fled.

Molly wadded the washcloth and hurled it into the layer of bubbles, then slapped the edge of the tub.

Damn! Another fire alarm!

"There is no fucking fire!" she told herself softly. "No smoke, no smell—only the alarm."

But she couldn't be sure. And she wasn't the only one in the apartment.

Sighing, she dutifully climbed out of the tub and dried off with a thick towel. Then she opened the hamper and dug out the clothes she'd just thrown into it.

By the time she was dressed, she could hear Michael crying beneath the din of the clanging alarm bell.

He became quiet immediately when she picked him up. He rested his head on her shoulder, maybe going back to sleep despite the clamor. This wasn't his first fire alarm; he'd attained a veteran's nonchalance.

Michael was getting heavy fast, but she decided against the stroller. If he became too burdensome, she could always put him down and he could walk.

In the corridor she saw a knot of neighbors waiting by the elevator. Elderly Mrs. Grace from down the hall. A middle-aged married couple, Irv and Rachel Teller, who lived in 2G. The young blond man Molly thought was an actor grinned at them as he walked past still buttoning his shirt. He swung open the door to the landing and Molly heard his rapid footfalls on the stairs.

Molly sniffed the air and glanced toward the ceiling. Still no scent or sight of smoke. It would have surprised her if there had been. These repeated false alarms were becoming wearisome. She remembered David speculating that the faulty wiring causing the alarms could itself start a fire. He'd been joking, perhaps, but maybe it was possible. She decided to write a letter to the management company and add her voice to the tenants' numerous complaints about the malfunctioning alarm system.

"Take the stairs," a thirtyish, heavyset woman, whose name Molly had never learned, said to her roommate, a tiny, thin blond woman about forty. "You know we're supposed to take the stairs and not the elevator in case of fire."

"There is no fire," Irv Teller told them in disgust. "It's the faulty wiring again. They keep promising to fix it but they don't. It's the second false alarm this month."

Both women stared at him as if he hadn't spoken, then followed the young actor down the stairs.

"So where's your husband, Molly?" Rachel Teller asked.

Molly shifted Michael's weight against her. "Working late tonight."

"Uh-hum," Rachel said.

"Too bad," Irv said sarcastically. "He'll miss all the excitement."

A few more tenants arrived simultaneous with the opening of the elevator doors. Obviously they wouldn't all fit in the elevator, so several of them made for the stairs. Molly, the Tellers, and three men and a woman Molly knew only to say hello to, rode the elevator down to the lobby.

When they went outside, Molly saw many of the other tenants standing in three or four tight groups across the street, staring glumly at the building. No one seemed to be seriously considering the possibility of a real fire.

Molly crossed the street and joined them, glad to put Michael down. Still sleepy, he stood leaning with his head pressed to her thigh.

The tenants were talking casually among themselves, about the weather, baseball, the sad quality of summer movie releases, about everything but the notion that the apartment building might be on fire. The night was warm, and Molly hadn't taken time to towel completely dry from her bath. Her clothes were sticking to her uncomfortably, and residue soap from the bubbles was starting to make her itch.

The alarm suddenly cut off, leaving the night in silence except for the usual neighborhood noises of traffic and occasional voices and laughter.

But nothing else changed. A police car cruised past, and one of the uniformed cops glanced with disinterest at the tenants, but the car didn't stop. The alarm wasn't the sort that summoned the fire department automatically, and apparently no one had phoned.

Even people in the surrounding buildings knew by now that most likely there wasn't a fire.

The tenants' attitude became one of irritation tempered by resignation. They were New Yorkers and conditioned to standing and waiting.

After a few minutes, one of the downstairs tenants who hadn't left the building appeared at the front door and yelled across the street to them that it was another false alarm and they could return to their apartments.

Several people groaned, as if disappointed that their homes and possessions weren't actually threatened by flames. They'd been fooled again. Slowly they crossed the street and began reentering the building.

Molly lifted Michael and joined them.

Michael went back to bed without an argument, and almost immediately he was on his way to falling asleep. *Something* was going right this evening.

Molly returned to the bathroom and lowered a hand into the bathtub to test the temperature of the water beneath the bubbles. It was still warm, and there were plenty of bubbles left.

She worked her damp body out of her clothes, dropped them back into the hamper, and lowered herself again into the tub. Trying to recapture her previous level of relaxation, she sank deeper and rested the back of her head against the cool porcelain. Enough bubbles had disappeared so that she could see patches of water now, but no washcloth. She fished around for it but didn't feel it.

Then she noticed its dark form floating just beneath the surface near her right thigh.

She reached for it, lifted it dripping from the water, and stared in horror.

It wasn't the washcloth.

It was the limp, dead body of Muffin.

Molly recovered from her shock enough to drop the dead cat and scramble screeching out of the tub. It was all one frantic motion and she felt the cat's claws scrape her stomach. She splashed water everywhere. Her bare feet slipped on the wet tile and she fell to the floor, bumping her knee on the toilet bowl.

Her leg throbbing with pain, she staggered from the bathroom, not looking back, her feet sliding and her toes curled to find traction by digging into the grouted spaces between the floor tiles. Bubbles had splashed up in her face and soap stung her right eye and blurred her vision.

By the time she'd reached the phone in the living room, she'd stopped screaming but her breath was rasping and her entire body was broken out in goose bumps and trembling. She'd never felt so horror-stricken and so vulnerable.

So naked.

Curled on the floor with the phone, it took her three fumbling tries before she punched out the number of the direct line to David's office.

46

They stood in the lobby of the Wharman Hotel near Columbus Circle. It was a small, mostly residential hotel, with wood paneling, a modest registration desk, and a single elevator with an old-fashioned brass arrow-and-numeral floor indicator above its door. Rates were reasonable because the Wharman hadn't the amenities of the larger hotels, no restaurants, bars, shops, or ballrooms.

The desk clerk was in his early twenties and sharply dressed in a blue suit, white shirt with red tie. He had neatly trimmed dark hair and a smooth complexion and looked more like a leader in the Young Republicans than a hotel employee. If there was a bellman, he was nowhere in sight.

Clutching Michael's hand, Molly stood off to the side near a chair and table and watched David check them in. At her feet on the waxed parquet floor were Michael's folded stroller, a suitcase, and a large duffle bag.

She found herself studying David's face. He was obviously under more strain than he usually allowed her to see. Like her, he was trying hard to hold everything together and keep his world from disintegrating.

The young desk clerk turned away from him to swipe his Visa card, and David quickly wiped a hand over his face, massaging his Adam's apple between thumb and forefinger as if his throat was constricted. His expression became placid and he glanced toward her and smiled to let her know he was thinking of her; he was hiding behind his facade again.

When he'd gotten the room key, he came over to her and lifted the duffle bag and suitcase. Without a word, she picked up the stroller and they went with Michael to the elevator.

David set down the suitcase and pressed the button with the Up arrow. After a pause, the brass arrow on the floor indicator trembled as if stuck on 12, then began moving spasmodically toward lower numbers.

"Did we remember to pack my electric razor?" David asked.

She knew he was trying to restore normalcy, to get her mind off what had happened to Muffin. The horror in the bathtub. Who had done it and why.

"I'm not sure," Molly said, not looking at him.

The arrow stopped at 4, then within a few seconds began lurching downward again.

"No matter. It isn't far. I can go back and get it, along with anything else we forgot."

"No!" she said vehemently. "You will *not* go back inside that apartment tonight. None of us will!"

The elevator arrived and they waited for a man cradling a bouquet of roses to make his exit, then they stepped in and David set the luggage at his feet and pressed the button for the fifth floor.

"Okay, Mol," he said reassuringly when the elevator door had closed. "Don't worry about it. I'll go into work late again tomorrow. We can go to the apartment together in the morning after dropping Michael off at Small Business."

"Julia," Michael said, at the mention of Small Business.

"All right," Molly said. "We'll do what has to be done there, then we'll get out. We don't live there anymore."

He leaned close and kissed her cheek. "Another thing we can do tomorrow is sign the lease for the new apartment."

The elevator door slid open, David stooped and picked up the suitcase and duffle bag, and they walked down a wide, gray-carpeted hall illuminated by indirect lighting set in carved wooden sconces on the pale green walls.

They stopped before the door to room 512.

David unlocked then swung the door open. He reached inside and flicked a wall switch.

After standing aside to let Molly and Michael enter, he followed with the luggage.

The room was small but high-ceilinged, well appointed with a dresser, desk, and a TV with a VCR on it on a wooden stand near the foot of the bed. Molly noticed right away there was no scent of tobacco smoke; David must have anticipated her wishes and asked for a nonsmokers' room. There was a large closet with sliding doors, one of which was a full-length mirror. What she could see of the bathroom was all gray tile and modern, with gleaming chromed plumbing and frosted-glass shower doors. Nothing like the apartment's old bathroom where Muffin—

She veered her mind away from vivid and disturbing images, concentrating instead on the room. It was cool and quiet, with light beige walls that were almost white. Here and there hung restful framed prints. Two of the prints were very stylized fox-hunting scenes, erect, red-coated riders on horses leaping over hedges to race over a green expanse of field bordered by trees. It was a bright, sunny day in the prints and everyone other than the fox was having a fine time. The room's carpeting was a dark green that matched the green in the fox-hunting scenes as well as the long green drapes and green, padded headboard. There was a small rollaway bed in a corner for Michael. The wall switch had turned on a tall brass floor lamp with a cream-colored shade that cast a soft light over everything.

"Just another hotel room," David said, hoisting the suitcase onto the bed to unpack, "but it looks comfortable."

To Molly it looked like much more than that.

It looked like sanctuary.

47

Molly knew Deirdre had probably left for work, but she still felt a sense of foreboding, a tingle of fear, as she crossed West Eighty-fifth Street with David to enter their apartment.

They'd overslept that morning. David had left the Wharman while Molly was getting herself and Michael dressed, and returned with some orange juice and a cinnamon roll from a nearby bakery for Michael's breakfast. After delivering Michael to Small Business in a cab, Molly and David had a leisurely breakfast on Amsterdam. The truth was, after what had happened to Muffin, and all that had gone on before, neither of them was anxious to return to the apartment.

But here they were, Molly nervously glancing up at their windows as they crossed the street, David staring straight ahead and setting a slow pace.

The building seemed to engulf her as they entered the foyer, but she said nothing as they walked to the elevator.

In the second-floor corridor, her heart was racing as David fit his key in the door to their apartment. Even the harsh grating of the key in the lock was now an unfamiliar sound. Full of their possessions though it might be, this place was no longer home.

David opened the door and entered first.

Molly saw him stop and stand still. She heard him mutter, "Good Christ!"

She went in and stood beside him. What she saw seemed to strike her in the stomach. It took her breath away and made her physically ill.

Then angry. Boiling angry.

The apartment had been viciously vandalized. Molly's desk drawers had been removed and the contents dumped on the floor. The desk itself was upside down. One end of the sofa, the end where Molly usually sat, had been slashed and the batting yanked from it to protrude in obscene bulges of cotton and horsehair from the gaping material.

David walked around slowly, staring in disbelief. "God! Look at this!" He used the toe of his shoe to nudge one of the desk drawers that had been hurled to the floor and lay upside down and broken. "What kind of sick, vicious animal would do something like this?"

"I'm not surprised," Molly said, barely containing her fury. "It was Deirdre."

David stopped and stared at her. "I don't know—"

"Don't, David! Goddamn you, don't tell me this wasn't Deirdre!"

She was glad he chose not to answer as they walked through the rest of the apartment.

"Notice?" Molly asked.

David nodded. "It's only *your* things."

It became increasingly clear that only objects connected with Molly had been vandalized. Her pillow was slashed. Her clothes had been pulled from the closet and ripped. Brush and comb and cosmetic bottles had been thrown to the floor. The T-shirt she usually slept in was draped from a drawer pull in tatters. Bright red lipstick was smeared wildly on her dresser mirror, as indecipherable as if it were scrawled in a foreign language.

Molly went to examine something glittering on the floor.

Shattered glass. A framed wedding photograph of her and David, which had been wrapped in paper on the back of a closet shelf, was broken from its frame and lay in the middle of the glinting fragments of glass. The image of a younger David, grinning in his tuxedo, was untouched. The smiling woman on his arm, Molly, had been shredded with a sharp blade.

Molly looked at him. "Who's crazy now, David?"

"Mol, I never said—"

"Never mind," she interrupted. "We both know what you thought."

In a way she was glad Deirdre had done this. Deirdre's duplicity, the danger that she posed, were out in the open now; no one could say they were merely in Molly's mind. What had been done to the apartment was an explosion of malice and violence that proved Molly was the sane one. Deirdre was mad.

"I'm sorry, Mol . . ." David was saying remorsefully.

Molly ignored him as they returned to the ravaged living room.

"I'm going to call the police," he said, and walked to the overturned desk. Near it on the floor lay the phone-equipped answering machine. He replaced the receiver, then gripped the machine and stood up. He paused.

Molly could see the glowing green digital numeral on the machine.

"There's a message," David said.

He propped the machine against his hip and pressed the Play button.

Beep.

Molly immediately recognized Deirdre's voice:

"Hi, David and Molly." She sounded jarringly normal and cheerful in the middle of such chaos. "This is you-know-who. I hope you like the way I redecorated your apartment. I guess you'll be busy for a while admiring it, making little personal changes. That's okay. Idle hands are the devil's playthings. And don't be concerned about Michael. I've already picked him up at Small Business, so you two can enjoy the rest of the day without worry."

Molly and David stood motionless for a few moments.

Then the full impact of what Deirdre had said hit Molly in a violent rush.

She was across the room in three strides and grabbed the phone from David.

"It's a bluff, Mol," he said. "We dropped Michael off at Small Business not much more than an hour ago."

But Molly was already punching out Small Business's number on the key pad. "Damn her! I'll kill her if she's taken Michael!"

David gently but firmly worked the receiver from her clutching fingers. She glared at him.

"You're in a rage, Mol. Let me talk. Let me see what Julia has to say."

She knew he was right. If Julia had let Michael leave the school, she didn't know what she might say or do.

She surrendered the phone to him then backed a step away and watched him hold the receiver to his ear and listen to the ringing phone at the other end of the connection.

Molly waited, fighting back her temper and fear for Michael. She could faintly hear the Small Business phone ringing, seeping from the receiver's earpiece.

"Yes, please," David said abruptly, tightening his grip on the phone. "I'd like to talk to Julia . . ." He stared inquisitively at Molly.

"Corera," she said, assuming he couldn't remember Julia's last name.

"Corera, please. I need to talk to her. Yes, I know, but it's very important."

He stood waiting, not looking at Molly, for more than a minute.

Then he grew rigid and stood straighter as the receiver returned to life.

"Julia. This is David Jones. That's right, Michael's father. Remember, his mother and I dropped him off at the school a little over an hour ago? We need to know if he's still there."

Molly saw his expression darken and her heart almost stopped.

After several seconds, he said, "I don't know. No, there is none. We don't know. Yes, thanks, Julia . . ."

He slammed down the receiver.

"What did she say?" Molly asked.

"Julia said Aunt Deirdre came to the school half an hour ago with a note from you saying there was a family emergency. She said they knew Deirdre at the school. She'd been there several times before to see Michael. Trusted her because Michael knew her and seemed fond of her."

"So they gave him to her," Molly said with a quiet rage. "She's got him! David, she's got our son!"

He was obviously alarmed by her expression, by the emotion vibrant in her voice.

"Mol, listen!"

It made her even madder that he would try to calm her. "You listen, David! I'm going to kill her! You hear me? I'm going to fucking *kill* her!"

"Jesus, Mol! Wait!"

But she was already out the door and in the hall. Fueled by a hate and desire she knew would scare her if she paused to think about it.

No time or patience for the elevator. She was aware of David following her as she strode down the hall to the door to the landing, then tromped up the stairs and down the fourth-floor corridor to Deirdre's apartment.

She began pounding on the door with her fist.

"Deirdre! Damn you! Open this door!"

She felt David grip her upper arms. He pulled her back so she couldn't reach the door.

At first she was enraged, thinking he was trying to restrain her to calm her. Then she saw his flushed features, the tightness to his jaw, the look in his eyes she'd seen only a few times during the early, sometimes vicious and hurtful arguments of their marriage. She knew he'd had time to assimilate what had happened and shared her concern and anger.

When he was sure she wasn't going to interfere, he took a step back and raised his right leg. Then he shot his foot out so the flat of it struck the door just below the knob.

The door gave but didn't open.

Molly felt like standing next to him so they could kick together. She actually moved toward him.

But he kicked again, with a loud grunt and much more force, and the doorjamb splintered around the lock.

The door flew open and bounced off the wall so hard it would have closed again if David's momentum hadn't carried him forward so that he struck it a second time with his shoulder. It hit the wall again, but not as hard. Brass screws and metal pieces of the lock clattered over the wood floor.

Molly and David exchanged frightened but determined glances.

She followed him into Deirdre's apartment.

48

The apartment was still disorganized from Deirdre's move, as if it had occurred only a few days ago. Molly took the lead despite David urging her to stay behind him, and they stormed through the apartment, satisfying themselves that it was unoccupied. They found themselves again in the living room.

For the first time, Molly looked around carefully at the mismatched and apparently secondhand furniture, the stacks of cardboard boxes against a wall.

Then the desk near the window caught her eye, and it took her a moment to realize why.

It closely resembled her own desk. There were the half-dozen reference books supported between quartz bookends, the green-shaded banker's lamp, the mug stuffed with pens and pencils.

Molly stepped closer to the desk and saw that the mug was exactly like hers, dark blue with a silver Statue of Liberty on it. Only the slight chip on the rim that marred her mug was missing on this one.

She began opening drawers.

"What are you doing, Mol?" she heard David ask behind her.

"Looking for some clue as to where Deirdre might have taken Michael."

The top drawer held only a stapler, a bottle of Liquid Paper, and a few household bills and receipts. Stuffed toward the back were some maps. A road map of Missouri. A street map of New York. A subway guide.

The second drawer contained only a shoe box.

Molly lifted the box out with both hands, noting that it was slightly too heavy to be empty. She set it on the desk and opened it.

Inside were a jumble of newspaper clippings weighted down by a videocassette. She set the cassette aside, then began lifting out the clippings and placing them on the desk.

She looked at them where they lay overlapping each other:

WOMAN PLUNGES TO DEA/POLICE ARE LO/TWENTY-STORY FALL FROM ROOFTOP RESTAURAN/RISTINE MATHEWS.

There was also a newspaper photo of what appeared to be a body lying beneath a bloody sheet.

"Look at this, David," Molly said.

But he was already standing behind her. He reached past her and rearranged the clippings.

They revealed the name of the woman who'd apparently plunged from the rooftop restaurant: Christine Mathews. It was her body beneath the bloody sheet.

"What do you think it means?" David asked.

"I'm not sure," Molly said. A fear like ice was moving beneath her flesh. "But I don't like it. I'm going to call the police."

As she turned her back to reach for the phone, she didn't see David pick up the videocassette and slide it beneath his shirt.

He quietly drifted into the hall leading to the bedrooms and bathroom. When he was far enough from the living room but could still hear Molly's muted, indecipherable voice as she talked on the phone, David withdrew the cassette from under his shirt. He put on his glasses and held it up to the light.

The label was neatly printed in capital letters with blue ink: 2ND HNYMN.

He looked around desperately. He couldn't let Molly find the cassette. And it couldn't be in the apartment if the police decided to conduct a search.

For now, he was stuck with it.

He slipped it back beneath his shirt, feeling its sharply defined angles press against his bare side beneath his ribs. Then he returned to the living room.

Molly was hanging up the phone after her conversation with the police.

———

She saw him in the corner of her vision and spoke to him. "They said—"

She and David both heard a slight noise and turned toward the door.

It was wide open, and Craig Chumley was standing in the doorway. His gray suit was wrinkled, his tie was loosely knotted, and there were perspiration stains on his pale blue shirt. He entered the apartment as if lost in a dream, glancing at the damaged door.

"What's going on here?" he asked. He was obviously confused and afraid.

"What are you doing here?" David asked before Molly could speak.

"I don't see where it's any—"

"Where are they?" Molly interrupted. Her rage erupted and she flung herself at Chumley, clutching his shirt with both hands. "Tell me!"

She lost her reason entirely, her place in time, as she tried to shake Chumley, to throw him to the floor, to kill him with the raw anger that devoured her senses.

Stunned, Chumley spun in a wild dance, giving in to Molly's efforts rather than fight her.

Finally she felt David's hands on her shoulders, pulling her away. Chumley gripped her wrists, not as hard as he might have, and gradually forced her arms back so she lost her grip on his shirt. The expression on his face was strangely kind as well as stricken.

She was in control of herself again, but breathing as if she'd run for miles.

"Calm down, Mol," David was saying. He was up against her back now, his body turned sideways, one arm lowered to encircle her waist. He took a few unsteady backward steps, dragging Molly with him.

David hugged her hard. "Easy, easy . . ." She could feel his breath in her ear.

She willed her body to relax. His grip on her midsection seemed to loosen. Or was it simply that she'd stopped struggling?

"Gonna be okay?" David asked.

"Yeah. If you can call it that." She was breathing easier. Her throat was raw. Her display of violence had achieved nothing; everything was the same, even the weight of her fear in her stomach.

"Deirdre's taken Michael," David said to the florid and flustered Chumley.

"Your son?" Chumley put his hand to his forehead as if he'd just been assailed by a terrific headache. "Oh, Lord!"

"What's your story, Chumley?" David asked. "The police are on their way here, and you'll be telling them soon enough."

Chumley moved his fingertips around to his right temple and bowed his head. His brow creased. Molly saw that his scalp was mottled beneath his thinning hair.

"I'm married," he said. "Have been for sixteen years. Deirdre made me forget that. Then, while she didn't actually threaten me, during the last few days she made it clear . . . if I didn't keep her on as an employee as well as a lover, my wife, Shirley, might find out about us." He glanced up for only a second. "Lately, we haven't been getting along."

"You and your wife?" Molly asked.

"Me and everybody," Chumley said despondently. "Friday evening, after Deirdre had gone home, a man named Stan Grocci showed up at my office. He was abusive, desperate. And he was searching for Deirdre."

"That's her former husband," David said.

"He said he was still her husband. He also said she was diagnosed as psychotic and dangerous after attacking and injuring a sales clerk with one of those spikes used to spear receipts. Later, she escaped from a psychiatric hospital in Missouri." He looked at Molly, then down at the floor again. "He also said there was an arrest warrant out for her in Saint Louis for the murder of a woman named Christine Mathews he became involved with while Deirdre was in the mental institution."

Molly's insides turned cold. "Jesus, David! The woman in the clipping! Deirdre must have pushed her from the roof!"

David was looking hard at Chumley. "You talked to Grocci Friday, you said. Have you seen Deirdre since then?"

"All weekend I thought about what Grocci had told me, wondering what I should do. This morning, when Deirdre came in to work, I confronted her with what he'd said."

"How did she react?"

"She denied it all and told me Grocci was the mental case and his accusations were preposterous. At that point I didn't really care. I knew I was in something I couldn't handle, so I fired her."

"And she went without a fight?" David asked incredulously.

Chumley smiled sadly. "Yeah. That should have alerted me to trouble. But I'd been thinking with my dick for so long . . ." He glanced apologetically at Molly. "Sorry."

"Think with your head now," she snapped.

"I noticed a while back that my files had been disturbed," Chumley said. "I think she made copies of some papers and took them with her, maybe even had them before I fired her. If she gives them to the wrong people . . . Well, I've been playing a little loose with my taxes. I came here to get the copies back, and to offer Deirdre money so she wouldn't go to the IRS or to my wife."

Molly didn't care about Chumley's troubles with his wife or the IRS. She didn't want to hear about them. She only cared about her son.

"Do you have any idea where she might have taken Michael?" she asked.

"No. I really know next to nothing about Deirdre."

There were noises in the hall. Voices. Footsteps.

Then, in the corridor outside the open door, a startling amount of dark blue. Cautious, emotionless eyes.

The police entered the apartment.

49

The uniformed officers listened patiently to Molly and David, then one of them made a phone call while the other gave Deirdre's apartment a cursory examination.

Soon afterward a pair of NYPD plainclothes detectives arrived. The shorter, heavier of the two, a graying man named Salter, with the face of an amiable but combative bulldog, was in charge. His partner, a much younger man named Marrivale, took notes while they listened to Molly and David.

At first Chumley refused to talk before consulting with his attorney, then at Molly's urging he changed his mind. With an air of doom and resignation, he told the detectives what he'd told Molly and David.

Neither cop showed any reaction to his story.

"Has anybody got a photograph of this Deirdre?" Salter asked. He had a rough, heavy smoker's voice. Three cellophane-clad cigars jutted from the breast pocket of his gray suit coat.

"Not even an old one," David said, glancing at Molly.

Salter looked at Chumley, who shook his head no. "Like I said, she's really not much more than a stranger to me—in a way."

The young detective, who had the wan, wasted look of an esthete, stared at Chumley until Chumley looked away.

"What about a photo of the boy?" Salter asked.

"I have several," Molly said. "They're downstairs in our apartment, if they haven't been destroyed."

"Let's go," Salter said. "It's time we looked at the destruction down there."

He accompanied them downstairs while Marrivale stayed behind and continued questioning Chumley.

In the elevator, Salter said nothing. Molly saw him glancing out of the corner of his eye at David, as if he were suspicious of him. She'd read that the police always suspected the parents first in the disappearance of a child. But this was different. They *knew* who'd taken Michael. A psychopath who'd left a taunting message on the parents' answering machine.

When they entered the apartment, Salter cautioned them not to touch anything. "The place will be dusted for prints," he said. "We want to know who's been here recently and handled whatever was vandalized."

Molly knew that made sense, but she felt somehow violated again, being unable even to touch her possessions in her own apartment. She and David stood near the center of the room with their arms at their sides, looking like awkward trespassers in their home.

Then Molly remembered that the apartment would never be home again—at least not the home it had been. She'd never be able to see it, to live in it, the same way. However the nightmare with Michael would be resolved, Deirdre had changed their lives forever.

Salter clasped his meaty hands together and looked around with his neutral, assessing eyes at the littered floor, the slashed sofa with its batting bulging from its wounds. "Somebody doesn't like you, all right."

"Deirdre," Molly said.

Sidestepping the contents of the desk drawers that lay on the floor, Salter walked over to the answering machine lying beside the overturned desk. He stooped and pressed the message button. Molly felt the boiling pressure of rage building in her again as they listened to Deirdre's message.

"You sure it's her?" Salter asked when the message was finished. He pressed his hand to the small of his back as he stood up. "The caller only identifies herself as 'you know who.' "

"Who else would it be?" Molly blurted.

"It's Deirdre," David said. "I recognize her voice. And Julia at Small Business Preschool said Deirdre was the one who picked up Michael."

"*Aunt* Deirdre!" Molly said.

Salter looked at her. "Deirdre was acquainted enough with the boy that he thought of her as an aunt?"

"Apparently," David said.

"Then the three of you were friends."

"No," Molly said. "She's my husband's ex-wife, for God's sake! We were civil, at first. Then it was just as I told you. She began tormenting me, sneaking in here, and she tried to kill me."

Salter looked at her the way he'd been looking at David in the elevator.

"Damn it!" Molly exploded. "A maniac has our son and you stand there looking at us as if we were the criminals. Do something! Do your fucking job!"

She felt spittle on her chin and realized *she* must look like the maniac, ranting and foaming at the mouth. David tried to pull her to him and hold her, but she pushed away from him, walked a few feet, and stood alone. She felt as isolated and ineffective as if she were frozen in ice with only her agonizing thoughts. When she gazed fearfully into herself, she saw only a deep darkness that pulled like a vacuum at her being. A devouring black hole in the space of her existence. What had happened to her life? It was all so horrible and hopeless.

The detective's lips were moving soundlessly. He was talking to her. She focused her mind and brought herself back to outer awareness.

"The photograph," Salter reminded her flatly. "You said you had a photograph of your son."

Later, in the hall outside Deirdre's apartment, Salter and Marrivale walked together to stand near the elevator, where they wouldn't be overheard.

"I checked," Marrivale said. "There's a murder warrant out for Deirdre Grocci, maybe goes under the last name Chandler, maybe Jones. She escaped from a psychiatric clinic in Missouri, and she's suspected of killing a woman named Christine Mathews in Saint Louis."

"A nutcase killer," Salter said. "And now they tell us she's snatched a kid."

"You don't think she did?" Marrivale asked, obviously surprised.

"Oh, yeah, I think she's got him," Salter said. "And I think maybe there's a lot more to it than we know."

"She sounds plenty dangerous," Marrivale said. His pale face tightened. "Jesus! That poor kid . . ."

"Yeah." Salter dug the photograph of Michael that Molly had given him out of his pocket and held it out for Marrivale to see.

"Poor kid," Marrivale repeated, staring at the photo with his head bowed. "He looks something like my sister's boy. About the same age." For a moment his expression hardened with fury.

"Some shitty world," Salter said, sliding the photo back into his pocket.

"Anything can happen anytime to anybody," Marrivale said. "And when it does, it usually isn't good."

"This time," Salter told him, "we've gotta see that it doesn't happen to this kid."

"It's too often the innocents who get hurt," Marrivale said. "They're like prey animals for the carnivores of the world. We have to protect them."

Salter looked at him, wondering for a moment if Marrivale might be too philosophical to be a cop.

50

Molly sat in a chair in the room at the Wharman Hotel that night and stared out the window, though her attention never reached beyond the reflecting pane that held her indistinct image, a woman mostly faded away, never changing expression and idly twining a strand of hair around her forefinger. She wished she could exist in that flat, opaque world that had no dimension or agony, that would disappear with the dawn.

After the police had taken her statement, then David's, they talked to Chumley again. And they listened again to Deirdre's message on the answering machine, then confiscated the cassette and slid it into a yellow evidence envelope. Another detective, who seemed to outrank Salter and Marrivale, arrived and was given the photograph of Michael that Molly had taken that summer in Riverside Park. He stared intently at it, then handed it back to Salter, who left to talk to Julia at Small Business.

Then they'd instructed Molly and David. At least one of them was to remain in their room at the Wharman. The police would be watching the apartment building. A policeman would be stationed inside their apartment, in case Deirdre returned there. He would also be monitoring and recording all phone conversations; any calls would be patched through, without the caller's knowledge, to the room in the Wharman. Molly and David were told to agree to any demands and terms for ransom money, and to ask to talk to Michael.

So after packing two more suitcases, they'd returned to the hotel room, which seemed to become smaller and more confining with every hour.

There was a ghost in the flat, reflecting window, pacing behind Molly. David, four paces one way, four the other, back to his starting point. She saw his reflection stand still and slam a fist into its palm, heard the impact of flesh on flesh behind her.

David resumed pacing.

"She'll know the police are watching the apartment building," Molly said in a flat, exhausted monotone. "She won't go back there. She's too smart. She was smarter all along than any of us thought. Scheming and smart and evil."

"The cops will find her," David said with more assurance than he could possibly feel. "They'll find Michael. If she calls the apartment, the cop there will listen in. They're ready for a phone call. They might be able to trace it."

"She won't phone," Molly said.

"She might demand ransom."

Molly laughed sadly, a broken expression of hopelessness. "Ransom! You still don't understand. It isn't ransom that she wants."

"What, then?" David asked.

"Didn't you read those newspaper clippings, David? Didn't you listen to Chumley? She's insane. She's dangerous. She's homicidal. And she has our son!"

David stopped pacing and stood in the center of the room. He appeared to try returning the gaze of her reflection in the dark windowpane, but there wasn't enough substance there and he turned away.

"Even insane people have their own kind of unique logic," he said. "It's only a matter of figuring out how she thinks."

"She thinks like an animal. A cunning, predatory animal that concentrates all of itself on getting what it wants."

"And you think she wants Michael?"

"He's only part of it," Molly said. "She wants you, David. She wants to become me. In some psychotic way, she wants to live my life."

He said nothing. Instead he walked over and stood behind her, then began massaging her shoulders. When she didn't respond, he bent over and kissed her cheek. She still didn't respond, watching the scene in the windowpane as if it were theater and didn't involve her.

He stopped massaging, lowered his arms to his sides, and sighed. "You're trembling, Mol. It's been a long time since we've eaten. You need something to keep your strength up."

She shook her head no. Dread filled her; she wasn't remotely hungry.

"You should at least have something to drink," he insisted. "I'm going to get some ice and try to find a soda machine. What do you want me to bring you?"

"Nothing."

"You've got to have something, Mol. Soda. A bag of pretzels or potato chips from a machine. Anything."

When she didn't answer, he went to the dresser, picked up the plastic ice bucket, and walked to the door.

She saw his reflection turn to face her.

"The door will lock behind me, Mol. I'll let myself back in with my key. I won't knock. If anyone knocks, don't go to the door. Promise me."

She remained silent. She simply had nothing to say to him, though she knew he was frustrated, near losing his temper.

"Dammit, Mol! This isn't helping Michael. Isn't helping you. Or me. We need you. Haven't you figured that out? We need you!"

She found herself standing up despite her great weariness. She looked at him, smiled feebly, and nodded.

He smiled back, looking immensely relieved. "Better, Mol. Much better."

Still carrying the ice bucket, he came to her and held her close. She rested her cheek against his shoulder and he kissed her forehead. His lips felt cool and dry as death.

"Gonna be okay here alone?" he asked.

She nodded, near tears. He was right. He did need her. Michael needed her. "Sure," she said. "Don't worry. Go ahead."

She watched him walk to the door, look back at her, then leave. He pulled the door tightly closed behind him so that the lock clicking metallically into place was loud and definite.

Molly stood still for a moment, then went to the dresser and studied her image in the mirror.

She shook her head in dismay. Her complexion was chalky, as if she'd suffered a long illness. There were dark circles beneath her eyes. Her hair was in wild disarray.

She attempted to rearrange her hair with her fingers, but it was futile. It simply sprang back up where she tried to smooth it down, and lay lank and lifeless where she tried to fluff it up. She opened the top dresser drawer, got out her cosmetic kit, and felt around inside it for a comb.

There was none. She and David had packed too hurriedly to remember everything they'd need. She wished now she'd asked him to go down to the lobby and see if he could borrow a comb from the desk. They probably kept a supply of courtesy toiletries for forgetful guests. If they had none, he might have gone to the drugstore down the street to buy a comb.

She glanced over at their empty suitcases stacked on a folding stand. It was possible that there was a comb in one of them from a previous trip. When they traveled, they were always buying things they'd forgotten, sometimes tucking them away in pockets or zippered compartments for the return trip then not remembering to unpack them.

She went to the stack of softsided luggage and checked inside the top suitcase. Found nothing.

Then she unzipped an outer compartment on the stiff fabric side of the second suitcase and reached inside.

Her groping fingers felt plastic, but it wasn't a comb.

51

David managed to wrestle two Pepsi-Cola cans and a bag of pretzels from the vending machines on the floor below. The ice machine was in an alcove across the hall. It gurgled and clunked as he approached, as if it had been waiting and was producing ice just for him.

After scooping ice into the plastic bucket, he managed to juggle everything so he could carry it, then walked toward the elevator.

He wasn't really worried about Deirdre learning where they were and showing up there. There was no way she could find out which hotel they'd chosen. Only the police knew.

He broke stride for a moment. And Julia? Did Julia know?

Well, it probably wouldn't matter. Still, he'd have to ask Molly if she'd talked to Julia, told her their location. Molly was right: Deirdre had the cunning and intensity of a carnivore on the hunt. If she decided to try locating them, she'd do anything.

He only hoped she wouldn't hurt Michael. That was something David told himself over and over wouldn't happen. God knew, he was aware of her kinkiness. She could enjoy inflicting pain. But he hadn't seen that kind of sadism in her, the inclination to harm a child.

He rode the elevator up a floor and got out. Balancing soda cans and pretzel bag in one hand, the ice bucket in the other, he made his way down the hall to the room.

Clutching the bucket under his arm and using his key, he entered, pushing open the door with his hip, his back to the room. He used his foot to close the door, turning around as he did so.

He dropped the ice bucket, unaware of it bouncing off his toe, or of the small, cylindrical chunks of ice scattering over the carpet. The shock of what he saw hit him with a palpable force that winded him.

Molly was sitting in the chair by the window again, hunched over and hugging her stomach. But now she was watching television.

The VCR's red light was glowing. Moans were coming from the TV. On the screen, David was on top of Deirdre. Her legs were locked around his waist, her fingers clutching his back like talons sunk into prey. She turned to face the camera and smiled wildly, the corruption of her madness gleaming in her eyes.

Dropping everything else he was carrying, David ran across the room and fumbled with the unfamiliar VCR controls.

Finally he found the power switch and the screen went blank. Then he ejected the cassette. He stooped and picked up a soda can, laid the cassette on top of the TV, and bashed it again and again with the can.

All his effort had little effect other than to crack the black plastic casing.

He tossed the can aside, then picked up the cassette and brought it down repeatedly and with all his strength on the edge of the dresser. The case separated, then shattered. David grabbed the tape and unreeled it, yanking it out until it draped in twisted ribbons to the floor. He bunched it all together between his hands, along with what was left of the cassette, and hurled everything into a nearby wastebasket.

He stood trembling, out of breath. What he'd feared for so long had finally happened. His world was as irreparably smashed as the videocassette. Gone from him and out of reach. Destiny. The harsh sounds of his struggle for air filled the room.

Then, standing there and staring at the broken cassette and the tangle of tape overflowing the wastebasket, his face flushed with abrupt realization.

He turned to confront Molly.

"Mol, I know where she is! I know where she's taken him!"

She was standing now, still hunched over, glaring up at him through her tears. She might collapse. She might fly into a rage.

She might become physically ill. He knew she was balanced on a fine edge.

She said nothing.

He stared at her in dismay. "Listen, Mol, please!"

"You *bastard!* Liar! Liar! Liar!"

She suddenly hurled herself at him, slamming him with her fists, kicking him, scratching at his eyes. One of the blows caught him on the forehead, momentarily dazing him. He reached out and pulled her in close, smothering her charge and hugging her tight, restricting her movements.

"I'm sorry, Mol! Jesus, I'm sorry! But I think I know where he is! I know where she's taken Michael!"

Her arms went limp. She stopped struggling and stepped back, looking at him as if he were a stranger who didn't interest her. The outburst and attack had left her mind and body exhausted. Her eyes seemed to stare at him from inside a final sanctuary where pain could no longer penetrate. He knew he'd done this to her, reduced her to this. He had to make it up to her and he could!

"Come on!" he implored. "I'll show you! Please, Mol, come with me!"

She continued to stare vacantly at him, emotionally and physically spent.

He gripped her arm just above the elbow and moved toward the door. She didn't resist, but he almost had to drag her as she accompanied him zombielike downstairs to the lobby, then out into the street.

He saw a taxi pass at the corner with its rooflight on and raised an arm, but it drove by without the driver seeing him.

Then a cab turned at the opposite corner and came toward them, rooflight glowing. Still with a grip on Molly's arm, supporting her, David waved his free arm wildly and saw the taxi swerve and coast toward them.

Salter saw the Joneses get into the cab. The husband seemed to be in a frenzy, the wife as calm as if she were drugged.

He started his unmarked car and steered it into the flow of traffic, staying well back of the cab but keeping it in sight. He was good at tailing cars; that's why Benning had assigned him to watch the hotel. The parents were always suspects when a child disappeared, so what had just happened wasn't a complete surprise.

It was, in fact, the kind of move Salter had been expecting. He was a twenty-five-year veteran and had developed the kind of radar for deception that only a gray and grizzled longtime cop possessed. He was fifty-seven and damn near too fat for the job, but his brain was better than when he was thirty-seven. It had struck him from the beginning that Mom and Dad were hiding something—especially Dad. The Joneses' instructions had been for at least one of them to stay in their hotel room at all times so they could field a ransom call if it came in and was patched through to them. Now here they were hightailing it away from the hotel together, Salter suspected to meet their partner or partners in the phony kidnapping.

He skillfully maneuvered the unmarked through traffic, then at a red light used the cellular to get in touch with Benning. It was always a possibility that the players on the other side were monitoring the regular police radio bands.

As the light went green and traffic pulled away, Benning came on the line.

Salter explained what had just occurred.

"Stay with them," Benning said. "There's been another development. A woman from where the father works was found dead in her apartment. Deep penetration puncture wounds made by a large instrument."

"God help the kid," Salter said.

"There might not be a connection," Benning cautioned him.

"Yes, sir," Salter said, knowing better. People in less extreme circumstances than the Joneses had murdered their own children. Or maybe whoever they were in this with—

"When they reach their destination, let me know," Benning told him, interrupting his thoughts. "If this is a phony snatch, we want them all in a neat bundle and we try to keep the kid from getting hurt."

"If he's alive," Salter said, tapping the brake, then cutting off another cab to round a corner and keep the Joneses' cab in sight. The cabbie behind him leaned on the horn. Salter wished he'd lay off; he didn't want to attract attention.

"Keep the line open," Benning told him. "I want to know what's going on, understand?"

"Yes, sir."

Salter said again, "God help the kid."

But softer this time, so Benning wouldn't hear.

52

They sat in the back of the cab, not touching each other, the varicolored light from outside playing over their faces in patterns of brightness and shadow created by motion. Something in the trunk rattled each time they hit a bump. There was a strong, spearmint scent in the cab, as if the previous passenger had been chewing gum.

On the other side of the cab's windows, heavy traffic, bright lights, flashed past rapidly in the night. David's face was tight with strain. Molly's was an emotional blank; she'd had more than she could bear and her system had shut down.

Tires screeched and a horn blared. The cab rocked as it veered, but it didn't slow. Momentary fear passed like a shadow over Molly's face.

Traffic at the next intersection was lodged in gridlock. The taxi reduced speed, then threaded its way through the maze of barely moving cars and miraculously found the clearance to accelerate with a roar as it jounced in a back-breaking race over the potholed pavement.

Salter pushed with all his might on the horn buttons, but the horn was silent.

"Piece of crap!" he said loudly. "Fucking city budget!" Too many of the unmarkeds were junk.

He cranked down the window. "Police! Out of the way!"

The well-dressed guy driving the Mercedes that had cut him off merely stared at him.

"Police!" Salter screamed again, and made a motion as if to flash his badge.

Now the guy in the Mercedes nodded and rolled down his own window. "I thought you said 'Please,' " he explained, before slowly driving into a narrow space between a truck and the curb and allowing Salter to pass.

Salter hit the accelerator and peered through the windshield at the street ahead, but he couldn't see the cab. The driver must be Mario Andretti or some such whiz.

"Shit!" Salter said, slapping the dashboard hard enough so that something broke loose inside it and tinkled down to make a sound like a coin revolving lopsided on a hard surface. The FBI was slated to enter this case in the morning. They'd love to hear about how the missing kid's parents got in a cab and disappeared.

He noticed there was noise coming from the cellular and picked it up.

"What the hell's happening?" Benning asked.

"They're gone. Jumped ahead of me in heavy traffic and I lost sight of them."

Salter expected to hear curses on the other end of the line, but Benning was silent. Maybe thinking about the FBI.

"I got the hack number," Salter said. "We can get the cab company to contact the driver."

"No," Benning said immediately. "Not yet. We don't want anything to happen that might spook these people while they're in the cab. We'll give them time to reach their destination, then have the cab company contact their driver and we can learn where he dropped them. Give me the cab's number."

Salter did, then said, "Still want this line kept open?"

"Why? So you can give me more bad news?"

Salter thought he'd better not say anything else.

He broke the connection and continued driving in the direction the cab had been going when it disappeared.

David gripped the back of the front seat and leaned forward to speak through the opening in the Plexiglas panel. "Faster! Can't you go faster?"

The driver, a swarthy man with a bizarre haircut bunched mostly on the top of his head, ignored him. In the strobe-light effect of passing lights playing over his face, there was an ominous glint in his eyes.

"Faster!" David urged again.

The driver glanced at him in the rearview mirror. "Don't understand. Faster? I go fast. Can't fly, go fast."

David squirmed with frustration. "Oh, Christ!"

The mirror showed another glance from the driver. "Pardon you. Not English, please."

David drew a deep breath, then exhaled and sat back in the seat, accepting the fact that he wasn't going to be able to communicate with the driver. "Okay, okay. Sorry. We'll get there when we get there."

The driver reached up and adjusted the mirror, and his eyes met Molly's.

The cab picked up speed.

Ten minutes later it came to a rocking halt in front of a tall apartment building on East Fifty-fourth near Second Avenue.

David and Molly piled out of the cab, David still clutching her arm. He dug a wad of bills from his pocket and tossed them in through the driver-side window. The driver retrieved them from his lap, quickly examined them, then stared after his two fares, who were hurrying to the building entrance.

David heard the cab pull away as he tried to remember the number code Deirdre had used to gain entry. He was good with numbers, and he thought he had it. He deftly pressed the buttons on a security keypad.

There was no result.

He gripped the handles of the thick glass doors and yanked on them, but the doors wouldn't open.

Then through the glass he saw the lobby elevator door open, and a man and woman dressed up to go out emerged and crossed the tile floor toward the street doors. The man was wearing a white dinner jacket. The woman had on a long violet dress and was carrying a small white purse on a gold chain.

David stood to the side as a shrill beeper sounded, and the man pushed open one of the heavy doors and held it for the woman. The man nodded to him, smiling, then rested a hand on the small of the woman's back as they walked on.

David grabbed the edge of the door as it started to swing closed.

Inside the lobby, he knew where they had to go. He guided Molly into the small, mirrored elevator and pressed the button for the thirty-fourth floor.

Molly leaned back against the reflecting wall and stood perfectly still.

David throbbed with rage and hope as the elevator ascended like a rocket.

On the thirty-fourth floor, the elevator door opened and Molly and David stepped out. An elderly man carrying a white poodle edged past them to enter the elevator, staring at them curiously as the door slid shut.

Practically dragging Molly, David made his way down the corridor.

She seemed to have figured out where they were now. She knew she was going to enter the place she'd seen on the videotape. Her step faltered, and for the first time since they'd gotten in the cab, she began to display deep fear and hesitancy.

But before she could summon up any resistance, they were at the door to apartment 34F.

David tried the knob. It rotated freely, but the door was locked.

"Okay," he said softly, "I'm getting good at kicking in doors."

He backed up a few steps, turned slightly sideways, and raised his right foot.

As he was about to kick, the knob turned and the door swung slowly inward about six inches.

Molly and David looked at each other.

David stepped in front of her, trying to control his fear, and reached out and nudged the door with his hand.

It made no sound as it swung open wide.

Molly's eyes bulged. David drew in his breath with a gasp almost like a scream.

A very tall, redheaded man was standing a few feet inside the doorway.

He was covered with blood and there was a knife protruding from his shoulder.

53

The redheaded man groaned and staggered out into David's arms.

David and Molly slowed his fall as he slid to the hall floor and sat slumped with his back against the wall.

David stared down at the injured man. "Is he the one who was following you?"

Molly nodded silently. She didn't seem to notice the blood on her hands and arms.

"He must have thought you might lead him to Deirdre," David said. He bent down to speak to the man. "You're Grocci! Stan Grocci!"

"That's right," the man managed to say. His voice was feeble but desperate. His eyes rolled toward the open apartment door. "Don't go in there! She's got the boy! She's done murder! She's crazy!"

Across the hall a door opened. A middle-aged woman wearing a pink satin housecoat peered out with curious dark eyes beneath long, artificial lashes.

The eyes blinked twice. Quickly she slammed the door, and the deadbolt audibly clicked into its shaft.

"She's sick," Grocci continued weakly. "Dangerous. She was in an institution, where she belonged. Then she got out, killed Chrissy . . ."

"Christine Mathews?" David asked.

Grocci bowed his head in what might have been a nod. Blood glistened on the right side of his face and neck. David saw a slash just above his hairline, like a dark worm beneath the strands of red hair, still trickling blood.

"It was partly my fault," he said, "but what was I supposed to do? The doctors said Deirdre would be in that place for years. I'd known Chrissy from my old neighborhood, so . . . things . . . they happened. Deirdre found out, she was jealous . . . Insanely jealous . . ."

David straightened up and took a step toward the open door.

"Don't go in there!" Grocci pleaded, raising a bloody arm. "She did this to me. I think she's killed me . . ."

David hesitated only a moment, then ignored Grocci and charged into the apartment. Molly was a few feet behind him. They dashed through the living room and into the bedroom where David and Deirdre had made love.

They stopped abruptly just inside the door.

Deirdre was cowering in a corner near the wide window where she'd enticed David as he'd gazed at the view. The window's white sheer curtains were open to reveal the jagged, brightly lighted Manhattan skyline. The night was clear and the city glittered like a galaxy that had fallen.

Deirdre's hair was blond and styled like Molly's, and she was wearing Molly's green dress and clutching Michael tightly to her. He appeared frightened, dazed, staring at his parents with dulled recognition and hope.

Molly and David stood where they'd stopped cold, fearing she might harm Michael.

Deirdre regarded them with calm green eyes that nonetheless held brilliant pinpoints of insanity that scared David.

"I came here to test you, David." Her voice was a sad monotone. "I knew you'd think of this place, but I hoped you might act to protect me. Instead you betrayed me." She glared at Molly. "You brought her." When she spoke of Molly, the hate in her voice echoed in madness.

David was aware of the abyss they all faced. He was gentle, coaxing. "I do want to protect you, Deirdre. That's why I came. Why don't you give Michael to me? I'll show you. I promise."

She continued glaring at Molly with eyes that blazed her hatred. "We don't need *her*, David. You never needed her. I came to New York to claim what I'd lost in life. I had no idea you were married. But it doesn't matter. You're rightfully mine! So is Michael, the child we should have had!" She loosened her grip on Michael to point a finger at Molly and took a few steps toward them. "Her life is rightfully mine!"

"That's in— That doesn't make sense, Deirdre. You know it doesn't make sense. Give me Michael. Please! Then we can talk, straighten all this out. I know you. You're not an evil person."

She held Michael tighter. "Of course I'm not evil. It isn't evil, and it isn't crazy, to take back what's mine and keep it. To keep it this time."

David involuntarily started forward, but Deirdre raised her forearm to a choking position on Michael's neck, and he stopped and stood motionless, fearful. Death was on the prowl here; ask Stan Grocci out in the corridor. Molly, who hadn't moved since entering the room, continued to stare vacantly at Deirdre.

Deirdre tightened her grip, and fear glowed in Michael's eyes. She widened her stance, as if tensing for action. "Don't come a step closer! Either of you!"

Sirens began to wail outside. Shrill loops of sound in the distance, but drawing nearer. David wondered if the woman across the hall, the one with the false eyelashes, had phoned the police.

"I'm crazy, remember?" Deirdre said. "We crazy women . . . we might do anything. We're mad as March hatters."

There was a blur of motion in the corner of David's vision.

Stan Grocci lurched into the room, past David and Molly. His shoes made scraping sounds on the carpet with each labored, dragging step. He was bleeding heavily and still had the knife in his shoulder. Though his movements were spasmodic and his progress slow, he was making his way toward Deirdre, his long features set and determined, his eyes fixed on her. In his right hand was one of the heavy onyx-bull bookends.

He was losing blood fast, getting weaker. His steps became even more faltering.

Deirdre merely stood staring at him, confident but wary, gauging his strength and waiting for it to expire.

Grocci's legs became rubbery, like a tiring boxer's in the late rounds. He began to weave. He stopped. His tall body swayed.

With a gurgling scream and a supreme force of will, he drew back his right hand and threw the heavy bookend at Deirdre.

It missed and shattered the window behind her.

Grocci fell with a dull thud on the carpet and didn't move. His determination had died, and now he was dying. He gazed with sad detachment at Deirdre through opaque and hooded eyes.

Wind howled through the window frame that now held only a few shards of glass.

While Deirdre was distracted, David charged.

She noticed him and reacted in time, not changing expression except for an added intensity in her eyes. Angling her body and holding Michael to the side, she expertly shot out a foot to kick David in the groin.

Pain rocked through him, clamping and twisting his insides in a vise, nauseating and paralyzing him. Clutching himself with both hands, he dropped to his knees.

Deirdre smiled faintly. "You didn't know what an athlete I am, did you, David? I'm very good. Running, martial arts . . ."

"And swimming," Molly said softly.

Deirdre stopped smiling and looked sharply at her, sensing that a balance had shifted. She knew the real enemy, the real danger.

Molly screamed and hurled herself at her, striking suddenly and with such unexpected speed and force that Michael was flung from Deirdre's grasp.

The two women grappled with each other, struggling, kicking, biting, gouging eyes. Molly's head banged against the wall, causing a burst of light along with the pain. It only made her fight harder. She tried to yank Deirdre's hair but it came off in her hand, revealing a wild red tangle plastered with perspiration to her scalp, making Deirdre look even more like the madwoman she was. Molly flung aside the blond wig and cracked Deirdre's jaw with her elbow all in the same motion. She continued to advance, never taking a backward step, driving Deirdre back.

The stunned but desperate Deirdre hacked at Molly's neck with the edge of her hand, but Molly's fierce attack kept her too close for Deirdre to gain leverage and inflict much damage. It was all happening too fast, too awkwardly, for Deirdre to set herself and use her fighting skills.

David saw what was happening and tried to stand up, but pain dropped him back to his knees.

Molly's advance was so determined and swift that both women

temporarily lost their footing and crashed against the wall, bouncing off the rough plaster and trying to regain balance. For an instant they separated, at last affording Deirdre fighting room. She yelled and raised her leg, wheeling her body sideways to deliver a crescent kick to Molly's head.

Molly was weaker than her opponent, but she was younger and a split second quicker. She leaned back and slapped Deirdre's flashing foot in the direction it was traveling, causing her to pivot faster and off balance on her toe and crash into the window frame, hitting her head hard on the steel upper sash. Dazed for a second, she sat down hard on the windowsill, teetering. Then she slid sideways away from the sill, toward dark space, bleeding where the glass shards had cut her. As she fell through the window, she scrambled frantically and managed to grab the marble outside ledge and hold on.

Molly staggered to the window and stared at Deirdre clinging to the ledge for life. The two women locked gazes. Deirdre was silent, her red lips drawn back from clenched teeth in what might have been a grin. Her eyes were ferocious.

Molly reached toward Deirdre's pale hands that were clutching the ledge.

Then she hesitated.

Deirdre was obviously weakening. Her splayed, whitened fingers almost imperceptibly began to slide over the smooth marble.

Molly's hands darted forward, then stopped and drew back slowly as Deirdre lost her grip and plunged thirty-four stories toward the street. For a few seconds she extended her arms, as if too late trying to catch the knack of flying. Then she tucked them in tight to her sides.

Molly leaned from the window and watched her all the way down, listening to her desolate, fading scream. Horror crossed Molly's face, an instant of revelation.

Then she became calm. She knew what she'd done. She'd been reduced to animal will, forced to play an uncompromising, primitive game outside the rules, one that had existed even *before* the rules. She'd killed to preserve herself and her family. Like a she-wolf protecting her brood. She didn't know if, under the circumstances, it was legal. If it was moral.

The legality didn't matter. No one else would ever know that she'd let Deirdre fall. That she might have saved her.

It was something she'd have to live with, and she knew that she could.

She scooped up Michael and went to David, who'd at last managed to gain his feet. Molly encompassed them both in her arms, drawing them to her and hugging them fiercely, harder and harder.

Her family.

54

Two weeks later, Molly and David were walking with Michael along West Eighty-sixth Street, near their new apartment. The morning was sunny and still pleasantly cool, and casually dressed West Siders out to enjoy the weekend crowded the sidewalks. Michael was seated in his stroller, quiet and content, as David pushed.

They were on their way to the small, fenced playground just inside the entrance to Central Park. David would watch Michael climbing and swinging on the equipment, while Molly sat on one of the benches and read the *Times*.

They were about to cross Central Park West when Molly glanced up at the crowd massed on the other side of the street.

She broke stride and her heart went cold.

A tall woman wearing a T-shirt, shorts, and jogging shoes emerged from the park and ran toward them, weaving through the people surging in unison now to cross the intersection as the light flashed Walk.

The woman's face wasn't discernible because of her long hair bouncing and swinging with each stride. But her running style was familiar, the effortless way she kicked far out with her tan, muscular legs, the graceful, easy manner in which she swung her arms.

Molly panicked and froze.

Then the woman was almost on them, hair flying, face of an angelic teenager. A young Audrey Hepburn.

She saw Molly staring, smiled curiously, and veered to run around them.

Molly returned the smile.

Then she and her husband and child continued their Sunday walk.